Keystone

Put a solemn Englishman into police uniform and thrust him into the crazy world of Keystone Film Studios in 1915 and you have the premise for Peter Lovesey's most exciting mystery novel.

The King of Comedy, Mack Sennett, insists on calling the new cop Keystone. But comedy swiftly turns to crime. Shocking things occur that are not in any script — a horrific death on a roller-coaster, a body in a bungalow, the disappearance of a girl, a shooting on a beach.

Keystone the Cop gets on the trail. His mission: to find the adorable and much abused blonde actress, Amber Honeybee. The action is threaded through the real stories of the silent comedy stars, Mack Sennett, Roscoe 'Fatty' Arbuckle and Mabel Normand.

Peter Lovesey has a flair for recreating the exotic and eccentric eras of the past. After his Victorian police series featuring Sergeant Cribb, came the brilliant 'twenties mystery, *The False Inspector Dew*, now matched by the thrills and verve of *Keystone*.

KEYSTONE

Peter Lovesey

Macmillan London

ISBN: 0 333 35044 8

First published 1983 by
MACMILLAN LONDON LIMITED
London and Basingstoke
Associated companies in Auckland, Dallas, Delhi, Dublin,
Hong Kong, Johannesburg, Lagos, Manzini, Melbourne,
Nairobi, New York, Singapore, Tokyo, Washington
and Zaria

Typeset in Great Britain by
MESSENGERTYPE
Chatham, Kent

Printed in Great Britain by
THE ANCHOR PRESS LIMITED
Tiptree, Essex

Bound in Great Britain by
WM. BRENDON AND SON LIMITED
Tiptree, Essex

ONE

'So you want to be a Keystone Cop?'

'Perish the thought.'

'Speak up, fella.'

'The answer is no.'

'Beat it, then.'

'Perhaps you prefer no thank you.'

'Go to hell.'

'I was told you are a monstrous bully, Mr Sennett. I am determined to ignore it.'

Mack Sennett raised his face above the rim of his bathtub and stared at me. It was a face familiar from a dozen movies. A bull-like face with glaring eyes. Grey hair sticking damply to the forehead. Rubbery, pouting lips that he twisted into imbecilic shapes when he played the rube in barnyard comedies. He was the head of Keystone Studios. The King of Comedy.

'You English?' he asked in a voice heavy with suspicion.

'Is there anything untoward in that?'

'What's your name?'

'Warwick Easton.'

Sennett pressed a knuckle to his ear and rubbed it. 'Did you by any chance say Keystone?'

'No,' I answered. 'What you heard was Easton.'

'You sure?'

'Emphatically.'

'What's wrong with Keystone, Easton?'

'It happens not to be my name.'

'Hogwash. When I was at Biograph a guy came for a

job, said he had experience at Pathé. We all knew he was lying. But he got the job. We always called him Pathé after that. What did you say your name is?'

'Keystone.'

'Better. But you still don't want to be a Cop?'

'That is my position, Mr Sennett.'

'What the hell are you doing here, then?'

'I was reliably informed it was your office.'

Mack Sennett gave a basso laugh that echoed round the bathtub. The tub was solid marble. It was so large it was practically a pool. It must have been five-foot deep. He was standing up in it. 'This *is* my office. You a gagman, Keystone?'

'I don't understand.'

'Gagman — a writer.' He pointed upwards. 'I keep four above this office, so I know exactly where they are. Writers need supervision. They have no telephone, books or other distractions. Just pens and paper. You sure you're not a writer?'

'I am an artist, Mr Sennett.'

'A what?'

'A variety artist.'

'Jesus Christ.' Sennett jerked back his head and hollered, 'Abdul!'

I was practically bowled aside by a massive figure responding to the summons. He was wearing yellow boxer shorts. I had been told about Abdullah the Turk. He was an ex-wrestler hired to massage the King of Comedy and run his bath-water. He lifted Sennett like a baby from the tub and stood him on the carpet.

'Cigar,' said Sennett. It was not an invitation. He closed his hand around the thick Havana that Abdul handed him. 'A variety artist, God help us. Let's get a look at you.'

He circled me. I wanted work. I submitted to the

scrutiny of this mother-naked, dripping man as if it were the Trooping of the Colour.

Several seconds passed before he discovered anything worth remarking on. 'You're tall.'

'Six foot two.'

'Who sent you?'

'One of your scouts, Mr Del Ruth. He watched me at the Empress.'

'So you're in vaudeville. What's your act?'

'I commence with a dramatic monologue.'

'Christ Almighty!' Sennett bit the end off his cigar. '*He commences with a dramatic monologue.* And you want to work in movies? Forget it, friend.' He padded into the adjoining room.

I followed him in. If I let him turn me down, I was jobless, an ocean and a continent from home. What I wanted was a character part, not a faceless future in the Keystone Cops.

The room was furnished with a rubbing-table and a brass spittoon.

I told him, 'I have a stooge in the audience who interrupts me. I challenge him to come up on the stage.'

'You horse around? Keep talking.' He heaved himself onto the rubbing-table and nodded to Abdullah.

'My stooge is short and fat, of course. He knocks me off my feet.'

'So you can do a pratfall.'

'After I hit the stage, I lie completely still. My stooge finds himself alone in front of the audience with an insensible man. He is unable to revive me. He tries to drag me off, but I'm too heavy.'

'I get the picture. What's the payoff?'

I blinked. The combination of cigar smoke and Abdullah's embrocation was painful to the eyes. 'He is too embarrassed to get off the stage. In desperation he

7

looks in my pockets for the sheet on which the monologue is written. He finds it. He walks to centre stage and clears his throat. He starts to read.'

'It's your laundry list,' Sennett said wearily. He propped himself up high enough to jerk his head and spit into the cuspidor. 'Goddammit, Keystone, that routine's as old as papering the parlour. Tell me straight: did Hampton Del Ruth really send you here?'

I had reached my limit. I was angry and I showed it. 'Am I the victim of a hoax?'

'What do you mean?'

'This so-called interview. It's bizarre. Preposterous.'

Sennett grinned at me. 'Don't you like the motion-picture business?'

'Is this what it amounts to — insults from a naked man?'

He guffawed at that. He hammered the rubbing-table with his fists.

I said, 'Candidly, I find your manners as offensive as your embrocation.'

He covered his ears. He was shaking uncontrollably. 'Don't say any more. You'll kill me. Keystone, I can use you. You sure as hell won't be another Chaplin, but I love your style. You're hired.'

'I don't understand.'

'You wouldn't,' Sennett chuckled. 'That's why you're so funny.'

The door was opened and a girl looked in. I recognised her face. Small, pert features framed by large black curls. Bold brown eyes. She was not embarrassed by Sennett's naked state. She said, 'Are you tied up, Mack?'

Sennett rubbed his eyes. He said, 'Mabel, I'm in stitches. Come right in. Would you believe this guy goes by the name of Keystone?'

She was Mabel Normand, first lady of the Keystone Company. She placed her child-sized hand in mine. 'How are you, Mr Keystone? Are you in movies, too?'

'It would appear so,' I replied, 'if what Mr Sennett said just now can be relied upon.'

'You got it, Keystone,' Sennett said. To Mabel Normand he explained, 'I just hired him as the newest Cop.'

'Congratulations,' said Miss Normand.

I shook my head. 'There's some misunderstanding.'

Sennett said, 'Don't start me off again.'

I would not be brushed aside. 'I came to audition for a character part. I don't wish to be a Keystone Cop.'

Sennett's mood abruptly altered. 'Are you ashamed to be a Cop, you lousy sonofabitch? Get this: every comic on the payroll started as a Cop, including me. What goes for Mack Sennett is good enough for some English dude — sorry, variety artist — who wants a break from vaudeville. Five bucks a day, Keystone. Take it or leave it.'

'Then I'll leave it.'

As soon as I had spoken, I went cold. Five dollars was an income. I had turned it down because I was ambitious. This was 1915. There were reputations to be made in motion pictures. I was talented, as I would prove to Sennett — if I gave myself the chance.

Mabel Normand must have read my thoughts. She told me, 'Don't let him railroad you. Do you have a job?'

Sennett said, 'Does he, hell? He was playing at the Empress.'

The Empress in Los Angeles was the last booking on the vaudeville tour across America. I had started on the road ten months ago in New York City. Sennett knew vaudeville. My act was not the sort that managers

9

re-booked.

Miss Normand gave me an encouraging smile. 'Why don't you work as an extra for a couple of weeks? No commitment on either side, just a chance for you to see us from the inside? Mack, what do you say to that?'

Sennett had lost interest. He gave a shrug.

Mabel Normand winked.

I nodded and smiled back at her.

I was launched in motion pictures.

TWO

Five days later I was on location in Exposition Park. I was only half-awake. My system wasn't geared to eight in the morning. Fortunately I was not required to do much.

With about fifty other extras on three dollers a day, I swanned around the amusement area masquerading as a member of the public. Watching us through the perimeter fence were the bona fide public, several hundred office workers, garage hands and shop assistants. When those crazy Keystone Cops were on the rollercoaster they had to be seen, even if it meant being late for work. And fired.

Mack Sennett was directing. He was carrying a megaphone. I was glad I hadn't set eyes on him before my interview. He was six foot one, with the shoulders of a boilermaker. As a boy of seventeen in the iron works in East Berlin, Connecticut, he had slammed home rivets with a ten-pound sledge-hammer. He looked all wrong in a three-piece suit and necktie. As if he knew it, he wore a Panama with the crown cut out. He laughed a lot. He was hated or adored by women.

He put the megaphone to his mouth. The fence vibrated. He was speaking to the men sixty feet above. 'Tell that sonofabitch he can start running when the damn car clears the top of the rise and not a moment sooner. Who is he?'

'Sullivan, Mr Sennett.'

'You hear me, Sullivan? The gag is all in the timing. You got five, maybe six seconds. Would I ask you to do this if it wasn't safe?'

There was ironic laughter from the film crew. The stunts

at Keystone were notoriously dangerous.

'How is the wind up there?' Sennett enquired of Sullivan, milking the joke for the benefit of his audience along the fence. 'What did he say? I didn't hear a goddamn word. Okay, boys and girls. One dummy run for Sullivan to get it right, and then we crank the camera. Did you get that, Harper?'

The cameraman perched on a sixty-foot tower of scaffolding beside the rollercoaster raised an arm.

'Everyone ready?' boomed Sennett. 'Rehearsal. Mabel? Harry? Get 'em rolling.'

An excited chorus from the fence acclaimed Mabel Normand as she appeared in view seated in a rollercoaster car. She was in a white lawn dress. She was laughing and blowing kisses to the crew while the car was transported slowly up the incline that would give the car its impetus. Her black curls under a small white hat bobbed to the rhythm of the ratchet mechanism.

Beside her sat Harry Gribbon, a hard-faced actor in silk hat and large moustache that stamped him indisputably as not to be trusted by an innocent girl.

In the rear were another couple, a blonde girl and a grey-haired man, both bit players. All eyes were on Miss Normand, so petite and vulnerable. The car reached the top of the rise and trundled around a bend before its first descent.

I looked up at the high section of the track in the centre of the ride. It was the longest and steepest dip. At the point where it levelled, the Keystone Cops were standing in two files, nightsticks drawn for the chase. They wore grey domed helmets and black tunics with rows of shining silver buttons. Their trousers were finely tailored to facilitate agility. They needed to be spry. They were standing on a catwalk one foot wide on either side of the track. Hazards in the shape of sun reflectors — discs faced with tinfoil,

four feet across, to maximise the light — were strapped
to the safety rail along the edges.

Someone signalled to Mack Sennett.

'Action!'

The Cops, brandishing their batons, started running up
the slope towards the high part of the ride. They seemed
oblivious that the car containing Mabel Normand and the
villain would reach the top and bear down on them any
second.

A woman close to me began to scream. Someone told
her it was only a movie, but others in the crowd started to
shout as well.

The car appeared and topped the rise with agonising
slowness. I had a clear view of what was happening in the
car. Harry Gribbon was forcing his attentions on Miss
Normand. He had both arms around her. She was strug-
gling to get free. The others in the car were too far back
to intervene. The silk hat flew up and the car hurtled
down the slope.

The Cops were halfway up. They raised their hands in
horror. They looked certain to be hit. With marvellous
precision, they flung their nightsticks to the wind,
crouched and gripped the side rails. They vaulted off the
catwalk and hung by their hands in space.

All but one. He was the slow one, Sullivan, the last in
line. He had barely started up the slope.

Instead of leaping to safety with the others, this dippiest
of cops was facing the oncoming car and holding up his
hands like an officer on traffic duty. Sensible at last to the
danger, he about-turned and started sprinting for his life
down the centre of the track. In seconds he was certain to
be overtaken. It was impossible already to escape the way
the others had.

Behind me, there was panic. Men were screaming with
the women. Many covered their eyes. Those who could

bear to watch saw the car close to within two yards of Sullivan.

He saved himself with a marvellous leap. Above the track at the point where it levelled was a metal arch with coloured lamps. It was almost ten feet high. He sprang with arms outstretched. He grabbed a handhold. He drew up his knees. The car with its passengers flashed underneath and on its way. It was a brilliant stunt.

'Okay, Sullivan, you got it right,' Mack Sennett announced through his megaphone. 'Take a ten minute break and then we do it for real. How did it look, Harper?'

The cameraman looked down from his tower and gave the thumb-up signal.

Meanwhile the car completed its trip and glided to a halt at the boarding stage. Harry Gribbon still had one arm round Mabel Normand, but she had stopped protesting. She was smiling at him. In the course of the ride, the hem of her skirt had crept almost above her knees. She appeared not to have noticed until now. She corrected it and stood up. Harry took her hand and helped her out.

She noticed me among the extras by the boarding stage.

I smiled back.

She called out, 'Changed your mind yet?'

I said, 'It's safer on the ground.'

'But much more fun up there,' she told me.

She was still the centre of attention. Her hair was being tidied by a woman with a brush. Another handed her a cigarette and lighted it. Mabel drew on it a couple of times, dropped it and moved away to speak to Sennett.

Her two attendants had to jostle with propmen and technicians in the crush around the King of Comedy. The hairbrush was taken from the dresser's hand.

Sixty feet up, the cops had hauled themselves over the safety rail and reassembled on the catwalk. Their nightsticks and several dropped helmets were hoisted to them by rope and basket. In full kit again, they sat in neat formation on the edge, dangling their legs and watching the cameraman adjust the angle of the light reflectors.

It crossed my mind that Mabel might be right. Perhaps it *was* more fun up there.

Close to me, a woman's voice cried out in protest. Mabel's dresser had tracked down the missing hairbrush. It was being put to use by the blonde I remembered seeing in the rollercoaster car. She was standing on a carousel to look in one of its many mirrors. She laughed and pushed away the dresser, who stumbled and almost hit the ground. It began a barney as hilarious as anything the crowd had seen so far.

Sennett missed it. He was laughing at something Mabel Normand had remarked. She was full of fun. Sennett guffawed and everyone around him was convulsed as well. He put his broad hand on the nape of Mabel's neck and ruffled her black curls. In the same movement he guided her towards the boarding stage. He hunched his shoulders to plant a kiss on Mabel's cheek. She was only five feet tall. She turned her face and took it lightly on the lips. She stepped into the car.

Mack Sennett's hand withdrew from Mabel's hair and grabbed the megaphone from his assistant.

'That's it. We're ready to go.'

Four and five deep along the fence, the public craned to watch the villain climb in beside Miss Normand. Moviemaking was a mystery to many. They could not fathom why she was so misguided as to take a second ride in such obnoxious company. Someone yelled to her to get out while she could. She smiled back and blew a kiss.

Sennett checked that everyone was ready. The car was given the push that sent it on its journey. It engaged with the machinery and climbed towards the sky. Miss

Normand waved and people cheered and Sennett bellowed lustily for silence. He wanted his instructions clearly heard.

He demanded order in his chaos. The gag, he had said, was all in the timing. At intervals along the track, studio assistants signalled the progress of the car. Sennett put the megaphone to his mouth.

'Action! Camera!'

The Cops scrambled up the slope in a glorious comic spectacle, little men in uniform insanely following their leader as the unseen car moved steadily up the other side. It surfaced at the top. They registered their panic. The car dipped for the descent. Mabel was battling for her reputation. The silk hat soared and fell.

'Now!' shouted Sennett.

The Cops grabbed the rail and swung to safety, all except Sullivan, the traffic cop. For a split-second he was the immovable object, left arm outstretched, right imperiously raised to halt the irresistible force.

Then he spun on his heels and raced for his life. Four or five strides to the point where he could leap for the arch and swing clear. The car closed rapidly.

Sullivan missed his handhold.

I had watched his face. He somehow seemed to pre-conceive disaster. Panic transformed his features. His eyes were alight with fear. His mouth gaped. His head went back. His hands groped for the arch without a hope of touching it, because he failed to jump. He simply failed to jump.

The car crashed into him a yard past the arch. It hit him with such force that it may have snapped his spine on impact. He was spreadeagled on the front and carried some forty yards, while Mabel Normand screamed and Harry Gribbon tried to reach across the safety bar to drag the man aboard.

He failed. The car swung into a bend and Sullivan slid clear. For two appalling seconds his body was suspended on the catwalk. Some people in the crowd believed that this was still a Keystone stunt. The figure toppled off the edge and dropped twenty feet. It hit a girder and flopped over it like cloth. It dropped again and hit the ground.

There were piercing screams, then silence.

I ran towards the spot. We all converged, Sennett and the crew, propmen and amusement park officials. The only service we were able to perform was to screen his body from the public. When we had covered him, I turned away. My legs were shaking.

The rollercoaster car had finished its fatal circuit practically unnoticed. Mabel Normand, lily-white, got out. Someone supported her.

The Keystone Cops hurried down the ladders lashed to the ironwork of the ride and ran across to have confirmed what they already knew.

Recriminations started in the crowd. It was too dangerous a stunt. It was indefensible to risk men's lives for entertainment. Some of these movie people were insane. They would try anything to turn a profit. They killed men and called it comedy.

An ambulance was driven in. The police arrived. Real cops in caps questioned Keystone Cops in helmets. They questioned Sennett and the actors who had ridden in the rollercoaster car. Mabel Normand was in a state of shock. As soon as she had made a statement she was allowed to leave in a chauffeur-driven car. The ambulance also left. A lieutenant borrowed Sennett's megaphone and told the public to disperse. There would be nothing else to see. In view of what had happened, the movie was abandoned.

A few doggedly stayed on. They saw the camera lowered from the tower. The rest of the equipment was brought down. Harper, the cameraman, was required to make a statement. Mack Sennett called him over and stood at the lieutenant's side. He made sure that he missed nothing.

Carloads of Keystone Cops were leaving. They moved out without the customary shouts and sounding of the horn. Harry Gribbon travelled with them. The blonde who had borrowed Mabel Normand's hairbrush sat uncomfortably beside the dresser who had retrieved it, in a landau stacked with costumes and the camera. The rest of us followed in three trucks.

Mack Sennett was the last to leave. When we pulled out, he and the cameraman were still in conference with the police.

THREE

I was standing by the bathtub again.

'You asked to see me, Mr Sennett.'

'How long have you been here now?'

'Ten days.'

'Like it?'

'Not much.'

'What's wrong with it, for Christ's sake?'

'As an extra, I don't get sufficient work. I was in the fairground picture, but it was stopped.'

'You don't have to tell me that.'

'I spend each morning standing with the others in that damned enclosure.'

'You objecting to the bull pen?'

'If I don't get picked, it's another wasted day. I've earned twelve dollars in ten days.'

'Changed your mind yet?'

'What do you mean?'

Sennett looked over the rim. 'There's a vacancy in the Cops. Report to Wardrobe for a uniform. I want you on the set tomorrow.'

I didn't argue this time. I went out into the sunshine.

The Keystone lot had started as a farmyard. It was a cluster of barns, bungalows, open stages, shops, studios, builders' yards and streets lined with paddy wagons and tin lizzies. Propmen and carpenters, actors and office workers went about their business with antlike urgency. Three or more comedies were always in production simultaneously, so every thoroughfare had its hazards of props, scenery and motor cars on the move.

'You look lost. Can I help?'

'I hope so. I was told to go to Wardrobe.'

'Fine. That's the way I'm going. You're new here, aren't you? What's your name?'

'Mr Sennett calls me Keystone.'

'Keystone it is, then. He's the gospel here. My name is Amber Honeybee. Don't say it's sweet — I've heard that a million times.'

Miss Honeybee was blonde and probably not twenty. She wore her hair in ringlets, like Mary Pickford. Her words came in bursts. She filled the intervals with piercing glances from her wide green eyes.

I seemed to know her face, but I couldn't place her at the studio. 'Amber Honeybee,' I said. 'It conjures all the fragrances of summer.'

'That's nice — real nice. Are you a poet?'

'Not by any stretch of the imagination. Almost the reverse. Is there anything more prosaic than a Keystone Cop?'

'You're one of the Cops? Since when? I thought I knew them all.'

'I was enlisted two minutes ago in Mr Sennett's bathroom.'

Amber gave a light laugh. 'He sees everyone in there, including ladies. That bathtub is Mack's pride and joy. It weighs two tons. It was brought here on a safe-mover's truck drawn by six enormous Percherons. Did you meet Abdul?'

'The masseur?'

'He used to be a wrestler. Mack likes to box, so they always start the morning beating each other with leather gloves. Then it's bath-time, and that can last two hours or more. Only an earthquake would get Mack out of his bath before he's ready.' She giggled. 'It happened once. There was some sort of tremor and Mack leapt out and raced across the lot pursued by Abdul. They didn't have a towel between them. This place is crazier than the movies we make.' Amber stopped and pointed. 'There's Wardrobe. Shall I come in and introduce you? They can be a little difficult in there.'

'If it's not imposing on your time, Miss Honeybee.'

'You've just got to be English. Do you know Charlie Chaplin? He was here.'

Before I could answer, we were in Wardrobe, hard against a sewing-table positioned to stop the casual visitor. Behind it was a woman of prodigious size. She was using a sewing-machine. Her plump hand guided the seam towards the jabbing needle at a rate that made my blood run cold.

'Winnie, this is Mr Keystone. He wants a Cop uniform.' Amber added with a wink to me, 'This place couldn't function without Winnie.'

'Another Cop?' Winnie said above the whirr of the machine. 'What do they think this is — the Los Angeles Police Department? I don't have unlimited uniforms.'

'It's terrible the work they give you,' Amber agreed, giving me a nudge.

'Deplorable.'

Winnie carried on machining. 'I wouldn't mind if they respected them. They come back in tatters, buttons missing, stained with Lord knows what. That's if they come back at all. I'm still waiting for the one the guy was wearing when he fell off the rollercoaster. You can't tell me they buried him in it.' She glanced up at me. 'He was a Cop.'

'I'm aware of that,' I answered evenly.

'And he was just the latest,' added Winnie as she stopped machining and with a flash of scissors cut the thread. 'The Devil only knows what goes on here.'

'Can you supply a uniform for Mr Keystone?' Amber asked firmly.

'This is a nut palace,' persisted Winnie, 'only they equip the inmates with automobiles and express trains.'

'He's wanted on the set tomorrow morning.'

'Men's costumes are back there. He's a long fitting. Try the end rack.'

Amber led me through rows of garments smelling of moth repellent. 'You have to make a friend of Winnie. Don't let her depress you.'

'It's all right. I knew about the accident in Exposition Park. I was there.'

'So was I,' said Amber. 'Horrible. I don't care to think of it.'

As she spoke, there flashed into my mind the image of the roller-coaster rising over the high point of the ride and hurtling downwards. Cops scattering to safety, all except Sullivan. In the car, the frightened faces of Mabel Normand, Harry Gribbon and two extras, one grey-haired, one blonde.

One blonde.

The blonde was Amber.

She said, 'These look like Cop tunics.'

'I'll try one. You're an actress, then, Miss Honeybee?'

'Amber. Yes, I'm in a minority at Keystone. There isn't much call for female leads, or much variety. The only roles we get to play are maidens in distress. The men have all the fun. Let's look at you. Hey, that's fine. Just dandy.'

'It's right for length, but far too broad across the shoulders.'

'That's no problem. They wear them loose. Really, it's all right. Let's find the pants. how did you come to Keystone?'

'In my motor car.'

'No, what I meant is . . .' Her eyes enlarged. 'You have an *automobile*?'

'I bought it two weeks ago, before I started here. After ten months on tour in vaudeville, I was ready for a fling. I blued my savings on it. No regrets: it's the perfect way to see the best of California. Here are the trousers. A long fitting for me.'

'Your very own automobile!'

'I'm thirty-four.'

'You don't look so old as that.'

'Inches, Amber. In the leg.'

'Oh.' She smiled. 'I wasn't concentrating. Find a pair that fit. Don't risk tripping over them.'

'Is there a changing room?'

'Through there. Listen, Keystone, I must dash. I have to get to make-up. We girls scarcely get a chance to breathe. Mabel and I keep saying we ought to take it up with Mack.'

'Mabel Normand? I met her.'

Amber's eyes narrowed. 'You did? Already?'

'She walked in when I was with Mr Sennett.'

'Uhuh. It figures.' She shrugged and smiled. 'Mabel and Mack are pretty close. Good luck with the Cops, Keystone, and take care. Let's have another talk sometime.'

I thanked her, and she turned so quickly that the ringlets twirled. Soon I lost sight of her among the racks of costumes.

When I had found some trousers that fitted, I went back to Winnie. She was using the sewing-machine again.

'These are perfect. May I take them?'

'You can take them off right now and put them on a hanger. You collect them from me when Mr Sennett really puts you in a movie. They'll be waiting.'

'I was told to be on the set tomorrow.'

'Mister, don't be kidded. You have to learn the business first. He wants you there to watch. He'll call you when he's ready. One of them will break a leg or something. Do

23

you have brittle bones?'

'I've no idea.'

She stopped the machine. She looked solemnly at me. 'That was a joke. Don't you know when people are making jokes? First thing you got to learn: look out for jokers.'

'I'm grateful for your advice.'

'Mr Sennett is as bad as any of them. Like when he wired a generator to the men's room and waited for Charlie Chaplin to go in. Mack switched on and Charlie staggered out a minute later.'

I pictured it and winced.

'The boys all swear that's how he learned the funny walk.' Winnie gave me a searching look. 'I guess that's not your line of humour. Just be careful, baby. And if you need advice, I'm the oracle here. It's no use asking walk-ons, however cute they look.'

'*Walk-ons*?'

'Bit players.'

'Are you referring to Miss Honeybee?'

'Who else?'

'Doesn't she play bigger roles?'

Winnie started turning her machine again. 'Sweetheart, Amber Honeybee has no talent whatsoever. She has as much prospect of a bigger role as my — aw, forget it.'

FOUR

Next morning I was early at the open stages where the shooting would be done. There were three, roofed with white linen sheets to diffuse the sun for scenes that were meant to be interiors. A gusty wind was getting under the material, causing it to swell and flap. Teams of carpenters and propmen toiled to build the sets.

Behind us loomed a square concrete structure like a castle keep. This was the tower where Sennett kept his writers and his bathtub. The first three storeys housed the 'office' with its tub and rubbing-table, the studio executives and the writers. The top floor was the observation room. Unlike the others, it was faced with windows on each side. Sennett liked to stand there, presiding over his personal Pandemonium. Any misdemeanour spotted from the tower could lead to summary dismissal. Even the cameramen made a point of looking busy, fixing magazines and polishing their lenses.

One of the sets was Police Headquarters. It was still in process of erection, yet it already had a flat incorporating a door and 'wanted' notices, and a desk and telephone had been deposited nearby.

I made enquiries. The director checked the cast-list. My name was not among the Cops. I tried the other stages. I was not wanted there. I decided to stand back and watch.

The watching lasted through the week. It was instructive, valuable, repetitive and tedious. I picked up bits of motion-picture jargon. I learned the functions of the various people on the set. I watched the famous fat man, Roscoe Arbuckle, and saw how gags were improvised and systematically perfected. I marvelled at the actors' patience while the shouts and laughter from adjoining stages bombarded their concentration.

Mack Sennett came by intermittently. He seemed preoccupied. He stood alone behind the camera, hunched, unsmiling, chewing pieces off a large cigar. The best efforts of the comics failed to humour him. I managed to catch his eye a couple of times. He looked away.

'Don't get depressed,' a girl's voice advised me after the fourth time this had happened. 'This is Mack's way. He believes his actors should learn the business first.'

Mabel Normand was so short that I had not noticed her at my side. She must have seen me glumly watching Sennett amble back towards his tower. She had come over from the set where she was working with Roscoe Arbuckle. They were setting up another scene there.

'I appreciate that,' I said. 'It's sensible. But wouldn't you agree that there comes a point when one learns more from doing the thing than simply standing by? I won't deny that any man would enjoy watching you for days on end, Miss Normand, but that's another matter.'

She didn't blush. She was evidently used to compliments. 'You should watch the others then.'

'I do. I think Fatty Arbuckle is astonishingly agile for someone of his size.'

'One thing else you'd better learn. He hurts easily. Nobody calls him Fatty. That's just the character he plays.'

'I shall address him as Mr Arbuckle if I have the privilege of meeting him. What do they call you, Miss Normand?'

She laughed. 'Mabel to my face, and Lord knows what behind my back.'

'How long have you been at Keystone?'

'Right from the start. I was at Biograph with Mack. Before that I was an extra with the Kalem Company.'

'You must have been young.'

'Sixteen.'

'Why did you leave Biograph?'

Her eyes shone and she made a chuckling sound deep in her throat. 'Romance, darling. I followed Mack. If you want to know what made *him* quit Biograph, it was genius. Well' — she giggled again — 'I guess frustration had a part in it.'

'Frustration with the management?'

'Don't misunderstand me. Mack will tell you himself that he is Mr Griffith's chief disciple. He spent hours walking with him, talking to him, learning the art of making motion pictures. And Mack directed some fine movies at Biograph. The problem was that he and Mr Griffith were too much alike. I promise you, Keystone, you could go from here to New York City and you wouldn't meet two guys as brilliantly creative and as maddening as Mack and Mr Griffith.'

'Maddening? In what way?'

'Always switching moods. One day like gods, inspiring everyone, the next grouchy, unapproachable.'

'Yes, I can imagine two men like that would lead to complications.'

She laughed. 'You said it. There was one day on location on the cliffs at Santa Monica. Mack had a walk-on part. He didn't mind: we all took turns at playing supers. What got to him was the lunch arrangement. Mr Griffith quietly tipped off the leading players that six hot steaks had been sent up from a restaurant in Venice. The lucky few moved off discreetly to a place apart. I can't help laughing when I remember it. When Mack sniffed those steaks and tumbled to the fact that he hadn't had an invite to the party, he was really mad. He started acting like an usher. "*Sandwiches this way, steaks over there. Not you, sir. Sandwiches for your sort. Line up with the rest.*"

Mack is not well known for speaking softly.'

'I'm aware of that. When did he leave Biograph?'

'The following winter. He got wind that two bigshots who ran the New York Motion Picture Company were in Los Angeles. You know there's only one hotel for movie people, the Alexandria. Mack put on a tux each evening and waited in the lobby until they saw him. They warmed to his ideas. They backed him. Some of us went with him. So the Keystone Company was formed.'

'Those bigshots must have been shrewd judges.'

She shrugged. 'Mack is very persuasive. And they took no chances. They gave Tom Ince a ten per cent stake in return for keeping tabs on Mack.'

'Tom who?'

'Ince. You're really new to movies if you haven't heard of Tom. He produced those beautiful westerns for the Bison Company, *War on the Plains*, *Custer's Last Fight*—remember? He has twenty thousand acres of gorgeous scenery out at Santa Monica, and a whole dummy town called Inceville. He was supposed to cable New York if Mack left town with the takings. Mack's as big as he is now.'

'So you were one of the pioneers.'

Mabel Normand rolled her eyes. 'You make me sound like a piece of history. I'm only twenty. I must go now.' She waved to the director who was calling. 'Remember no-one in the business knows comedy like Mack. He's foul-mouthed, grouchy and as daffy as a daddy-long-legs, but if you stick with him, and you have an ounce of talent in you, he'll bring it out. I'm going to marry him.'

That surprised me. 'Despite the fact that he is foul-mouthed, grouchy and whatever else you called him?'

She grinned. 'Mack and I are two of a kind. Ask any of those guys.' She went back to work.

The next day, something happened that tended to confirm it. Halfway through the morning, Mabel was called to Sennett's office. She was there an hour or more. The shooting had to be suspended. The crew were philosophical as they smoked their cigarettes. They said you couldn't hold a protest meeting every time the studio boss felt horny.

There was a false assumption here. It was evident in Mabel's eyes when she returned. They were red-lidded. Tears were running from them, washing the black liner down her cheeks. She announced to everyone, 'That man is impossible. I'm sorry everyone. For God's sake let's get back to work.'

Roscoe Arbuckle asked her what was wrong. He put his arm around her shoulders and walked her quietly away across the lot.

'That's the sweetest-natured guy in movies,' the senior propman commented to me. 'He'll calm her down, poor kid.'

'What do you suppose upset her?'

'Lovers' tiff. Wouldn't be the first time. She idolises Mack. Aims to marry him.'

'So she told me.'

'Can't see it happening myself.'

'A case of unrequited love?'

The senior propman gave me a speculative look. 'You're new around here, aren't you?'

'My first week at the studio.'

'Thought I didn't recognise you. Mabel has been starry-eyed about the boss since she was a kid at Biograph. He directed her first movies. She came to Keystone with him. It was his idea to put her in a bathing suit for *The Water Nymph*. The first Keystone release. Mack Sennett is no fool. He knew how Mabel looked out of her clothes. He was on a winner.'

'I see — I think I see. Love overcame discretion.'

'I know who you are! You do titles.'

'Titles?'

' "Meanwhile in the old barn . . ." '

'Ah — I understand. No, that is not my forte. I am on the acting strength. So you think Mr Sennett is not ready for marriage?'

'Mack a married man? I don't see it. Sure, they keep naming the day, but that keeps Mabel quiet. She's great box office. He doesn't want to lose her. There's a hundred grand net profit on each two-reeler Mabel makes. Why should he get hitched? He has women beating on his door begging to be billed in movies. He's doing fine.'

'I presume he has a conscience.'

The propman shook his head, then nudged me with an elbow. 'He had a Constance, if I remember right.'

I didn't think it funny. 'So Miss Normand is deceived?'

The propman stared at me. 'How did you get here, buster — on the *Mayflower*?'

I walked away.

Presently Roscoe Arbuckle returned with Mabel clinging to his arm. He signalled to the make-up girl. The crew and actors prepared to start again. No more was said about the interruption. Mabel was popular. Real sympathy surrounded and encouraged her. She was quiet between takes, but she managed to perform with spirit for the camera. Not once did she glance towards the tower, where a brooding figure stood and watched.

On Friday evening a new notice appeared on the studio bulletin board: the cast-lists for the following week's productions. The eager and anxious studio employees crowded in front of it. Information was relayed to those unable to get near enough to see.

'Mack Swain is back with Chester. Roscoe again! He works so hard he's losing weight.'

'The Cops are still in business. Shall I call them over?

Booker, Chase, Conklin, Hayes, Keystone — who the heck is Keystone?'

'What was that?' I asked. 'Did someone mention me?'

'If your name's Keystone, pal, looks like you got your Cop badge. Are you insured?'

'Hey,' said someone, 'Mabel isn't listed.'

'What do you mean? She's got to be there somewhere.'

'Okay, wise guy. Where?'

'He wouldn't axe Mabel. Who has he got for leading ladies, then? Mae, Minta. Who's this, for God's sake — A. Honeybee?'

'That must be Amber. Blonde, pretty, plenty of pep. You sure about that? Amber never had a billing before. She's just a walk-on.'

'Not any more. She's right up there with Roscoe and the Cops.'

'Is that a fact?' said Roscoe Arbuckle from the rear. 'It's news to me. Who is Amber Honeybee?'

FIVE

'Keep it clean,' said Winnie as she handed me my uniform. 'Which company did they put you in?'

'Number Three. *Kidnap in the Park*.'

'Lousy title. Who's in it?'

'Roscoe Arbuckle, Mack Swain.' I paused. 'And Amber Honeybee.'

She grinned good-naturedly. 'Keystone, you're just a little new on the scene to make a monkey out of Winnie Armstrong.'

I said solemnly, 'Madam, when I make a statement it is true.'

Winnie searched my face as thoroughly as if it were a costume I had worn. 'I believe you really mean it. No, it can't be true! Amber in a leading role? The boss is really off his trolley this time. Who's directing this benighted show?'

'Mr Murray Brennan.'

'That figures. Murray is so nice they unload all the junk on him.'

'What do you mean by that? This is my first performance too, you know.'

'Better not be late, then, sweetheart.'

On the second floor of the players' building was the main dressing room. I found it full of half-dressed Keystone Cops.

'Here he is,' announced one withered in appearance, in nothing but an undershift reaching almost to his knees. 'You must be Keystone.'

'That's correct. Good morning, gentlemen.'

32

The veteran glanced around the room. 'You mean that lot?' He held out a bony hand. 'Welcome to the fun factory, Keystone. I'm Frank Hayes, excused dangerous stunts on account of my age.'

Another Cop stepped forward. 'Harry Booker. With me, it's the back.'

'Edgar Kennedy. The right leg.'

'Charlie Chase. The left.'

'Chester Conklin. Feet.'

'Slim Summerville. The nervous system.'

They roared with laughter.

'Great to have a fit man on the force,' said Hayes, clapping me on the back.

I crashed forward and hit the floor like an axed tree.

'Geronimo!' peeped Hayes. 'What did I do?'

'Out like a light,' I heard one of them say. 'Better get some water.'

As they crowded round, I rolled over and sat up. 'In my case,' I said calmly, 'it's shock.' I got up easily and hung up my uniform.

'Boy, oh boy!' said Hayes. 'That was sharp. In thirty years of vaudeville I never saw a front fall as sweet as that. Keystone, welcome to the Cops.'

I thanked him. I was still not fully reconciled to joining them, but they were a friendly bunch and I had no reason to unload my discontent on them.

While I changed, I tried to learn some names. Slim Summerville was easy — a lamp-post of a man whose clothes threatened to slide off him. Slim's comic foil was Chester Conklin, five foot in his shoes, with eyes like ping-pong balls and a droopy false moustache. I had seen them often on the screen. Frank Hayes, too, was one of the longer-serving Cops, and by the look of him he had served a long time somewhere else before he joined them. He must have been well past sixty, skinny, pink-faced and

33

acutely proud of the peaked cap that made him senior man.

We moved off together and assembled on the largest outdoor stage. Our director was already there in conversation with the cameraman, Jake Harper.

'Come on,' said Hayes. 'He'd like to meet you.'

So I was introduced to Murray Brennan. He shook my hand with a firm no-nonsense grip. 'How are you? Your first picture? I can promise you some laughs. Nice to meet you, Keystone.'

Our conversation had to end there. I liked his voice, redolent of Ireland and draught Guinness in comfortable pubs. His shape was keglike, too. That hadn't stopped him from dressing as a film director should. Boots and jodphurs, white shirt, red bowtie, black and white check cap. Between the bowtie and the cap was a pudgy freckled face with blue eyes magnified by pebble glasses.

By the time I rejoined the Cops, Brennan was standing on a chair addressing us through a megaphone. He began with introductions. 'Amber Honeybee's pretty face', he told us, 'is well known around the studios, and her name will soon be equally familiar, as Roscoe Arbuckle's newest leading lady. There they are together, folks.'

We all looked to where Arbuckle stood with Amber, who was in a maid's blue and white costume. They both smiled and Amber gave a modest wave.

The next to be introduced was an infant boy called Arnold, who at two years old, Brennan told us, was already a veteran of three motion pictures. Arnold's mother held him high. Arnold sucked his thumb and looked malevolent.

'Finally,' said Brennan, 'there's a new officer on the roll of the Keystone Cops. I'm not kidding when I say his name is Keystone. Would you stand up, Keystone?'

Behind me Charlie Conklin said, 'Hold on to him, fellas

— don't want him to fall.'

While they laughed, I rose and touched my helmet.

'Thank you,' said Brennan. 'Sounds like the Cops have already taken you in hand, Keystone. Now let's talk about the movie. It's a simple kidnap story with the usual chase. Amber plays a nursemaid. Her employer sends her to the park with baby Arnold. There, Amber is distracted by a fat guy fooling with the ducks. No prize for guessing who plays him. While this is going on, the heavy — that's Mack Swain, of course — steals the kid. Fatty pursues him in his old tin lizzie while Amber calls the Cops. Naturally, when they come on the scene, they arrest the wrong guy. The heavy makes off in Fatty's automobile with Amber and the baby. The cops take up the chase, with predictable confusion. But Amber is not so loopy as the lawmen. She has left a trail by unravelling the wool from baby Arnold's clothes. The story reaches its spectacular conclusion in the villain's hideout. He has bound and gagged poor Amber.' Here Brennan paused.

The company obliged with a shout of, 'Ooh!'

'And the baby has no clothes left.'

'Aah!'

'But when the Cops arrive, he takes baby on the roof.'

'Ooh!'

'You've got the drift, boys and girls. We shoot interiors today, tomorrow morning. In the afternoon, we're on location in the park. Wednesday, on the roof of a house on Allesandro Street. Thursday is reserved to re-shoot anything we don't like in the rushes. Friday is the chase.'

Slim Summerville explained to me, 'It's studio policy to shoot the chase on the last day.'

'Why is that?'

He mimed a man on crutches. 'So they don't have to re-cast the movie.'

I grinned, but I was fairly certain he was serious.

KEYSTONE

'We won't be wanted for a couple of hours,' Chester Conklin told me. 'Care for a game of poker with the boys?'

'Thank you, but I don't altogether care for gambling.'

Summerville smiled. 'You picked the wrong job, Keystone. See you later.'

I watched the rehearsals for the opening scene. The set was the interior of a handsome drawing room. The lady of the house was played by Alice Davenport, an actress of dowager appearance. The script required that she should be exasperated by little Arnold's tantrums. The child filled his role impeccably, seated in the middle of the set, punishing a rubber duck by beating it repeatedly against the floor and finally hurling it at Alice Davenport. She pulled a bell-rope.

Amber made her entrance. She sailed in like Bernhardt as Cleopatra.

'Stop there a moment, ladies,' Brennan told them. 'Amber, my dear, I love the costume. Could you also convey your servant status through your movement?'

'You want me to curtsey?'

'No, my dear, just play it with a little more restraint. Let's try it again from when Alice rings the bell.'

Alice rang the bell eleven times before Amber succeeded in toning down her entrance to a passable imitation of a nursemaid.

'Fine,' said Brennan patiently. 'We'll move on. Alice, would you give the maid her orders, please? Move upstage a fraction, Amber. We want to see the child as well.'

After they had rehearsed it once, he said, 'I liked it, Alice. Amber, my dear, it would carry more conviction if you looked at Alice while she spoke to you.'

'Don't you want to show my face from different angles?' Amber asked.

'That's not the point, my dear.'

'I don't like to contradict you, but it is. If you only show my left profile, the audience will get the wrong idea.'

'And what's that, Amber?'

'They'll think I'm just the servant.'

Brennan glanced at his script. 'That's what you are, my dear.'

'Mr Brennan, there's something I'd like to clarify right now. Am I the leading lady in this movie?'

'That is my understanding.'

'In that case, will you kindly allow me to make contact with my public?'

'What do you mean, exactly?'

'This is my debut as a leading player. I intend to be noticed from the start.'

'You're telling us!' murmured Alice Davenport.

'Did you say something?' demanded Amber.

'Ladies, let's take a break at this point,' Brennan said rapidly. 'Would someone remove this child, so we can hear ourselves?' He stepped forward for some private conversation with his cast.

The cameraman, Jake Harper, commented to me, 'Relax. At this rate, you won't be working at all today. Maybe I won't either.'

'The matter seems a crucial one,' I said. 'Perhaps a few minutes now to reach an understanding will save hours of discussion later.'

Harper jerked his head aside and spat on the ground. 'He'd damn soon reach an understanding with that one with the end of a strap.'

'You're speaking figuratively, I presume?'

'Presume anything you like, pal.'

It presently grew obvious that Murray Brennan was coming under stress. He produced a spotted handkerchief and held it to his forehead. He asked repeatedly for water. Scene One had looked straightforward in the script, but it was turning out to be a minefield. Amber was determined to dominate the stage, whatever direction or advice he gave her. The rehearsals mounted up. Little Arnold grew more fractious than the script required. Alice Davenport announced that she was wanted on another stage. She had been scheduled for one scene only, and it ought to have been shot inside an hour. Brennan did his best to pacify her. He had someone fetch an icecream for the child. By lunch the scene was still not ready for the camera.

When we returned from lunch, Alice Davenport was missing. She arrived ten minutes late, with Mack Sennett at her side. They spoke to Brennan. There were histrionic gestures from Miss Davenport. Brennan took off his cap and rotated it in his hands. Sennett swayed and growled. On the set, Amber passed the time playing peek-a-boo with little Arnold.

The consultation ended. Brennan put the megaphone to his mouth. 'Prepare to shoot Scene One. Take your positions, please.'

Jake Harper said in disbelief, 'You want me to crank it like it is?'

'That's what I said.'

Harper shrugged and got behind his camera.

Sennett stood back to watch. He hunched his shoulders and let his head jut forward, like Hackenschmidt the wrestler. No-one went near him.

'Action! Camera!' called Brennan, then, 'Hold it! Something's wrong.'

There was a paralysing moment when everyone believed that our director's nerve had snapped.

'The duck!' he said. 'The kid hasn't got his rubber duck.'

The tension eased, but only briefly. An embarrassed search was mounted for the toy. Everyone but Sennett joined in. He watched without a flicker of amusement. I made a private note that there were things at Keystone that were comical and there were things that were not. It was wise to know the difference.

After five minutes, one of the crew was despatched to the Edendale General Stores to buy a replacement duck. Morale was sinking. Suspicions of a wrecker in the company could not be discounted.

When it was finally shot, the scene did little credit to the morning's work. Amber appeared to ignore or forget all that had been agonised over in rehearsal. She reverted to her Cleopatra entrance. She simpered at the camera. When the moment came for her to lift up Arnold, she held him with his back to the camera. As she exited, she bounced the child against the door, through trying to keep her face in shot.

'Cut,' said Brennan in a voice of deep despair. He turned towards Sennett with his hands outspread.

Sennett said, 'Print it.' His blank face dared anyone to challenge him. He ambled off towards the tower.

'That's all I wanted to hear,' said Alice Davenport. 'Nothing personal, Murray. 'Bye, everyone.'

The order was given to strike the set. While the propmen worked, disbelieving actors and camera crew debated whether Sennett's mind had wandered while the scene was played. He usually demanded something near perfection. The scene had been a travesty. A theory was advanced that he would cut it from the picture, that Alice Davenport had convinced him it would never work.

Looking as fragile as a fat man can, Brennan called his company together. The new set was the villain's hideout.

'The chase is over at this time,' he told them. 'The kidnapper has brought the nursemaid and the child to this house. The scene requires that Amber is upstairs, bound hand and foot, and gagged.'

'Should help a little,' Jake Harper commented to me.

KEYSTONE

As it emerged, there were no serious problems. Mack Swain, a Falstaffian figure with an exaggerated black moustache, played his customary role as heavy. He worked well with Arnold. He improvised a comedy routine by trying to snatch the duck away from the child, to send it with the ransom note. Arnold would not be parted from it. He kept hold of his duck and grabbed the note, tearing it to pieces. He tweaked Mack Swain's moustache. The fight between the big man and the kid brought peals of laughter from everyone around the stage. Brennan had sensibly told Harper to crank it from the start, so it was filmed first time.

The next sequence featured the Keystone Cops. We were supposed to strike terror into Swain by running past the window.

'Do we have the Cops?' asked Brennan without much confidence.

'Just one, apparently,' said his assistant.

Everyone looked to me for an explanation.

'The thought occurs to me,' I improvised, 'that it might be comical to show a single helmet move stealthily past the window at the level of the sill. We could repeat it several times.'

'Say, that's not bad,' said Swain. 'I could do something with it.'

'Let's try it, then,' Brennan said and added wearily. 'Who wants to break up the studio poker school just to shoot a motion picture?'

So I went behind the scenery and practised creeping past the window, crawling back unseen, and repeating the manoeuvre. Mack Swain soon developed a routine. The first time, he scarcely moved an eye to register that the helmet had moved across. At the second sighting, he twitched his head like a chicken. At the third, he turned it slowly, following the movement. He then dived under the

40

kitchen table.

We tried variations. Once I passed the window in the reverse direction. another time I turned my head to look inside.

'Shoot everything,' Brennan told his cameraman. 'We can tidy up this scene in the cutting room.'

By the finish, most of the absent Cops had returned to the stage. They joined in the laughter at my capers and Swain's reactions. 'You guys can thank Keystone for letting you off the hook,' Brennan lectured them when it was over. 'Next time any of you goes missing, I'll have the boss show you the gate.'

No-one believed him. He was too soft-hearted.

When I left the players' building at the end of the day, Mack Swain stepped in beside me.

'Just out of interest,' he said, 'You knew that window routine would get some laughs, didn't you? It was in your mind before I said a thing.'

'Is that of any consequence?' I said.

'There are guys with burlesque in the blood. Not many.'

'I'm glad to hear it. It sounds distressing.'

Swain smiled. 'Don't deny it, Keystone — you're a natural clown. Why don't you speak to Sennett, see if you can get a character part? You're going to be wasted in the Cops.'

I tried to look surprised.

SIX

'Isn't anyone going to untie Miss Honeybee?' I asked.

Amber was lying on the bed with her wrists lashed to the posts and her legs pinioned by a belt. A silk scarf was tied across her mouth. A three-handed poker game was in progress at the opposite end of the bed. The remaining Cops were lounging and talking baseball.

As no-one appeared to be interested, I repeated the question.

'Can't do that,' said Frank Hayes. 'Murray wants another take. Care for a peppermint?'

'For Heaven's sake,' I said, 'she's trying to ask us something.'

Hayes turned to look at her. 'Sorry, Amber. These are extra strong, sweetheart. Definitely not with a gag across your mouth.'

Brennan came over to us. I thought he was concerned about Amber, but he simply wanted another take. 'One more time, my darling,' he told Amber.

'Come on, guys,' said Hayes.

I looked at Amber. The urgency had gone from the green eyes. They had a glazed appearance, as if reconciled to what was happening. I shrugged to register futility and she returned a nod. I joined the others off the set.

This time we got it right. Nightsticks in hand, we tumbled through the door and started a frantic search for Mack Swain and little Arnold. The point of the sequence was that in spite of opening the wardrobe, searching on top and behind, rolling back the carpet, peering under the bed and climbing over it to look out of the window, not

42

one of us noticed Amber. We all ran out and slammed the door. but it opened again and one Cop came back. He was Slim Summerville. He stood in front of the mirror and straightened his helmet. Then he ran out again.

'Cut,' ordered Brennan. 'That's good enough for me, boys. Nice to be back on schedule. Get some lunch now. This afternoon is free for you. I want to shoot the park scene. That's just Mack, Amber, baby Arnold and a couple of extras. No Cops.'

'And tomorrow we do the rooftop sequence?' said Hayes.

'Allesandro Street. Which of you can walk on stilts?'

There was hesitation, then Slim Summerville said, 'I have this irrational fear of heights.'

Hayes said, 'My knee joints ain't so good these days.'

Brennan's eyes narrowed. He was smiling and it pushed his cheeks upwards. 'Don't feed me that old corn. Listen, guys, this is a damn good stunt. The Cops place a ladder against the side of the house and start climbing to the roof to save the kid, but the rungs are rotten. Three of the cops do pratfalls, and one is left up there. Then the sides of the ladder start to separate. Get it? He keeps his footing on a couple of stumps, and, what do you know, he's walking on stilts. Terrific gag — who's doing it?'

To a man, the Cops turned and looked at me.

'What do you say, Keystone?' asked Brennan.

I glanced towards Amber. 'I say it's insensitive in the extreme to keep Miss Honeybee shackled to this bed while we discuss tomorrow's stunts.'

'Christ, she went clean out of my mind!' said Brennan, genuinely perturbed. 'Amber, honey, how could I do this to you? Quick, you guys, untie the lady.'

The Cops did as they were asked. Brennan helped. By tacit agreement it was left to him to loosen Amber's gag. Shaking his head and babbling apologies, he fumbled with

43

the knotted scarf until it fell away.

Instead of the howls of execration everyone expected, all that Amber said was, 'May I have a drink of water?'

'Water for Miss Honeybee!' commanded Brennan with the force of a man astonished to have recovered the initiative. 'See it has ice in it. You wouldn't like something stronger, Amber? Gee, your poor wrists!' He took one of her arms and massaged it with his fingertips. 'You must let me take you to lunch. My wife is coming in. I know she'd love to meet you.'

'That's kind,' said Amber with a tone of voice suggesting she was about to add something else. She turned her eyes in my direction. 'Could Keystone join us, please?'

'Sure,' said Brennan. 'Anything you want, my dear.'

This caught me by surprise. Even in America I wasn't used to luncheon invitations from attractive actresses I scarcely knew.

'Thank you,' I said. 'I'm honoured.'

I don't mind admitting I was intrigued as well. The first time we had met she was simply someone who had helped me find my way. Americans were like that, women as well as men. Only this was more positive than help. Amber had made it obvious that she desired my company.

My senses quickened. I was suddenly, acutely, absorbedly aware of her. Her neck. The exposed part where her ringlets had been lifted and fitted under the nursemaid's cap. Wayward hairs so fine that they stirred each time she moved. So blonde that it took the sunlight to discover them.

'Easy, Keystone,' said Frank Hayes. 'Even your buttons are steaming over.'

We were given a table at the smart end of the studio restaurant. Amber and I were introduced to Murray Brennan's wife. Louise was younger than her husband, about thirty-five. A pale, long, well-powdered face under a large lilac-coloured hat. Beryl-blue eyes that hardly blinked at all. Light brown hair in artificial curls. A parasol to match the hat. Pastel pink gown and gloves.

Murray told her, 'Amber is our newest leading lady and Keystone is our newest Cop. Aren't you pleased to meet them?'

'If it means we are spared the company of a certain uncouth individual, I'm more than pleased,' Louise said, turning her eyes to another table where Mack Sennett was holding court.

'Careful dear,' Murray cautioned her. 'He may shout a lot, but he isn't deaf, you know.' He signalled to a waitress. 'We'd better order — I don't have too much time.'

'That's nothing new,' said Louise. 'I'll have the fish, and ask them not to smother it with sauce.' She turned to to Amber. 'I home you aren't compelled to work the appalling hours my husband does.'

'It doesn't worry me,' said Amber. 'I don't think of it as work.'

'I expect you're very good at it. Are you?'

Murray interjected, 'Amber and Keystone, I'm going to have the T-bone. How about joining me?' When the order had been placed, he said, 'Something I meant to ask you, Amber. I don't think you're from California, are you?'

'Boston, Massachusetts. My father is a publisher.'

Louise smiled approvingly. 'Ah, I thought I recognised the name.'

Murray asked, 'And how will your Papa like having a famous movie actress for a daughter?' He beamed at Amber.

Louise gave him a sharp look.

Amber said solemnly, 'Actually, he won't be very pleased about it.'

'That's too bad. Has he seen you in a picture?'

She shook her head. 'Father doesn't care for comedies.'

Louise said, 'I expect he prefers something of more substance. So do I.'

'Me, too,' said Murray. 'But a job is a job.'

'Murray ought to be making serious motion pictures, not slapstick,' Louise went on. 'What do you think, Mr Keystone? I guess it's no use asking a Keystone Cop to take my side.'

'Only a very new one, ma'am,' I said. 'I think comedy — or rather the playing of comedy — is a serious business. It's certainly serious to a performer if he isn't getting laughs. I suppose we're all obliged to use whatever talents we are born with. If it happens to be comedy . . .' I gave a shrug.

'I can't agree with that,' said Louise. 'Goodness, if Murray thought like that, he'd never have become a director. You can't possibly know all the talents you possess.'

'Some of them take a long time and plenty of hard work to develop, dear,' said Murray. 'That's specially true of comedy. I mean performing, not directing. Just because I'm a walking history of the motion picture business, it doesn't mean everyone wants to be.'

'How did you start?' I asked him, spotting a smoother avenue of conversation.

'With a bang. San Francisco. August, 1906.'

'The earthquake?' said Amber.

Murray nodded. 'I didn't fancy sorting out the good stock from the damaged in my father's drugstore, so I cleared the place, rented fifty chairs from the funeral parlour across the street, and opened a nickelodeon. Sure was the right time to be in moving pictures.'

Louise said, 'One year later, he had three more nickelodeons in the city, and he married me.'

'I couldn't go wrong,' said Murray, smiling at her with genuine affection. 'Louise was even smarter, though. She could see more profit in running the film exchange that

46

supplied the movies to us, and as Los Angeles is the market-place for motion pictures, we moved down here. I made some bucks, but that was a cut-throat business. Gee, the tricks those creeps would pull if I didn't watch them — duping, bicycling — '

'What's that?' Amber asked.

'Bicycling? I rent a film for showing at a nickelodeon, okay? The manager is a wise guy. He sub-rents it to the nickelodeon two blocks away and hires a boy on a bicycle. The film is bicycled all day between the two theatres. And I only get one fee. Well, I could live with small-time sharks, but the joy went out of the exchange business when the companies started to combine and swallow up the independents. I happened to know Tom Ince and he suggested I go into the production side. He got me into Keystone.'

'As a start,' emphasised Louise.

'To learn the business,' added Murray.

'Two years ago,' said Louise.

'Is it as long as that?' said Murray.

Louise ignored him, turned to Amber and said, 'We have two lovely daughters aged five and six. The elder is called after my first name, Louise, and May was my family name. I want the very best for them.'

'Naturally,' said Amber.

The food arrived and the conversation moved on to pictures that had impressed us. Murray was rapturous about *The Birth of a Nation*, but neither Amber nor I had seen it, and Louise preferred costume dramas such as *Ivanhoe*. Amber confided that her ambition was to appear in a serious historical role. I noticed Murray's eyes widen, but he said nothing when Louise announced that she was sure Amber would go on to play all the great romantic roles.

I, too, reserved my opinion about Amber's professional future. I was busy speculating on a possible romantic role in modern dress, and — let's be truthful — out of it. I can't remember contributing much intelligent conversation.

When the waitress came to take the order for desserts, Murray looked at his watch and asked us to excuse him. He had to discuss the next day's shooting schedule with the office. He told us not to hurry. There was plenty of time before Amber would be needed in the park.

Louise announced that she, too, had an early afternoon appointment, but she would look forward to meeting us again. I got to my feet so smartly that I had to steady the table.

I was alone with Amber. A pulse was jabbing in my head. My mouth was dry. In seven years of music hall and vaudeville I was not without experience of girls. Any man who has stood backstage crushed among dancers dressed in little more than fleshings — and got accustomed to it — has the right to feel surprised by a physical response to an actress dressed in the uniform of a nursemaid. Amber excited me like no girl I remembered.

We ordered coffee.

She said, 'I want to thank you for being so concerned about me this morning.'

'Don't mention it. I should be thanking you, not only for including me in the luncheon party, but for taking Murray Brennan's mind off the potentially painful matter of who is to walk on stilts tomorrow.'

She smiled as she remembered. 'Could you do it if you have to?'

'As it happens, yes, but I would rather not.'

'Because it's dangerous?'

'Because it displays a want of tact. I've had a bigger share of the spotlight than is judicious for a new recruit. I could easily antagonise the other Cops.'

Amber shook her head. 'They don't want to do it.

They're a frightened bunch of guys.'

I disagreed. 'I think that's just their style of humour.'

'It isn't, Keystone.'

I guessed what was in her mind. 'You're referring to the accident in the amusement park.'

She nodded gravely. 'But I don't want to talk about it. I get bad dreams still.'

I stared into my coffee. 'Well, let's forget the accident. Did you know the man?'

'Just a little. His name was Sandy Sullivan. He came from up the coast. They always pick the newest Cop to do the really dangerous stunts, like jumping off a moving locomotive or running into a blazing building. The other Cops were happy to let Sandy have the spotlight, as you put it. Most of them have families. He didn't.' She leaned back in her chair and added casually, 'How about you?'

'What about me precisely?'

'Do you have a family?'

'A mother and father in England, if that is what you mean.'

'No wife and children?'

'No wife and no children.' On an afterthought I added, 'Is that dangerous here?'

Amber gave a shrug. 'Like I said, Sandy Sullivan was alone in the world. No-one outside the studio came to the funeral. Mr Sennett fixed it all and paid the check.'

'I should think that was the least he could have done. I presume he was responsible for the stunt?'

She nodded. 'He and his writers, I guess.' She glanced towards the clock. 'Keystone, I've got to dash now. It's my big scene in Griffith Park this afternoon and I don't mean to be late, whatever Murray says.'

I got up to pull back her chair. 'May I drive you there?'

Her eyes shone. 'Would you? I'd love to ride in your automobile. And you could watch me play my scene. I'm sure I'll do it better if you're watching. I get the feeling not everyone in the company is so sympathetic.'

I said, 'I expect they're just a little envious. Don't let them undermine your confidence.'

SEVEN

From the way she performed in Griffith Park that afternoon, Amber's confidence remained rock solid. It was the confidence of everyone around her that crumbled.

The scenario was simple. Amber, as the nursemaid, was to bring Arnold in his baby carriage to a bench beside the lake. Unnoticed by her, Mack Swain, the heavy, was to follow them, darting from tree to tree. At the bench, Amber would stop to rest. She would catch sight of Roscoe Arbuckle, in his character of Fatty, among the ducks down by the lake. He would be making faces and mimicking them. She would rock with laughter at his antics. Fatty would notice and play up some more. Flirtatious looks would pass between them. Meanwhile, the villainous Mack Swain would hook his walking stick over the handle of the baby carriage and pull it smoothly out of sight. Panic would then follow when Amber discovered it was gone. Then she would spot it running down the slope towards the lake. She would wave and scream to Fatty, who would make a dramatic sprint and catch it at the water's edge. Proudly, he would trundle it back to her, only to discover it was empty, except for a note saying *Ransom $100 or Else* . . .

They started to rehearse.

'Cut,' called Murray. 'Amber, my darling, when you get to the bench there's no need to consult the fates about whether to sit down or not. It's no big deal to take a rest on a park bench.'

'Don't you like the way I play it?' said Amber tonelessly.

'Sure, honey. It's just that we don't need the hesitation there and the hand on the side of your face and the movement of the eyes. Couldn't you just arrive at the bench and sit down?'

'I happen to think that it's a dramatic moment.'

'Deciding to sit on a park bench?'

'If I didn't sit down, the baby would not be kidnapped.'

There was a pause. 'That's true,' said Murray in a voice that was trying to be generous. 'Yes, I see what you are driving at, but would you try it my way, honey?'

'Would you quit calling me honey? I don't like it.'

Murray turned pink. 'Sorry. Let's move on, kids. We'll pick it up from the moment after Amber has sat down.'

The action switched to the edge of the lake where about fifty ducks and waterfowl had been recruited as extras with a breadcrumb bribe. Arbuckle in the character of Fatty gambolled among them, belying his 270 pounds, extemporising duck behaviour that convulsed the crew and underscored his reputation as the funniest fat man in the world. He worked up a rivalry for a piece of bread with one belligerent old mallard that finally chased him out of shot in precisely the direction he had planned, so that the back view of his duck waddle seemed to be mimicked by the bird.

'The only actor in the business who can steal a scene from an animal,' Mack Swain remarked to me. 'The guy should be in front of the camera all the time.'

'Where did he learn to be so funny?'

'Search me. His childhood was no joke — real poverty and regular thrashings from his father.'

I nodded. 'Actually one of the surest recipes for success.'

'I don't follow you.'

'Practically all the great comedians from Dan Leno to Charlie Chaplin suffered appallingly as children.'

'Is that a fact?' He looked confused.

'There is a connection,' I pointed out. 'The art of slap-stick is taking punishment with style.'

He frowned and considered what I had said. 'Now you mention it, I took some beltings as a kid. How about you?'

'I have to thank my English public school for making me a comedian.'

'Plenty of beatings, huh?'

'In abundance. But here I am at Keystone, so it was all to my advantage, as they never failed to reassure me.'

Mack Swain grinned at me. 'I guess that wasn't how it struck you at the time.'

The activity at the water's edge finished. Murray Brennan and his crew moved up the slope towards the park bench to rehearse Amber's reactions to what had just been going on. Amber waved to us as she passed.

'She a friend of yours?' asked Swain with an ominous note in his voice.

I was cautious. 'That would be putting it too strongly. We've exchanged a few words and I gave her a lift in my motor car. I'd call it an acquaintanceship.'

'Keep it that way.'

I stared at Swain for a moment. 'Why do you say that?'

'Another great truth about comedy. When you make it to Keystone, don't fool around with Sennett's latest.'

'Amber? I thought Mr Sennett was engaged to be married to Mabel Normand.'

'So did Mabel. Have you seen her around the studio this week?'

'No — but surely that is not surprising when she has no part in a production.'

'Have you asked yourself why? Haven't you noticed that your acquaintance Amber is just a little short on talent — as an actress, I mean — to be offered a leading role? How do you think she got to be playing opposite Roscoe?'

'I haven't given it a thought.'

'Maybe you should, Keystone.'

'I can't believe Mr Sennett would set his reputation as a film producer at risk for the friendship of a pretty woman.'

'No?' Mack Swain turned his head.

I followed his gaze to the park bench where Murray was trying to coax some semblance of real laughter from Amber. There was no denying it. Her performance was lamentable. She was failing to deliver anything more spirited than a Mona Lisa smile.

'I got nothing against Amber,' said Swain, 'except she can't act to save her life. She's like a piece of Chippendale, elegant and wooden. I say bring back Mabel Normand.'

My eyes were still on the rehearsal. 'They appear to be looking for someone.'

'Jeez, it's me! I should be in this scene.' Swain ran over to them, blurted an apology to Murray, and ducked behind the bush where he was supposed to be in hiding.

They resumed. Swain used his walking stick to hook the baby carriage away while Amber exchanged flirtatious looks with Fatty Arbuckle. Like the laughter, the flirtatious looks proved difficult. Amber overplayed them. As Murray patiently explained, he wanted coyness from her, the shy glance and the quick, self-conscious smile. They tried it many times. At one point he asked her to get it into her head that she was a nursemaid. He almost added, '. . . not a whore.' The word was forming on his lips. Amber glared at him. He managed not to say it.

Time was running out. At this rate, they would still be in rehearsal when they lost the sunlight. More from exigency than satisfaction, they moved on to the next phase. Amber was to notice that the baby carriage had gone. She was to panic.

She succeeded in standing up and clapping her hand to her forehead, but otherwise she was about as panic-stricken as a polar bear in snow.

They sent the baby carriage rolling down the slope towards the lake. Amber performed ballet movements with her arms.

'We'll have to crank that as a long shot,' Murray told Jake Harper.

'Why stop at that?' enquired the cameraman.

'Quit it,' snapped Murray. 'You're not the comic here.'

Murray needed to assert some authority. It was showing less and less. He let the rehearsal limp its course without another interruption, then ordered an immediate take. It was as if he had decided to cut his losses and finish the movie as soon as possible.

They took the shot of Amber walking the baby carriage through the park. She stopped beside the bench and started to glance towards the camera.

'Sit down!' bellowed Murray.

Amber was so surprised that she obeyed.

'Did you get that?' Murray asked Jake Harper.

'You didn't have to shout,' protested Amber. 'You ruined my performance. I'd like to do another take.'

Murray had gone to speak to Harper. He turned his head and said, 'No need. He got it. Mack, would you remove the baby carriage?'

'Did you hear me, Murray?' said Amber. 'I want to do the shot again.'

'Okay, fellers?' said Murray, ignoring her. 'Let's go see the ducks.' Megaphone in hand, he set off towards the lake.

'Come back!' called Amber. 'I demand another take.'

Other people had started following Murray down the slope.

'Please, Murray! Just once more.'

Murray stopped, half-turned, stared at Amber and said, 'Dry up.'

'You brute! You fat, insensitive brute! Why are you doing this to me? You hate me, don't you?'

He strolled on, nearly out of earshot.

'Murray, I didn't mean that. *Please*!'

He had almost reached the lake. The ducks were scrambling up the bank to meet him.

Amber was in tears. 'I hate him!' She turned and saw the cameraman still cranking. 'What are you doing?'

'Murray's orders,' said Harper indifferently.

'Cut!' shouted Murray through his megaphone. 'Did you get that, Jake?' He started walking back again.

'What's going on?' screamed Amber. 'You had no right to film me then.'

'Orders,' repeated Harper.

Breathing heavily, Murray came back. 'Amber, you just gave us our panic sequence. Beautiful.'

'You tricked me, you skunk! I was upset. What could I have looked like?'

Murray grinned contentedly. 'Like I wanted you to look, like a wonderful actress, like a nurse should look when a baby is snatched away from her. Don't be upset, my dear. When you see the rushes, you'll be proud of it, I promise you.'

'It was a dirty, underhand trick.'

'Sure,' said Murray affably. 'And I apologise. Take a rest now. I really mean to film the ducks this time.'

'I feel sick. I'm going home.'

'As you wish, darling. We can shoot the rest tomorrow.'

'Don't count on it, Murray.' Amber looked around and her eyes lighted on me. 'Keystone, would you drive me home, please?'

EIGHT

Amber said, 'You're a gentleman.' Then she was silent. We both had to change our clothes, so I drove her to the studio. While I was waiting in the entrance of the players' building, Chester Conklin happened to come out.

'Care for a beer?'

'Thank you, but I'm waiting for a lady.'

'Nice work. Anyone I know?'

'Miss Honeybee. She felt unwell in Griffith Park, so I agreed to drive her home.'

'Amber?' Conklin grinned. 'Don't get ideas, Keystone.'

'Ideas?'

'You'll find out.'

I watched him go. I remembered what Mack Swain had said. Everyone seemed to be in awe of Sennett. I was not convinced that Amber had got her leading role by making up to Sennett. It was all too cynical.

Just the same, I would be a fool to ignore them altogether.

Amber appeared again, wearing a pongee duster and a wide-brimmed straw hat. She was carrying a bulging carpet bag. I took it from her. She smiled her thanks. She seemed to have shed her anger with her studio costume. She had lined her eyes and put on lip rouge far more subtle than the greasepaint. She said without preamble, 'Where shall we go first?'

I blinked, frowned and smiled in rapid sequence.

'You have the advantage of me. I'm a stranger to Los Angeles.'

She giggled. 'Who would have guessed? Come on, let's

take a look at the ocean.'

We drove through Beverly Hills to Santa Monica. The breeze gusted around the windshield. Amber grasped her hat with both hands and gave delighted cries.

'That's Inceville.'

I stopped the car. Below the road along the beachfront, intersecting streets of dummy houses made of scaffolding and plywood formed a whole movie village. Miners' shacks and western-style saloons shared the site with gothic gingerbread and an English Castle. A brigantine was anchored in the bay.

'Mr Ince makes costume movies five and six reels long,' said Amber wistfully. 'Real movies, not stupid slapstick. I'm going to be his leading actress.'

'Is he aware of this?'

'Not yet. First he has to see me on the screen. He part-owns the Keystone Company. Would you like to walk along the beach?'

As soon as we reached the sand, she put a hand on my shoulder and drew off her shoes and stockings. I politely took an interest in some seagulls.

'Aren't you going to take off yours?' she asked me.

'It wasn't my intention.'

'You'll spoil your shoes.'

'I could try walking on my hands.'

She took me at my word. 'I'll turn a cartwheel if you can.'

'Really?' Without another thought, I dipped and up-ended myself. My back arched gently and I balanced there on my hands. Then I circled her.

She clapped her hands. 'I don't believe it! Beautiful! Here I go, then!' In a flurry of white lace and pink flesh she cartwheeled zestfully along the beach until she collapsed laughing in the sand.

'Bravo!' I said, squatting at her side. I believe my pulse

was racing faster than hers.

She reinstated decorum by covering her knees. '*Bravo*— I adore that! Who but an Englishman would come up with a word like that?'

'Who but an American lady would turn glorious cartwheels on a public beach?'

'Did I shock you, Keystone?'

'I was enchanted.'

'I guess I was inspired by your hand-walking. Pardon me for mentioning it, but I'd never have taken you for an acrobat. Can you do other tricks?'

'Only with a safety net.'

'Are you serious? I can't tell. You hardly ever smile. You're the most unpredictable guy I've ever met.'

'Is that disturbing?'

Amber considered for a second. 'No, it doesn't trouble me. It's kind of stimulating.' She stood up and brushed the sand off her clothes. 'You want to walk along the beach?'

'If you stop worrying about my shoes.'

She laughed. 'I won't mention them again. What were you doing before you came to Keystone?'

'I was on tour, in vaudeville.'

'Right across America?'

'Yes. Out from New York through Chicago and all the other places.'

'As an acrobat?'

'A knockabout comedian.'

'That's a tough way to earn a living.'

'I enjoyed it while it lasted — more than the audiences did, unfortunately. There is not much prospect of working my way back in the opposite direction.'

'Do you want to go back?'

'My country is at war. In a few months I shall have earned enough to make it to New York again. I'll sell the car and book my passage to Southampton.'

'Just to get yourself killed in France?'

'It could be over before I get there.' I changed the subject. It was becoming morbid. 'How about you, Amber? What is your reason for being at Keystone?'

'Like a lot of other girls, I had a dream about working in the movies, so I came to Los Angeles and found myself standing in the bull pen with hundreds of other would-be actors every studio I tried. Like I told you, I want costume parts, but the only place I could get work was Keystone. Mack makes more movies per week than any other company. In six months I have graduated from crowd work to bit parts to leading lady.'

'You have a lot to thank Mr Sennett for, then.'

Amber looked away. 'Would you like to eat?' she asked unexpectedly. 'There's a dinky little roadhouse up there that sells shrimps with pretzels.'

It was a wood building so close to the cliff edge that it might have featured in a Keystone movie. We were the only customers. The shrimps were heaped high on thick white china plates, and there was iced beer to drink. The sea spray and the exercise had laid a deeper colour on Amber's cheeks. Her green eyes caught the flicker of the oil-lamps. Hardly a word was said, or needed to be said. Far below the open window the ocean purred and sighed.

'Keystone, that was far too much,' Amber told me when we got outside.

'The food?'

'The tip you left him. You don't hand over a dollar bill in a two-bit joint like that.'

'It was all I had.'

'You had no change?'

'It must have fallen out of my pockets when I stood on my hands.'

Amber shook with laughter. She gripped my arm and

pressed her head against it. 'I'm so glad! I was afraid you were too perfect to be true.'

'Try me,' I said. With my fingers I gently raised her chin. She curled her arms around my neck and responded to the kiss.

'You'd better drive me home.'

'You'd better tell me where you live.'

We drove to a bungalow in Santa Monica. I turned the motor car into the drive and stopped.

Amber said, 'Would you care to come in? I don't believe you've met my mother.'

I gave her a mock frown. 'I wouldn't like to think you were teasing me.'

'Why do you think I said it, then?'

'You want to make me smile.'

'I'll put it another way. How would you like some coffee?'

'That would be delightful.'

I helped her out of the motor car. She had the doorkey in her hand, but the front door was opened first.

I stared.

Amber said, 'Mother, this is Mr Keystone.'

NINE

Mrs Honeybee was shorter than Amber, with similar fine blonde hair which she wore plaited and coiled. A few silver strands blended almost invisibly in the tight-packed arrangement. In conversation, slight lines of strain appeared at the edges of her mouth and eyes, but she was animated and attractive.

'I do wish you had told me, darling,' she gently chided Amber. 'We're not usually so disorganised, Mr Keystone.'

The disorganisation amounted to a few copies of *Moving Picture World* that she scooped off the sofa and into the piano-seat. Everything else was tidy. It was furnished like any other sitting room except for an extra emphasis on the performing arts — a toy theatre, a phonograph and a harp.

'That girl!' she said with affection in her voice when Amber had gone to make coffee. 'Six months at the studio and she hasn't told me a thing about you.'

'That's hardly surprising, madam. We only met last week.'

She smiled knowingly. 'I understand. Amber thinks of nothing but her acting, and you must be far too occupied with more important things to take time walking around the studio lot meeting up-and-coming actresses. It's such a hive of industry. I've been through your gates on more than one occasion, Mr Keystone.'

'My gates?'

'I met your studio manager, Mr Sennett, such an exceptional man, wouldn't you say?'

'Madam, I am one of the Keystone Cops.'

'There's no need to sound apologetic. It's no bad thing for the top man to get to know what happens on the studio floor.'

I shifted my position on the sofa. 'I am sorry to disappoint you. I am not by any stretch of the imagination the top man. Almost the reverse. My name is Warwick Easton. For his own reasons, Mr Sennett calls me Keystone, and that is all. I am not the owner of the studio. I am an English actor compelled to scrape a living scrambling over roofs and being hit by custard pies.'

She flushed deeply, gave an embarrassed laugh, and said in a rush, 'Lord save us. What'll that girl do next?'

With helpful timing, Amber entered with a tray of cups and said, 'Keystone drove me back from Griffith Park, Mother. Wasn't that kind?'

'*Drove* you?'

'In his automobile.'

'Automobile?'

'It's called a Brush. It's bright red and handsome, with beautiful brass lamps.'

'That is not the point, Amber.'

'Oh, Mother, it is. I wasn't well. I could never have travelled in the streetcar.'

'You're ill?'

'I was, wasn't I, Keystone? He took me to the beach to get some air.'

Amber's mother looked as if she could use some air. 'He took you to the beach?'

'That's what I said. And after that, he bought me supper in a roadhouse.'

'He did?'

I thought she was going to reach for the smelling salts.

'So the least I could do was ask him in for coffee. Black or white, Keystone?'

'Black, if you please.'

Amber's mother said in a small voice, 'I ask myself why I bothered to leave my husband and come to California.'

With an effort at conversation, I asked, 'Are you from another state?'

'Didn't Amber tell you? What did you find to talk about in all that time?'

Amber said, 'We're a New England family.'

Her mother said, 'My husband Tom is one of the Honeybees of Boston. The publishers — you must have heard of them. He has a wonderful old office on Park Street and we all lived in a large house on Huntington Avenue, until Amber took it into her head to come to California and work in motion pictures.'

Amber called from the kitchen, 'Mother, you encouraged me.'

'What if I did?' Mrs Honeybee shouted back spiritedly. 'As I see it,' she told me confidentially, 'every mother has a duty to make the best of her children's talents, even at the cost of personal sacrifice. Tom didn't agree, so I left him. We haven't heard from him for over a year.'

'I'm sorry to hear it.'

'Amber is worth it. Between ourselves, she's no Sarah Bernhardt, but she's prettier.'

'Unquestionably.'

'Oh, so you have noticed,' Mrs Honeybee said with the relish of a prosecuter tricking out an admission of guilt. 'I think it's time you told me a little more about yourself, Mr Keystone. You're not a married man, by any chance?'

Amber reappeared with a coffee-pot. 'He has eleven children and he's twice divorced. Mother, don't be so embarrassing. Are there any cookies? I couldn't find them out there.'

'Of course there are.'

When Mrs Honeybee had gone to the kitchen, Amber whispered, 'She's a little anxious, but she's the sweetest mother anyone could have.'

The cookies arrived before any more could be said. The conversation turned to the filming of *Kidnap in the Park*. Amber gave a selective summary of the day's events. It was as if she had mentally put it through her private cutting room. Anything remotely touching on the difficulties with Murray Brennan was omitted.

I finished my coffee and thanked them. I got up to leave.

'Amber will see you out,' said Mrs Honeybee with an understanding smile. 'I may be a jailer to my daughter, but I try to temper it with mercy when I think it is safe to do so. Such a novelty to meet you, Mr Keystone. I hope you come again.'

By the car, Amber held both my hands and said, 'Thank you for what you didn't tell her.'

'I have a mother, too.'

She kissed me lightly. 'I'd better go now.'

'Wait.' I went to the trunk and opened it. 'Don't forget your bag.'

She laughed as she took it from me. 'It's so enormous. You should see me take it on the trolley.'

'Will you be using it tomorrow?'

'I have to. It has my make-up, hairbrush, everything.'

'Would it help you to leave it in the car?'

'What a wonderful idea!' She delved inside and took a few things out. 'You sure it won't get in your way?'

I shook my head. 'It's my guarantee of seeing you tomorrow.'

I closed the trunk and went forward to crank the engine.

TEN

At 6.30 in the morning Mack Swain was astride the roof of a house on Allesandro Street with the infant Arnold in his arms. Harper, the cameraman, was on a tower of scaffolding close by. Murray Brennan was directing from the street. He was trying to persuade the child to look distressed and frightened. Arnold was not co-operating. He had never been taken on a roof before. He was patently delighted to be there. All week he had scowled and whined and refused to be adorable. Now he was laughing and waving to the people on the street. Murray was suffering this new infliction with the patience of a Job. He could have solved the problem by ordering Swain to slap the waving arm or pinch a leg, but he did not. He was a decent man. And he had Arnold's mother in attendance.

We Cops sat waiting on the Keystone paddy wagon. It had been agreed that Al St John would do the stilt-walking. I imagined this would take the spotlight off me, but Chester Conklin was determined it would not.

'Keystone, how did you make out last evening?'

'I beg your pardon?'

'With Amber. How did it work out?'

'Keystone with Amber?' said Slim Summerville. 'Hey, what's this?'

Other conversations gave way abruptly to this hot topic.

'He gave her a lift in his automobile,' said Conklin, as innocent as it was possible to be behind his false moustache. 'Did she enjoy the ride, Keystone?'

'He took Amber for a ride?' said Frank Hayes, making innuendoes with his eyebrows.

I said firmly, 'I am sorry, gentlemen. Much as I appreciate your interest, my personal and private life is not a topic for general discussion.'

'You mean you want to keep the discussion on a professional footing?' said Hayes.

'Exactly.'

'So where did you go — did you find a good location?'

'An interior, maybe?' said Summerville, quick to follow up.

'Any interesting angles, unusual shots?' said Hayes.

The paddy wagon shook with merriment when Conklin, saucer-eyed, added, 'Maybe even a double exposure?'

Stiffly, I said, 'I fail to see what is so remarkable in my leaving the studio in the company of an attractive actress.'

'Shall I tell him, boys?' said Hayes. 'Keystone, you're not unique. Three or four of these ugly apes around you have at some time dated Amber. Sooner or later —'

'Later, in my case,' put in Summerville.

'. . . each of them thought he had achieved the ultimate,' Hayes went on. 'He got invited home. And what happened?'

'We met mother,' said Conklin.

'Ah,' I said, as understanding dawned. 'So did I.'

I let them quieten down, and added, 'But which of you were offered cookies?'

The rooftop sequence was eventually completed. Arnold got restless and, as Mack Swain tightened his grip, Jake Harper cranked some lovely footage of the bawling child.

The Cops came on. We clambered out of the bedroom window and hoisted Chester Conklin on to the roof. He slid down the tiles and saved himself by clinging to the gutter. Much of the clowning was improvised. The ladder stunt was tried repeatedly without complete success, but Brennan seemed to know when we had reached our limit, and called a stop. He would magic something out of all the takes when he reviewed them in the cutting room. He had the consolation of a virtuoso performance on the stilts by Al St John. It drew applause from everyone, even Swain, still on the roof, which nearly brought disaster as baby Arnold tipped abruptly to one side. Whether Swain was fooling I did not discover.

Back at the studio for lunch, I was met by Amber just inside the gate. My fellow Cops whistled and shouted encouragement. Amber laughed and made as if to shoo them off.

'They're a bunch of kids,' she told me. 'How are you today? Did you complete the shooting?'

'I understand we finished, yes.'

'That's good. It means Murray is free to shoot the last few scenes in the park this afternoon.'

'You've decided to continue, then, in spite of yester-day?'

Amber shrugged. 'I'm not too proud to see good sense. What would I gain from backing out? Sure, here I am again, ready to go — which is why I wanted to catch you. My bag.'

'Of course.' The Brush was parked on the main street through the studio. I led Amber to it and lifted the bag from the trunk. 'It's heavy, isn't it?' said Amber as she took it. 'I'd like to take out a couple of things and leave them in here.' She widened her eyes a fraction and a quick smile passed across her lips. 'That's if you haven't changed your mind.'

'Certainly not.'

'You're sweet. When I saw you with the other guys, my heart sank for a moment. I got the feeling they'd been talking about me.'

It was better not to deny it. 'Is that so bad? Men do discuss the prettiest girls.'

The troubled look lifted from Amber's eyes. 'Flatterer!'

'Nothing was said that could offend you.'

'I guess you must have heard that I've been out with a couple of them, Slim and Chester? Oh, and Willie Collier. They're regular guys and fun to be with.'

I nodded tolerantly. 'Amber, I'd consider it an honour to take you to a better place for dinner this evening — unless you prefer the roadhouse?'

She blushed and bit her lip. 'That's really generous, Keystone, only I promised someone else.'

'I see.'

She laughed nervously. 'I guess it seems like I'm always out with some guy or other. This isn't like that. As a matter of fact, I'm invited to the Arbuckles. Have you met Minta, Roscoe's wife? She's a lovely person. Keystone, I'm sorry.'

'So am I.'

'Shall I see you in the park this afternoon?'

'I'm afraid you won't. There's a rehearsal call for all the Cops. The man who has devised the car chase proposes to explain it to us. I was told that this was one meeting I would miss at my peril.'

'That's true,' said Amber earnestly. 'I'd hate anything to happen to you.'

I really think she meant it.

ELEVEN

All seats in the projecting room were taken for the rushes of *Kidnap in the Park*. Murray had invited everyone associated with the movie to view the footage shot so far. At noon, Mack Sennett would be given his private showing. If there were squalls ahead, most people liked to be forewarned. Three days' shooting had created a chronic nervousness about this picture. But you could never tell with movies. Just as a stunt hilarious to shoot could flop in the projecting room, occasionally a few judicious cuts could turn a lustreless performance into what Sennett called a yell.

It was studio policy to cut and edit by repeated reference to an audience. Anyone seen idle on the Keystone lot, a pay-clerk, typist or delivery-boy, was liable to be drafted to watch the tenth or twentieth version of a gag. There was no need of conscripts in this morning's audience. The actors, cameramen, make-up artists and mechanics sat in apprehensive silence. The only absentee of note was Amber.

The projector rattled. Images flickered on the screen. As take succeeded take, it emerged that, by artifice and ingenuity, Murray had salvaged something from his skirmishes with Amber. Her performance was not to be compared with Mabel Normand, but with judicious cutting it promised to get by. And the surer talents of Roscoe Arbuckle and Mack Swain would unarguably lift the movie. Fatty among the ducks had even this jittery audience laughing, and the scene with Swain baffled and

bemused by my movements past the window scored
belly-laughs in plenty. At the end of the reel there was
spontaneous applause.

People turned to look for the director. He was no
longer in the room.

'Murray left before the end,' said one of his
assistants. 'He was called to Mr Sennett's office.'

Most of the audience waited, wanting to affirm their
faith in their director. He returned in twenty minutes,
looking ashen. A few people started clapping, but it
died. It was clear that something was extremely wrong.

Murray raised a hand for silence. He spoke softly,
spacing out his words. 'Please listen carefully. I've just
come from Mr Sennett. Something has happened that is
going to cause us to suspend the shooting of this movie.'

'Oh, no!' cried someone in the audience. 'It's going to
be terrific, Murray. It's a darb!'

'Would you hear me out?' said Murray. 'This is no
reflection on the quality of your work or mine. It's
something that happened last evening concerning a
leading member of the cast, something tragic, violent,
unexplained. I only heard of this myself in the last few
minutes. The County Police are in the office asking
questions. I'm not at liberty to say any more at present.'

'Who is it, Murray?' asked Chester Conklin.

'Amber?' said Mack Swain.

I felt as if volts were passing through me.

Murray gave a nod, but said, 'I didn't answer that
question. Any further statements will be issued from the
office. Some of you may be asked to help, so please
don't leave the studio just yet.'

Amber.

Something tragic, violent, unexplained. What did he
mean? I got up and bolted after Murray. People were

leaving their seats, getting in my way. I pushed them angrily aside. I reached the door. He was ahead of me, striding towards the tower.

'Murray!'

He turned, looked at me and shook his head.

TWELVE

Winnie of Wardrobe had got the salient facts. She had been in the front office when the police had arrived. Now she was outside, ready to talk. I hammered her with questions. In no time there was a crowd of people with me agog to hear her information. 'Will you give me room? Yea, I know what happened, and if you stop crowding me, I'll tell you. I don't know who gave you the idea that Amber is hurt, but forget it. She's okay, from what I heard. What I mean is that she isn't hurt. I wasn't told what kind of state she is in. Pretty upset, I guess. Her mother is the one who bought it. She's in the morgue, poor soul.'

'Dead? What happened?' I demanded, overwhelmed that Amber was unhurt.

'I'm telling you. Someone slugged the poor old lady.'

'She's not that old. She can't be more than forty-five.'

'Do you want to hear what I got to tell you, or not? They have this bungalow in Santa Monica. Late last evening one of the neighbours hears some kind of argument going on in there. There's screaming. He figures there is something violent happening, only the curtains are drawn, so he can't see. He knocks on the door. No answer. It's quiet by this time, but the lights are on, so he figures someone must be in there. He goes down the street to Ocean Avenue to find a patrolman. Have you ever tried to find a patrolman when you wanted one? After maybe twenty minutes he gets back with this cop. They knock on the door and Amber answers. She is in her night-things. Her breath stinks of alcohol and she is unsteady on her feet. The cop asks if everything is okay and Amber answers sure. She doesn't know a goddamn thing about the screaming. The cop decides to take a look around. The first door he opens, he finds Mrs Honeybee lying in a pool of blood beside her bed, stone dead.'

'Someone hit her?'

'That's the way it looks. A fractured skull.'

'And Amber didn't know a thing about it?' said Chester Conklin.

'So she told the cops. They're holding her at police headquarters. She's been there all night.'

'They figure Amber killed her own mother? Why would she do that?'

'Who knows? I guess that's what the questions are about.' Winnie's mouth clammed shut and her small eyes darted left and right. She had told all she knew and now she was assessing the effect.

I, for one, was feeling angry.

I said, 'I was at the bungalow the evening before last. Amber and Mrs Honeybee were on very cordial terms. The idea that Amber would attack her mother is preposterous.'

'She'd been at the bottle,' said Frank Hayes.

'She had been out to dinner with Roscoe Arbuckle and his wife. I expect they had a glass or two of wine.'

'Roscoe? Is he mixed up in this?' said Chester Conklin.

'Some people get pretty ugly after a couple of drinks,' persisted Hayes. 'Even girls.'

I glared at him and said, 'Speculation as ill informed as that is perilously close to slander.'

'What's your theory, Keystone?' asked Mack Swain.

'It's not for us to theorise. The least that one can do as a friend and fellow-actor is keep an open mind. I hope Amber has a lawyer with her.'

'Some hope!' said Hayes. 'You ever been picked up by the cops, Keystone?'

'We ought to make sure she gets a lawyer.'

'Just how do you figure to do that?'

I wasn't sure myself, but I meant to find a way. 'I'll talk to Mr Sennett.'

'There's no sense in that,' said Conklin. 'Sennett will tear you up and smoke the pieces.'

I set off at a brisk step towards the tower.

I found Mack Sennett pacing his office in a purple bathrobe.

'Mr Sennett.'

'Get out of here.'

'I would appreciate a few minutes of your time.'

'I said beat it, sonny.'

'I think Miss Honeybee needs a lawyer.'

'And you, my friend, are going to need a doctor,' snarled Sennett, coming at me with his fist clenched.

I stood my ground. 'Perhaps you would prefer me to raise the matter with Mr Ince.'

'What did you say?'

'Mr Thomas Ince. I believe he has an interest in the company. He won't wish to see its reputation smeared.'

Sennett put his face within a couple of inches of mine. 'Just what are you driving at, fella?'

'If what I hear is true, Miss Amber Honeybee is under suspicion of causing her mother's death. She has been subjected to a night of interrogation at police head-quarters.'

'So what? She must be suspect number one.'

'If this ordeal persists, she may be persuaded to put her signature to a confession.'

Sennett tossed back his head and laughed. 'So that's the size of it? A murderess at Keystone. You figure the publicity would hurt us? You don't know people, buddy. We'd treble our takings on any goddamn picture Amber has appeared in.'

I shook my head. 'That's not the point at all, Mr Sennett. I believe Amber to be innocent, and I intend to prove it. What will it do for the reputation of the company if one of its leading actresses is unjustly charged with murder and you refuse to give a cent to help her?'

Sennett hesitated. He closed one eye and squinted at me. 'What did you say your name is?'

I heaved a long sigh. 'Does it really matter? You know me as Keystone.'

'I remember now. Okay, Keystone, let's lay our cards out, shall we? What's your interest in Amber?'

'With due respect, that is the question you should answer.'

Sennett said thickly, 'What the hell does that mean?'

'What matters, Mr Sennett, is how much interest *you* have in Amber.'

Sennett grabbed me by the necktie. 'All right, you son-ofabitch, you've said enough.'

'I meant "you" in the corporate sense,' I told him quickly. 'Does the Keystone Company have any interest in Amber? Is it going to help her now?'

The pressure on my throat relaxed. 'You're right, you ugly punk. I ought to beat the crap out of you for insubordination, but you're right. Fix it with the office. The best attorney they can raise. And Keystone . . .'

'Mr Sennett?'

'I don't advise you to lock horns with me again.'

Inside ten minutes, Frank Madison, one of the most experienced lawyers in Los Angeles, had agreed to go at once to police headquarters and find out what was going on.

Before I left the office, Roscoe Arbuckle came out of the room where he had been facing questions from the detectives. He let out a long breath and sank into a chair. 'Those guys are unshakeable. They are convinced that

Amber attacked her mother in some kind of alcoholic frenzy. I don't see it. I don't see it at all.'

'Had she drunk much?' I asked him.

'Dinner wine. A couple of cocktails. Maybe three or four. Enough to make her happy. A little unsteady when I walked her home. We have a house on the beach two blocks away, so I walked back with her. It was early, about eleven. That doesn't sound like a drunken party, does it? Minta and I just had this idea of a quiet dinner with the girl away from the pressures of the studio. She took some punishment this week and I didn't want the kid to feel depressed.'

'Was it as friendly as you planned?'

'Sure. It was a nice evening. Amber is inclined to be a little too aware of herself on stage, but she relaxed. She laughed a lot. We all did.'

'Did she mention her mother at all?'

'Not once. Say, do you know something about this? The dicks in there asked the same question.'

'I would like to help Amber if I can,' I answered. 'I can't believe she attacked her mother.'

'Nor me. I know Mrs Honeybee — knew her, I mean. She was a charming lady. Some of these stage mamas are dragons breathing fire. She was not. Say what you like about Amber — and I said a few strong things this week — she was devoted to that mother. She had no reason to hurt her.'

'Did you escort her all the way home last night?'

'Right to the front door. I helped her unlock it, but I didn't go in. She thanked me and kissed me on the cheek and went right inside. That's the kid that those guys in there want to pin a murder on. A killer driven wild by liquor. Bullshit.'

'What do you think happened?'

Arbuckle gave a shrug. 'Some kind of accident?'

KEYSTONE

The door of the inner office opened and a pock-marked face looked out. A secretary got to her feet.

'We'd like to see some jerk called Keystone. Would you find him, sweetheart?'

'I think the officer means me,' I told the secretary.

'What do you know?' said the detective. 'He must have been expecting it.'

The senior detective was speaking on the telephone, a huge man, almost as huge as Arbuckle, only older, with cropped grey hair and jet black eyebrows of diabolic shape. His crimson necktie had a shark's tooth motif. 'What?' he shouted down the mouthpiece. 'Who is he? Madison, that shyster! How did he get on the case? . . . He does, does he? Tell him from me that we're holding her on suspicion pending the medical report. She's answering certain questions, okay? . . . Yea, soon as I can.' He slammed the phone on the hook. 'What's your name?'

'Warwick Easton.'

He glared at his assistant and said, 'What the hell?'

'He said his name was Keystone, Chief.'

'A contracted and foreshortened form,' I explained.

'You trying to be smart with me?'

'It's bound to cause confusion on occasions, officer.'

'Don't give me lip. What do you do here?'

Something told me to be wary. 'I'm, er, on the acting strength.'

'You in this movie Fatty Arbuckle is in?'

'Roscoe, actually.'

'What?'

'Roscoe, officer. He doesn't care for Fatty.'

'Answer the question,' said the pock-marked man.

'Yes is the answer.'

'Who are you playing?' asked the Chief.

I hedged again. 'An anonymous character. No name as

78

such.'

'Comic, huh?'

'Trying to be.'

'He's stalling, Chief.'

The Chief eyed me like a predator. 'Let's have it straight — are you a Keystone Cop?'

'Is this relevant?'

'Because I've always wanted to meet one of those creeps who get cheap laughs making decent men in uniform look like . . . look like . . .' the Chief ground his teeth, unable to go on.

'Asses?' I suggested.

The Chief jerked as if I had thrown a punch at him. 'What did you say?'

'Asses, officer. Long-eared domestic mammals related to the horse.'

'He's English, Chief.'

There was a moment while the Chief regained control. 'All right, smart-horse — ' A triumphant grin was flashed at pock-face. 'Let's get down to business. How long have you been at Keystone?'

'Just ten days.'

'And before that?'

'I was touring. I am a vaudeville artist.'

'No fixed address. Get that down,' said the Chief to his assistant. 'Been in America long?'

'Almost two years.'

'Passport?'

I took out my pocket-book and handed over a British passport.

'No picture here. This could be faked.'

'It has my name and description. May I have it back now?'

'When we finish with you.' The Chief tossed the passport across the room. 'Get on to headquarters, Chick. I want a check on this.'

Chick reached for the telephone.

'Where are you living?' asked the Chief.

'I'm renting an apartment down the street.'

'Number?'

'178A.'

The Chief looked thoughtful. 'Do you have some means of transportation?'

'I possess a motor car.'

The Chief's voice was pitched higher with each question. 'You know Amber Honeybee?'

'Yes.'

'She a friend of yours?'

'Yes.'

'Lover?'

'That's a damned offensive question.'

'Answer it.'

'For heaven's sake — I only met Miss Honeybee last week.'

'And took her in your motor car,' sang out the Chief with a meaning that had nothing to do with motoring.

I gripped the chair in an effort to control my rage. It was in the balance whether I would strike the Chief. I got up and crossed the room to his assistant.

'Where are you going?' asked the Chief, and there was a note of apprehension in the question.

'May I have my passport?'

'Sit down, Mr Keystone. I been up all night. You got to make allowances.'

'I'm not prepared to listen to vile insinuations.'

'You drove Amber Honeybee back to the bungalow on Monday evening, right?'

I stood in silence, waiting for my passport. Chick was still using the telephone.

'We need to know what happened.' As I still said

nothing, the Chief added, 'Okay, I take back the vile insinuations. I'm uncouth. Now can we start over?'

I remained standing where I was, but I half-turned and said, 'I was invited in for coffee. Mrs Honeybee received me. When I had disabused her of the notion that I owned the Keystone Company, we had a cordial exchange about my personal circumstances and theirs, and then I left.'

'How were things between Amber and her mother?'

'They had an obvious and deep affection for each other.'

'You sure about this?'

'Amber remarked to me herself that she had the sweetest mother anyone could have.'

'This was your first visit to the bungalow?'

'Yes.'

'The first time you had driven Amber home?'

'Yes.'

'Did you suggest another meeting?'

'I invited her to dinner the next night, but she explained that she was going to the Arbuckles.'

'So you knew about that. Who else knew?'

'I have no idea.'

'You see that it could be important?'

Across the room, Chick hung up the phone and gave a nod.

The Chief said, 'Seems you're clear with Immigration. One more question, Mr Keystone. Where were you last evening between the hours of ten and twelve?'

I ground my teeth. 'In my apartment.'

'Anyone with you?'

'Certainly not.'

'Too bad. It's just your word, then.' The Chief motioned to Chick to return the passport. 'That's all for now.'

'Not quite all,' I said. 'When do you propose to allow

Miss Honeybee to return home?'

'Why do you want to know?'

'She must be exhausted and distressed by now.'

'She can't go home before my boys have finished in the bungalow. She was resting at headquarters until some bonehead sent an attorney to see her.'

'When you do release her, I will collect her in my motor car.'

'You're getting in this up to your neck, aren't you, Keystone? Or are you in it already?'

I didn't condescend to answer.

THIRTEEN

Madison, the attorney, called the studio at 2.30 to say that Amber would be free to leave in a short time. I had asked the office to contact me as soon as anything was known, so when Amber did emerge from police headquarters, pale and obviously under strain, I was on the steps to meet her. My motor car was waiting on the street.

'I took the liberty of booking a room for you at a quiet hotel at Pacific Palisades,' I told her. 'You shouldn't be disturbed there.'

'You're very thoughtful,' said Amber in a tired voice.

'There are policemen at the bungalow, but I expect you'd like to collect some things, if you can bear to go back there.'

'Yes, I shall need my night things.'

No more was said as we drove to Santa Monica. Amber closed her eyes. Her blonde ringlets flicked against her face. She let them.

There was a uniformed officer at the door of the bungalow. A lieutenant was inside. He agreed to admit us both. While Amber was in her bedroom, I took a glance into Mrs Honeybee's room.

'Is this where it happened?' I asked the lieutenant.

'Mister, that's no coffee stain.'

I looked at a dark patch on the honey-coloured carpet beside the bed. 'A head injury, I gather.'

'Yup.'

'Were there any other injuries?'

'Not that I heard.'

'Did they find the implement used by her assailant?'

The lieutenant studied me in an unadmiring way. 'No, Mr Sherlock Holmes, sir, they did not.'

I let the sarcasm roll off me. 'It's not inconceivable, is it, that she could have fallen and struck her head on the sharp side of the washstand there?'

'Would you like to examine it with your little old magnifier?'

I went to see whether Amber was ready. She was sitting on the bed in her room, staring at the wall. She had made no attempt to pack her things.

I asked her gently where she kept her nightdress. She pointed to a chest of drawers. I opened the top drawer. The things were in disarray as if they had been stuffed in there without concern about the possibility of creasing. I found a satin nightdress. From the lower drawers, which were also in a mess, I took out a change of underthings and put them in the carpet-bag with the nightdress. In the closet I picked out a day dress dark enough to pass for mourning wear. I packed her toothbrush and washthings in a towel.

I said, 'We're going now.'

Amber got up and left the room with me.

When we arrived at the hotel, I carried the things to her room. She lay on the bed dressed as she was. I drew the curtains and pulled the cover over her. I told her I would call for her next day towards lunchtime. She nodded. She may have tried to smile.

I drove downtown and located Madison's office. The lawyer was in the outer room speaking to his secretary. He looked over his glasses at me.

'What can we do for you?'

'I am from the Keystone Studio, enquiring about Miss Honeybee.'

'Who are you exactly?'

I hesitated. 'I am known as Keystone.'

Madison held out his hand at once. 'How are you, Mr Keystone? I guess I should have recognised you. I don't get to socialise enough with you movie people.'

I entered smoothly into the spirit of the false assumption. 'Don't apologise. If you could get to all the parties, it wouldn't speak too well for the state of your practice. Mr Madison, we were all extremely impressed by your prompt intervention in this distressing business.'

'Don't mention it. There's nothing I like better than making policemen jump. We're in the same business, Mr Keystone.'

'They held her for questioning for an excessive time. Do they have a case against her?'

'Nothing that will stick yet. What kind of girl is she, by the way? How does she fit in at the studio?'

'She has just been given her first leading role.'

'Good actress, huh?'

'Mr Sennett must believe so. He arranges all the casting. What I — what we — would like to know is whether the police found anything to implicate Miss Honeybee.'

Madison indicated that he preferred to answer in his office. We moved through and he closed the door.

'Cigar? I forgot — it's Sennett who actually eats these things. Mr Keystone, I'll be frank. The probability is that your pretty little blonde is guilty as hell. The cops are working on the well-attested principle that these things are usually domestic. There's no evidence of a break-in. Amber didn't notify the cops. She was in her nightdress when they called. She'd been drinking. She claims to have returned to the bungalow by 11.30, and the fat guy —'

'Roscoe Arbuckle.'

' . . . corroborates it. About this time the neighbour heard the screaming, but no-one can be precise about the time. It's give or take ten minutes. The only certain timing is the patrolman's. He was alerted by the neighbour at a quarter of midnight. The neighbour isn't sure how long it took him to find the cop. My private hunch would be that it was actually less than the twenty minutes he has estimated. When you're looking for a cop and can't find one, every second drags. So it's not impossible — in fact, it's arguable by a competent attorney — that Amber gets home the worse for liquor around 11.20, has a screaming row with mother and knocks the lady down. By midnight when the patrolman calls, she has closed the door on mother and changed into her night things. She's a trained actress. She can carry on from there.'

'In that case, why is she at liberty?'

'She admitted nothing and they don't have *prima facie* evidence. When the preliminary medical report came in, I was able to point out that it was not inconsistent with an accident. Mrs Honeybee was one of those individuals with an exceptionally fragile skull. She was lying beside a washstand with a marble top. If she had fallen and hit her head on that, it could have killed her; probably did, in fact.'

'So you *do* think it was an accident?'

'No, Mr Keystone, I think Amber pushed her, else why would she have screamed?'

'Perhaps it was Amber who screamed.'

Madison grinned at me. 'Whoever screamed, it's manslaughter.'

FOURTEEN

At noon next day I drove back to the hotel in Pacific Palisades. I was not needed at the studio. Some of the more experienced Cops had been drafted into other movies, but I would have to wait and see if I was listed in the next week's productions.

For once I was grateful to be unemployed. I needed time with Amber. Time to gauge her state of mind. To see if she had yet adjusted to the shock of her mother's violent death and the cruel aftermath of interrogation by the police. I hoped she had got some sleep. There were vital things that needed to be said, and questions asked. One thing was certain: the full truth about what had happened had yet to be uncovered. For Amber's sake — for both our sakes — I meant to get that truth.

But I knew it would be futile — not to say inhuman — to interrogate her like the police.

She was in the elevator when I opened it. She was wearing the dress I had picked out for her the previous afternoon. Although she was pale, her expression was alert. She was clearly pleased to see me.

She kissed me lightly on the mouth. 'All those things you did for me: I want to thank you, Keystone. I wasn't functioning at all.'

'That was to be expected. You were suffering from shock. How do you feel today?'

'A whole lot better than I would have done without you. You looked after me so well. Even the change of clothes. It makes me blush to think of it, but that was really thoughtful.'

'Forget it, Amber. What have you had to eat?'

'Nothing yet.'

'You must be ravenous. I shall take you somewhere for lunch.'

There was a fish restaurant a block from the hotel. I ordered salmon for Amber and king crab legs for myself.

'I called my father in Boston,' Amber told me. 'We haven't spoken on the telephone since Mother and I left home, but I had to tell him.'

'Is he coming out?'

'He's going to try. He told me to arrange the funeral as soon as possible. He'll pay for it. He's very businesslike.'

'I expect he was disturbed to hear the news.'

Amber shook her head. 'He took it very calmly, like one of his books had got a bad review. Keystone, I don't know anything about funerals. Would you help me?'

'Of course.'

'You may think this sounds callous, but I mean to see that Mack Sennett doesn't axe my movie. You don't think he is planning anything like that, do you?'

'I don't think anyone is capable of fathoming Mr Sennett's mind.'

'He hasn't stopped the production?'

'It has been suspended for the present.'

She tightened her mouth. 'Maybe this is just the excuse he wanted.'

'On the contrary. The rushes were very well received.'

'By Mack?' She reddened suddenly, and looked amazed.

'By the company.'

Her face fell. 'They were just looking at their own performances.' She sighed heavily. 'Keystone, why did this have to happen now?'

'Do you wish to talk about it?'

'No.'

I must have raised my eyebrows just a fraction.

Amber tried to explain herself by adding, 'I've been over it all with the police a dozen times. What's the point? It won't bring Mother back.'

'There must be some explanation.'

'Don't *you* believe my story either?'

'Amber, of course I do. But what does it leave us with? An accident?'

She stared at me. 'Why not?'

I had not intended to raise the subject so obviously or so soon, but now I had started I couldn't very well hold back.

'Correct me if I'm wrong, but I formed the impression that you took particular care of your clothes.'

'What does this have to do with it?'

'When I went to your chest of drawers to collect your nightdress, it looked as if a whirlwind had been through there, every drawer.'

She coloured deeply. 'Gentlemen weren't meant to look in there.'

'My supposition was that someone had been through the bungalow and disarranged the drawers.'

'You mean a thief? Nothing was missing that I could see. Mother and I had nothing worth stealing.' She gave a light, nervous laugh. 'I'm sorry to shatter your illusions, Keystone, but I have to admit I'm not the tidy lady you took me for.'

'Is it possible that someone could have broken into the bungalow? It was a warm night. Presumably windows were open somewhere?'

Amber pushed her plate aside. 'Keystone, I appreciate what you're trying to do, but, believe me, it isn't going to change anything. I don't want a big investigation. I just want to give my poor mother a decent burial and get on with what she would have wanted me to do, which is making movies.'

I cursed myself. I had spoken far too soon. 'I'm sorry. I have a very dogged side to my character. Some people call it cussed. Let's talk about your life in Boston. Where did you go to school?'

We finished the meal without any more speculation about Mrs Honeybee's death. I suggested Amber should remain at the hotel until after the funeral. The studio would pay for her stay there.

'Is there anything else you need from the bungalow?'

'Not today. I'll take a walk there tomorrow. I need to occupy myself. But there is something else. When I picked up my bag from the automobile, I left a few things in the trunk.'

I remembered. 'A pair of shoes, the *Saturday Evening Post* and somebody's birthday present by the look of it.'

'Oh, the parcel?' She smiled. 'Nothing so nice, I'm afraid. Just a few cooking pans I bought downtown. I need the shoes, but I don't require the pans just now. Would they be in your way if I left them in the trunk?'

'Of course not. They're no trouble to me, but don't forget about them altogether.'

'I won't.'

When we walked back to where I had left the car I remembered the shoes she wanted. I opened the trunk, which on the Brush was literally a travelling trunk mounted on the chassis at the rear.

'Are you sure this is not a bomb?' I joked, as I moved the parcel aside. Something inside the paper rattled.

'I told you what it is,' she answered with a serious expression. 'Do you think I would want to injure you?'

FIFTEEN

Late that afternoon I drove to the studio to check the castings for the following week. Mack Sennett was by the bulletin board. He was playing the patriarch, chatting affably to all comers through a nimbus of cigar smoke.

'It's going to be a lighter week for you,' he announced as if he were giving me good news. 'I put you in Mabel's latest — a zippy little seaside caper. The Cops come in at the end and get hopelessly entangled with the bathing beauties. Only one day's filming, but, boy, it should be wild!'

'One day isn't much.'

'I figured you would need time off to bury Mrs Honeybee. We got news this afternoon that the medical examination indicates an accident. The poor lady fell and cracked her head on a marble washstand. There's a full autopsy in the morning, but the cops are ninety per cent sure that nothing criminal took place. Amber is in the clear.'

'That was never in doubt.'

'Not in a million years. If I appeared to be a little shaken at the time, it was just that I know the damage bad publicity can do. Dead mothers are not good news, Keystone.'

'I thought you were concerned for Amber.'

'That, too,' conceded Sennett before expanding on his theme. 'Mothers are something special in the movie business. You can never joke about a mother. You can try, but it won't get a laugh. Fathers are another thing. So are mothers-in-law. You can do anything this side of torture

91

and get a laugh with a mother-in-law.'

I wasn't interested. 'What will happen about *Kidnap in the Park*?'

'Amber's movie?' Sennett drew thoughtfully on his cigar. 'Has she been asking you?'

'Naturally she's interested to know.'

'It wasn't finished. Roscoe didn't shoot the chase.'

'That is the way it stands,' I commented pointedly.

'Goddammit, what does she expect?' demanded Sennett, casting geniality aside. 'We can't shoot the lousy chase without her. She's got a funeral coming up.'

'I rather think that when the funeral is over —'

'She'll have to be in mourning,' broke in Sennett. 'She can't start playing comedy again. That would be a son-of-a-gun thing to do.'

'She says it was her mother's dearest wish.'

'She does?' Sennett dropped the butt of his cigar and crushed it with his heel. 'Listen, I got Roscoe starting another movie Monday morning. The cast are scattered to the winds. This is crazy, Keystone, crazy.'

'She sees it as her golden opportunity to make her name.'

'I know, I know.'

'One day would get it finished.'

'Are you trying to put the screws on me as well?'

'I am trying to be constructive, Mr Sennett.'

Sennett uttered a profanity, but not at me. He had spotted Mabel Normand moving jauntily but purposefully towards him up the studio street. He said, 'Tell me, Keystone, am I nuts, or am I really being persecuted?'

Mabel was in a blue silk blouse that made a tidal motion over her chest. 'Howdy, it's Keystone, isn't it? Howdy, Mack. I came to see my cast list. Too bad about last week: Amber, I mean. Wasn't that just tragic?' She smiled wickedly. 'I mean what happened to her mother, not her acting.'

'That's unworthy of you, Mabel,' Sennett admonished her.

'Yes. Miaow! But I did stay away all week. I could have stood around the set and gloated, couldn't I?'

'You made your feelings plain without that,' answered Sennett.

She asked him coaxingly, 'Aren't you happy to have little Mabel back?'

He softened slightly. 'It's been a darned long week.'

'How about you?' she said in a generous effort not to exclude me. 'Did you enjoy your debut as a Cop?'

'Immensely. What it will look like on the screen is another question.'

'Darling, it won't arise,' she gently pointed out. 'The movie is as dead as Amber's mother, rest her soul. Isn't that so, Mack?'

Sennett took off his panama and ran a hand through his grey hair. 'We were just discussing that.'

'What do you mean — discussing it? What is there to discuss? She was a disaster. Alice Davenport told me.'

Sennett asked stiffly. 'Since when has Alice Davenport taken the decisions here?'

Mabel's brown eyes widened in amazement. 'I don't believe this! You're not still hipped on Honeybee?'

'You know it was never like that, Mabel.'

'I know you for a sucker, Mack Sennett.'

'Let's discuss it some other time.'

'Do you know what I did this week while I was un-employed?'

'I have no idea.'

'I'll tell you, then. I went downtown and bought myself a wedding dress.'

Sennett mouthed the words, 'A wedding dress?'

'If you recollect,' said Mabel through her teeth, 'you

93

and I are engaged to be married. I know you have other things to keep you busy, principally blonde, but I foolishly supposed you might soon be getting around to naming the day.'

I told Sennett, 'I think it's time that I was going.'

'I think it is,' he answered wearily.

SIXTEEN

I was at Amber's side at Pasadena railroad station when her father stepped off the Pullman.

When Amber had kissed him, she said, 'Daddy, this is Keystone. He's a friend from the movie studio.'

'Pleased to meet you. This is Deirdre Holland. She's my secretary. How about a porter?'

I said, 'I can manage those.'

'No,' said Deirdre. 'We'll use a regular porter.'

It amused me slightly. My official reason for being at the station was to help with luggage, but I didn't argue. Amber had asked me to be there, and what she wanted, I would do. Besides, I was interested in her father.

Mr Honeybee took off his homburg and fanned his face. It was a face as smooth and neatly finished as his pinstripe suit. His silver hair was beautifully groomed.

His secretary Deirdre also looked immaculate, apparently unwearied by the five-day railroad journey from the east. Her mass of charcoal-coloured hair under a black straw hat emphasised the whiteness of her skin. Probably she was thirty-five, a decorative, swanlike creature, not to be provoked.

In the cab, Amber said, 'The funeral is tomorrow. Keystone made the arrangements.'

'Are you the undertaker?' Mr Honeybee asked me.

'No, Daddy,' said Amber. 'I told you — he's an actor.' Her eyes met mine. 'And a very considerate friend.'

Deirdre, seated next to Mr Honeybee, asked, 'What time is the funeral?'

'Two in the afternoon.'

'That's good. I can use the morning to see about the bungalow. I understand your mother had it on a lease.'

Amber gave Deirdre a look that was less than pleased. 'It's paid up for the next six months. I intend to go on living there.'

Deirdre ignored her and remarked to Mr Honeybee, 'I can negotiate a rebate.'

'Just what do you mean by that?' asked Amber with her voice pitched ominously high.

Mr Honeybee explained, 'I want you to come back with us when this is over. Deirdre will attend to all the arrangements. Did you have a contract with the movie people?'

'Daddy, I am not going back to Boston.'

'My dear, you can't stay here alone.'

Deirdre added, 'This is no place for a single girl.'

'What do you know about it?' Amber demanded. 'Daddy, let's get this straight. I am a motion-picture actress. I came here to work. I will not be moving out of California.'

'We'll discuss it later,' said Mr Honeybee. He groped for a topic that excluded California and the movies. 'How many will be coming to the funeral?'

'Only three outside the family. Keystone and Roscoe and Minta Arbuckle.'

'That fat comedian?' said Deirdre with distaste.

'Mother was very fond of him.'

'He's going to look rather out of place, to say the least.'

Amber said, 'As you won't be coming, that needn't bother you.' She added, just to twist the knife, 'A family funeral is no place for a secretary.'

'Tom,' said Deirdre acidly to Mr Honeybee, 'I think you'd better tell her.'

Mr Honeybee sighed and looked embarrassed. 'I wish it could have waited. Amber, my dear, when this is over, after an appropriate interval, Deirdre and I intend to be married.'

Amber gave a mocking laugh. 'Oh, boy, that's rich! And she's come all the way from Boston to see your first wife buried.'

'Amber, that's a damned offensive thing to say.'

'Not so offensive as what has obviously been happening back in Boston. I'm just thankful Mother never knew about it. If this woman shows up at the funeral tomorrow, I'll push her face against the nearest tombstone. I mean that, Daddy.'

'Ass-hole!' said Deirdre.

'Here is your hotel,' I said as if I had not heard.

Deirdre did not appear at the funeral next day. It was a simple, moving service at the only church in Santa Monica. Amber held her father's arm. After it was over, she walked with him along the sea front.

Later she returned to the bungalow alone. I was still there with the Arbuckles.

'Daddy went back to his hotel,' she told us. 'We had a heart to heart. He's reconciled to my career in motion pictures, and I shall say no more about his . . . his private life. They should be on the train tomorrow. Thank you for being here, all three of you. I needed your support.'

'We were honoured to be here,' said Roscoe. 'Well, I guess you want to be left in peace now.'

Amber said, 'Not at all. I've had all the peace I want sitting in that miserable hotel. I want to get back to work as soon as possible. Roscoe, what's happening about our movie? When can we shoot the car chase?'

Arbuckle looked down. 'Sweetheart, I can't say. That's something you should ask Mack Sennett.'

'Haven't you discussed it with him?'

'To be candid with you, I figured it was shelved.'

Quickly, I explained, 'I spoke to Mr Sennett. He is aware that you would like to get the picture finished. It appears there is some difficulty in getting everyone together.'

Amber said, 'Shucks, he can do it by snapping his fingers. Did you tell him that?'

I shook my head. 'The conversation was curtailed by the arrival of Miss Normand.'

'Mabel? What did she want?'

'So far as I could gather, a wedding.'

Minta said, 'Oh, my!'

Roscoe asked, 'What's the matter, dear?'

'Just studio gossip, but it could spell trouble. Mack and that friend of Mabel's, Mae Busch, were seen together more than once last week. Everyone knows Mack and Mabel are supposed to be engaged. I don't know why women are so sneaky with each other, even so-called friends.'

'It's the fatal charm of men,' said Roscoe with a grin.

'Mack Sennett?' said Minta disbelievingly. 'He can be fun, but I don't find him attractive. He's uncouth. Amber, wouldn't you agree?'

'Sure,' said Amber quietly. 'I agree. But he also has the power to make or break us. That's Mack Sennett's fatal charm. I don't care about Mae Busch or Mabel Normand. I'm going to see him in the morning.'

SEVENTEEN

The seaside picture I was in was directed by a former Keystone Cop, Charles Avery. When the company, including the Sennett Bathing Beauties and a strong contingent of the Cops, had assembled on the beach and the camera was set up, someone pointed out a member of the public lying on the sand too close to the area reserved for filming.

Avery turned to me, as I happened to be standing near him, and said, 'Would you ask the guy to move out of camera range — but politely?'

I strolled across the sand towards the white-suited, panama-hatted figure propped on one elbow looking at a magazine. I wondered if my uniform would startle him. You don't expect to be cautioned by the police for lying on a public beach.

Deliberately, I couched my words as amiably as possible. 'I say, would you mind awfully . . .'

I didn't complete the sentence.

The man was motionless. He was not even breathing.

I put out a hand to touch his shoulder and he slumped face down into the sand.

I jerked back with that sense of horror you experience on contact with the dead. I had the shakes. To calm myself, I took a couple of deep breaths. I knelt beside him and rolled him back towards me.

I was looking into the crudely painted sackcloth face of a studio dummy.

One of their practical jokes. I tried to smile.

The dummy twitched and half sat up. The shock convulsed me. I yelled and leapt away. The dummy fairly skimmed across the sand to where Slim Summerville held the rope that he and Conklin had attached to its leg and hidden under the sand.

I was told that my reaction was the most satisfying outcome to a practical joke since Charlie Chaplin had staggered out of the ten-volt urinal. Avery and his crew, the Keystone Cops and the Sennett Bathing Beauties had watched the entire performance.

Good form demanded that I smiled and took my humiliation like a man, and this I tried to do, but I am bound to admit that inwardly I smouldered. I was furious with them and more furious with myself for getting caught. At that moment I was ready to resign from the Keystone Cops. If we had not been on location, I would probably have handed in my uniform at once.

Instead I had the consolation of being surrounded by the Bathing Beauties, all giggling and agog to know how completely I was taken in. The girls were in black tights and sleeveless, but by no means, shapeless tops. It was a good thing I was used to waiting in the wings with chorus girls. The proximity of all those bosoms jigging with amusement might otherwise have sent me quite berserk.

Mabel Normand, as the leading lady, wore candy stripes and bloomers to just above the knees. She was laughing as she told me, 'We felt really mean, knowing what the boys were planning, and watching you go off so obligingly, but we couldn't spoil their fun, now could we?'

'Obviously not,' I answered, trying to match her smile. 'I should have been more alert. The newest Cop must expect to cop it, mustn't he?'

They laughed in chorus.

'Do you know the girls?' asked Mabel. 'This is Olga, Myrtle, Julia and Mae.'

I shook hands with each of them. Something made me

say, 'Mae — I know the name. Would it be Miss Busch?'

The slim brunette whose hand was still in mine, said, 'Why, yes. How do you know my name?'

I really couldn't answer. I shook my head. 'I imagine someone must have mentioned it.'

Mae Busch had fashionable heavy eyebrows. She raised them slightly. 'I hope it was in a nice connection.'

'I'm sure it was.'

Mabel Normand said, 'If it was Mae, it must have been. She only has nice connections.' The Bathing Beauties giggled, and Mabel wagged her finger like a schoolmarm. 'Now, girls, don't let me down. You know exactly what I meant. What is so amusing?'

The question was left unanswered. Charles Avery was calling a rehearsal. In the tradition of seaside comedies, this one was rich in spectacle and action, and destitute in plot. It involved a deckchair Casanova, Harry Gribbon, pestering Mabel Normand and attracting only the attention of the Cops. A frantic chase along the beach would end with the entire constabulary falling off the pier. After three rehearsals, a picnic lunch was taken.

Summerville called across to me, 'I should check the sandwiches. You don't know what you might be eating.'

Before we finished lunch, Charles Avery got up to make an announcement. 'Word has just come down from Mr Sennett. This is to ask everyone who was in the cast of *Kidnap in the Park* to report Saturday morning, 7 a.m., Main Street and Allesandro, to shoot the final scenes.'

'How about that?' said Chester Conklin. 'I was positive he'd dumped it.'

'A certain lady wouldn't let him,' said Frank Hayes.

'Who do you mean?'

'Blonde, cute little ringlet curls.'

'Amber?' said Conklin.

Summerville said, 'What do you know about it, Frank?'

Hayes glanced in my direction and then said, 'It's obvious. She's ambitious. She wants that movie badly.'

'Yeah, but what's her pull with Sennett?'

'Who knows?'

Summerville said, 'She ain't his kind of girl. She's nice, only she's nice, if you know what I mean. Maybe he feels sorry for her, with her mother killed like that.'

A few looks were exchanged, all sceptical of Mack Sennett's sympathetic nature.

'He was dating Mae last week,' said Conklin.

'Keep your voice down,' Hayes quickly cautioned him. 'Mabel could be listening. She and Mae are bosom friends.'

Conklin eyed the girls, 'I'd say there's ample evidence of that.'

Hayes laughed. 'Chester never noticed dames were different until he saw Madame Tetrazzini at the San Francisco opera.'

'Did you say *Tet*razzini?' Summerville asked.

'Aw, come on! This is deteriorating fast,' said Conklin. 'What do you think, Keystone — or have we silenced you for good?'

I shrugged. 'There's nothing useful I can say.'

'But you know Amber. What's her secret? How does she get through to Sennett?'

The question had filled my thoughts for days. Now that it was asked like this I decided it was time to air my views, if only to test them on an audience. I'm afraid I sounded more pontifical than I intended or anyone expected: 'You ought to know by now that I refrain from idle gossip. If you want my serious opinion, it is this. Amber is intelligent, ambitious, beautiful and, to use an old-fashioned word, chaste. She intends to succeed in moving pictures, and she believes that Mr Sennett holds the key. Other young women — I shall not be specific — have observed

102

that Mr Sennett is susceptible to feminine allure. That way is not for Amber.'

'It's a well-worn track,' said Hayes.

'Exactly. She is too high-principled to go along it. She relies on something else.'

'You don't mean talent?'

There were groans all round. I gave Hayes a withering look. 'Amber has an extraordinary sense of purpose. She wants to be an actress more than Mr Sennett wants to stop her. He capitulates. That is her secret, as you put it.'

'She dominates him?'

'What other interpretation is there?' I considered a moment, and answered my own question. 'Ah, yes. The devious way — through blackmail. What do you suggest? A compromising photograph? A letter? Can you imagine anything like that embarrassing a man whose indiscretions are a legend?'

'Some people think she has the screws on him,' said Conklin.

'Yes, I expect they do. I expect they would like to stop her. I think they may have tried already.' I glanced around the circle of interested faces with their exaggerated false moustaches. 'Gentlemen, now that Mrs Honeybee is dead, Amber is alone. She needs support. She may even need protection.'

'She can count on us,' said Summerville.

'She has the Keystone Cops on her side,' Hayes confirmed.

There were murmurs of 'You bet.'

Chester Conklin pointed his finger at me and said, 'But don't you kid yourself you get protection, Keystone. You're still the new boy, so watch out!'

Later, I remembered that advice.

The filming on the beach concluded with our chase along the pier. Everyone had to take a drenching because, as the Cops in full cry sprinted after Harry Gribbon, the Bathing Beauties ranged along the pier leapt off in panic. The whole thing had been lengthily discussed, walked through and rehearsed without the actual jumps. We were committed to a single take. Aside from the discomfort of performing in saturated clothes, we had in mind the coldness of the water. Anyone who says bathing on the Californian coast is pleasurable has a better circulation than mine.

To everyone's relief we satisfied Charles Avery in one take.

There were just three small bathing huts along that strip of beach. Out of chivalry we Cops had to allow the ladies to use them first. The afternoon was getting cool by then. Even at two people to each hut, it would be a long time before I had my turn.

My motor car was on the headland above the beach. I decided I would rather motor home in wet clothes than stand shivering another twenty minutes there. I told the others, picked up my things and set off over the sand towards the cliff steps. If no-one was about, I planned to use the car as my changing room.

From higher up the cliff the small, dark-suited figures with long shadows, waiting patiently around three poky bathing huts, looked just a little absurd. The girlish screams that started each time one of the figures hammered on a hut-door reinforced my alienation. I really found it difficult to share their fun. On the battlefields of Europe, men in thousands were laying down their lives. Yet would a bird's eye-view of what was happening in the trenches look any less ridiculous?

I reached the headland. About ten other vehicles were parked there, some no doubt belonging to the Keystone staff. I went over to the Brush, unfixing buttons as I walked. My boots were chaffing, so I used the running-board to bend over and untie them.

I hadn't even loosened the lace when I was hit. Something struck my head with massive force.

Redness blocked my vision.

Blackness.

Then oblivion.

EIGHTEEN

It was not at all like waking up.

I was in total darkness. My eyes were open and I couldn't see a thing.

I had a raging headache and I couldn't move. Well, hardly. I could rock a couple of inches back and forth. When I did, my clothes felt strangely cold against my skin.

Clammy.

In my body's warmest areas, crotch, armpits, the clothes were dry. The clamminess was worst where the fabric had been out of contact with my skin.

I wanted to feel the outside of the clothes, but my hands refused to function. I strained to move them.

They were tied behind my back. Tied to my ankles.

I was lying on my side with my legs forced up behind me to meet the strap of whatever it was that gripped my wrists. A neat, efficient, excruciating method of restraint.

My face was hard against some sort of floor, wooden by the smell. And gritty. Musty, coarse and damp.

Why?

And how?

The dampness triggered an image in my brain. Falling into water. I shut my eyes and fought the headache and struggled to remember. The ocean. Wading through waves. Shouting to the others.

Others? The Keystone Cops. Thank God for something definite. I remembered climbing the cliff steps and reaching my motor car. Something had hit my head.

There, rational thinking stopped. Concussion, however serious, didn't account for my present problem. Trussed tighter than a turkey and shut up somewhere.

But where? I needed to explore the void around me. Constricted as I was, I could make small movements by rocking and pivoting on my hip. It hurt me, yet the impulse to explore was overwhelming. I clenched, braced and willed myself across the floor until my forehead came in contact with a wall.

Wooden again, but ridged. Vertical strips of bare wood, probably tongued and grooved.

I got a splinter in my forehead as a souvenir.

I wriggled the length of the wall until I reached a corner. Not far. The same vertical strips. I edged along for what I estimated was five feet before the top of my head touched the transverse wall.

Actually it was a door. I felt the draught from under it against my face. No chance of pushing it open. I moved on.

By this laborious process I mapped my prison. Probably square. No more than five feet either way.

Bare. And wooden. A box? Too big for a coffin, anyway.

I took a breath and shouted, 'Anyone there?'

It nearly split my head. I didn't shout again.

I strained against the strapping round my wrists. Not a hope of slipping free. Instead I was conscious of a stiffening in my thigh. The first sign of cramp.

What now? Keep the circulation moving. Change position. If I could force my backside into the space between my arms it might be possible to get up into a kneeling position.

I tried it, made it, achieved more mobility and with a mighty effort got my head and shoulders off the ground. Houdini himself would not have been ashamed of that. I was on my knees.

I felt better upright. My thinking process sharpened.

Information snapped together. Five foot square. Wooden, with a door. Damp. The gritty surface on the floor.

Sand. I was in one of those damn bathing huts on the beach.

Another practical joke? Would even the craziest of the Keystone Cops have thought it funny to brain me, tie me up and shut me in this freezing place in my damp clothes?

Someone had done it.

Bastard.

No point in burning up energy in anger. *Think*. How long had I been here? I had no idea except that my body heat had dried parts of my clothes, and outside it was dark, because I couldn't see daylight under the door.

If I waited until morning, someone would come by. Someone, some time, would want to use the hut.

Who in California hated me enough for this?

I knew I was not good at making friends. Most of my life, people had described me as stand-offish and aloof. That was my temperament, though. I preferred to call myself reserved. Oddly, it had proved an asset in the music-halls. I was a natural straight man. In America, with my British ways and accent, I was even more of an outsider. I provoked amusement and occasionally derision. But real animus — the hatred implicit in my present situation — was something I had not encountered there.

I tried to think of enemies.

Obviously someone from the studio. No-one outside knew where to find me. Film locations were kept secret from rival companies, who were not above pirating a scene with hidden cameras.

The only member of the Keystone staff I had crossed swords with was Mack Sennett. The man was certainly a bully and a tyrant, but if he really hated me, he could sack me. Attack by stealth didn't seem Sennett's style.

One of the Cops? As a group they had welcomed me,

but suppose there was one who harboured some resentment? I knew the unwritten law that the new arrival shouldn't seek the limelight. That window scene with Swain might have made someone jealous. Too late to explain that it wasn't of my seeking.

Who then? Frank Hayes, the veteran, clinging to his status as the senior Cop, but fearful that an addition to the squad meant he might be retired? Slim Summerville, the tall man, worried for his job because I had a similar physique? Or little Chester Conklin, whose humorous remarks were often edged with malice?

Mack Swain even? Or Arbuckle? I was getting into realms of fantasy. But one thing was real: in the so-called fun factory of Keystone lurked violence and malice.

If no-one wanted to use the bathing huts when it was light, I could be there another day and night. The filming on the beach was finished. It could be a week or more before anyone at Keystone registered that I was missing. This could really be my coffin.

Was I hallucinating when I believed I saw a streak of grey appearing under the door?

Daylight.

By degrees it strengthened. Feeble as it was, it enabled me to see.

The first discovery was something light in colour suspended from a clothes-hook above my head. Fabric, striped in pink and white. Candy stripes. Mabel Normand's bathing-costume, discarded and forgotten. One more missing garment for Winnie to complain about.

The fleeting thought of Mabel standing wet and naked, towelling herself in this place where I was trapped, was curiously comforting. Best kept a fleeting thought, however. To exorcise the image, I switched my thoughts to Amber, at this moment surely lying in her bed, blonde hair fanned across the pillow, the ribbons of her satin nightdress perhaps unfastened at the neck. Innocent, warm, caressable. Oddly, in my predicament, I was sexually aroused. Not a bad way to raise the body heat and promote the circulation, but no assistance in escaping from a bathing hut.

I looked up and made my second discovery — an obvious one if I had given it some thought. Reasonably enough, the door was meant to be fastened from the inside, with a bolt. And the bolt was open, as it had to be, seeing that I could not have fastened it myself.

So it was reasonable to assume that my attacker had rigged up something on the outside to hold the door in place.

A wedge, perhaps? Or a piece of driftwood jammed against the door?

If I could get some leverage and hit the door, there was a chance of moving the obstruction. My legs were of no help, clamped to my wrists. But if I could utilise it, I had the movement between my trunk and thighs.

I scrabbled round so that my back was against the door. No good. Without trying it, I knew I couldn't bear the pain of my bruised head meeting solid wood.

Pause for second thoughts.

If I turned the other way and lay on my back, I could still employ the pincer movement. My feet would hit the door.

Each manoeuvre stretched and rasped the skin around my wrists and ankles, but it had to be endured. I twisted back to face the door and let myself topple backwards. Touched my head on the floor and nearly blacked out with the pain.

Same objection. Sore head against hard wood.

Another think.

The solution stared at me. Mabel's bathing costume. Get it off the hook and use it as a pillow.

Once again, the agony of getting off my back on to my knees. I shuffled across the floor and strained to reach the costume. Touched it with my head. Tried to get it moving. Eventually, by leaning on the wall and shifting my weight to my feet, succeeded in raising my head a fraction higher. Gripped the costume with my teeth and worried at it like a dog.

A seam or something ripped. The costume fell and so did I, luckily on my side.

With my teeth I folded it to make the pillow. Lay on my back again and tried it out. The pillow dulled the pain enough. I brought my knees against my chest and thrust my feet against the door.

I was wearing Cop boots. They hit the door quite hard.

It felt rigid.

I skewed round slightly to concentrate the blows as close as possible to the jamb. Absolutely solid. It seemed as though the thing was held there by a rock.

I battered it until my feet ached and my head could take no more. Not a hint of movement. I was angry and exhausted.

I lay still and groaned.

What else could I try? Nothing, till I got some strength back.

In ten or fifteen minutes, I had another thought. Not brilliant, but worth trying. Instead of battering the door where it logically should open — and would not — I would attack the hinges. I couldn't see them. They were on the outside.

I wriggled over, set myself ready, braced and kicked.

Perhaps my assault on the other side had made some difference. There was definitely movement. I conjured up a mental picture of rusty screws wobbling in the wood.

Encouraged, I renewed the attack, cracked a dozen blows in swift succession.

The movement grew. The door was giving by about an inch. I rested for a minute, then took it up again.

Progress was slower than I wished. It must have taken nearly an hour before I felt something snap and saw a wedge of light inside the hut. Sunlight reflected off the sand.

I struggled up and examined the gap I had created. Pushed my heel in, leaned on it, felt it give some more. Cried out in elation. Didn't mind the pain.

The top hinge held for six or seven minutes more.

Then I felt it go. I turned, shoved my feet against the jamb and thrust myself backwards through the gap.

Exquisite. My backside settled in sand.

I wriggled out, blinked, opened my eyes on a totally unpopulated beach. Still shackled, but triumphant. Not least because beside the hut was an empty whisky bottle. My captor's sustenance after jamming a heavy metal bar against the door?

Anyway, I had a use for it. Smashed it against the bar, wedged the jagged edge against my heels and used it to cut the strapping between my wrists. A slow and bloody job, but rewarded with success.

My first action was to stretch out on the sand and blissfully straighten every limb. Then I ran down to the sea and bathed my wrists.

For the first time since I had regained consciousness, I thought of my motor car. Would it still be standing on the cliffs? Was it stolen? Was that the motive for this attack?

I crossed the beach and started up the cliff steps, fully twelve hours, I judged, since I had previously made the climb. My attacker must have brought me down them some time in the evening. A strong man, if he managed it alone. Unless there was an easier descent. I didn't feel inclined to explore.

All I wanted was to get home, wash and sleep for a

couple of hours.

The Brush stood in shining isolation on the cliff-top. I was so delighted I broke into Daisy Dormer's music-hall refrain, 'I wouldn't leave my little wooden hut for you-oo'. It hurt my head and reminded me how fragile I was feeling.

My clothes were on the floor in front of the passenger seat, but I didn't bother to change. Cranking the engine was all the effort I could make. Mercifully she engaged first time. I climbed in and rattled through the sleeping suburbs at speeds approaching forty-five. It was still not 6 a.m. when I reached home.

At the door I felt in my pocket for the key, then remembered I was still in uniform. Went back to the Brush and picked up my trousers.

The key wasn't there. Tried the other pocket. The jacket. Still no key. Curse it! Damn thing must have fallen out.

My landlord had once told me where he kept a spare, under a brick in the backyard. I said a silent prayer of thanks as I located it. And another prayer that it would actually fit the door.

It did.

My furnished apartment was on ground level, three rooms sublet in a small house on Allesandro Street for thirty dollars a month. Convenient and comfortable. Or had been when I left it.

I unlocked the door and found it devastated.

Every drawer of every chest had been pulled out and the contents thrown across the floor. The mattress had been slashed, my suitcases ripped open, my piano accordion torn in two. My clothes lay covered in a scattering of flock and feathers.

Yet there was money on the bedside table left un-touched.

And beside it was the missing doorkey.

I was so exhausted I didn't care about an explanation. I simply registered that I had been condemned to spend the night in that fetid beach hut so that my attacker could possess my key and vandalise my home.

I walked through the debris to the bathroom.

I vomited. Washed. Spread a towel across the slashes in the mattress.

And slept.

NINETEEN

Something was happening, prompting my consciousness, lifting me out of sleep.

Warmth on my face.

The sun? I was aware without opening my eyes that it was day, and probably afternoon. I was hot.

It was not the steady heat of direct sunlight. There was movement in it, soft stirrings of air, regularly spaced, like someone breathing.

I could hear it, too. Hear someone breathing.

I opened my eyes and saw Amber staring down at me. Her face was furrowed in concern.

'Keystone, whatever happened?'

I didn't answer. In my drowsy state, the senses functioned, but the memory refused.

I said, 'Kiss me.'

She still looked anxious, but she lowered her face until her blonde curls slid across my forehead and her open lips touched mine. They moulded to the shape of my mouth, pressed and squeezed with a force that was a revelation to me.

I returned the kiss. I was so distracted that I scarcely noticed that my right arm lay between us until I felt the quick beat of her heart against my hand. Perhaps I deceive myself in saying that I tried to slip the hand away. It met the firm pressure of her breast and moved no further.

'Keystone, no more.'

'You're beautiful.'

'Please, Keystone.'

'You certainly please me, Amber.'

She flushed and drew away. 'Then try to understand me.'

'I thought I did.'

'I have never been with a man like . . . like that.'

I noticed a moistness on her lashes, darkening them.

'Are you afraid?'

She shook her head. 'But when it happens, I want it to be beautiful.' She hesitated, and looked at me with eyes that underlined her words. 'Don't you?'

I tried to draw her to me, but she tensed.

She said, 'What happened to your apartment?'

I remembered, looked around the room, understood what she was telling me. We were lying in a ruin, the squalid wreckage of my personal possessions. Pieces of flock were sticking to our clothes.

'How did you get in?'

'Through the door. The key was in the lock.'

'I must have left it there. I was all in. What time is it?'

'Three in the afternoon.' She straightened her hair. Both of us knew that the moment had passed.

'Why did you come?'

'I thought I would see you at the studios today, but you weren't there. I had to have some still pictures taken, so when I finished I decided to come by and see if your motor car was outside.' She took one of my hands in hers and seemed on the point of saying something affectionate when she caught sight of my arm. 'Your poor wrists! Darling, you've got to tell me about this.'

I told her everything, showed her the marks around my ankles and let her examine the swelling on my head. She offered to apply a cold compress. I thanked her and said I thought a wash and shave would see me restored to health again. I got up and picked a clean shirt off the floor.

When I came back from the bathroom Amber had made the room habitable by folding the contents of the drawers and putting them away.

'I think the accordion is beyond repair.'

I picked up the pieces. 'Yes. It was an old friend, but it's no good now.'

'You must be hungry. Is there a place where I can cook you something?'

I smiled my thanks. 'Through there. Bread. Eggs. Tomatoes.'

'I'll see what I can do.'

While she was in the kitchen, I checked my possessions. The damage was chiefly to the accordion, the suitcases and the mattress. Nothing was stolen. My few articles of value and the money had been left.

Amber came in with coffee and a plate heaped high with scrambled eggs on toast.

'I've checked my things,' I told her. 'Nothing is missing.'

'You're certain?'

'Positive.'

'Will you go to the police?'

'I don't know. I'm not sure what it will achieve. My encounters with them haven't given me much confidence.'

Amber ran her fingers over one of the slashed suitcases. 'Such wanton destruction.'

'I don't think so.'

'What?'

'I don't believe this was capricious. As I see it, it was the outcome of a pretty elaborate plan. There were three stages. The first was to attack me on the cliff, hit me from behind and knock me out. Stage two was to transfer me to the hut, probably after dark, tie me up and trap me there.'

'And then break in here while you were helpless in the hut?'

'They didn't need to break in. They had my key. They let themselves in and set to work without disturbing anyone in the house.'

'But why, Keystone?'

'I'm still not sure. The trouble they took suggests a purpose. I can't believe it was just to vandalise my apartment. They were looking for something. Hence the ripping of the mattress and the damage to the cases and the accordion. These could all conceivably have been used to hide something of value.'

'What?'

'I've no idea. I haven't anything worth hiding. Amber, I want to ask you something. I asked it once before and you didn't precisely answer me.'

'What do you mean?' The colour was draining from her face. I hated causing her distress, but I had to know. 'That night your mother died, someone searched your room, didn't they?'

She hesitated. 'And you think . . .?'

'Amber, I'm trying to make sense of the inexplicable.'

'Yes,' she said. 'Someone had been there.'

'You didn't see them?'

'By the time I got there, they were gone.'

'Did you tell the police?'

'No.' She looked steadily at me. 'I didn't.'

'But the person who was there may have been responsible for your mother's death.'

'Yes.' There was a note of finality in the word.

'Amber, we've got to find them.'

She said in a voice more interested in other things, 'I guess you won't feel like riding in the chase scene now.'

'What?'

'Saturday. My movie. Remember?'

I had never met a girl so single-minded.

TWENTY

When I reached the rendezvous at Main Street and Allesandro I learned that it was just a blind to keep the police department guessing. Studio employees had been out since 7 a.m. stacking barrels of liquid soap behind a building at the corner of 8th Street and Figueroa. It was no use seeking police permission to turn public streets into skid pads; it had to be done by stealth.

We were driven there in a convoy of tin lizzies that made sufficient racket to wake up all Los Angeles. Just off Figueroa Street was a patch of open ground where the studio mechanics were working on the paddy wagon. They disappeared in dust as our drivers made a spectacular circuit of the place before screeching to untidy halts.

In theory at least, we knew what to expect. I was resolved to play an unobtrusive part in the proceedings. For one thing my body wasn't ready for more punishment, and for another I was hazy about the details of the chase. True, I had been present at the meeting when it was discussed, but in the ten days since, a few other things had occupied my mind.

Murray Brennan signalled to us to congregate around him. He wanted to get started right away.

'It's a typical Keystone chase,' he told us through his megaphone, 'and it was all explained to you last week, so the only pile-ups ought to be the ones I scheduled. We have time to rehearse each sequence once in slow time, and then it has to be for real. I have two cameras on the street and one mounted on a wagon, and I intend to keep them rolling, so whatever goes wrong, say your prayers and keep moving. Okay, boys and girls, let's see you in your vehicles ready to go.'

'Keystone!'

I glanced across at Amber, already seated in the Model T Ford the rest of us were about to chase. She was waving.

I went over.

She looked animated, clearly excited by the prospect of the chase. Her eyes were several shades more vivid than I had ever noticed before. 'I'm so pleased you came,' she told me. 'How are you now?'

'Fine,' I said, not wanting to involve Mack Swain in a discussion of my recent problems. He was in the front seat, at the wheel. Amber had young Arnold at her side. 'There's something wrong, you know,' I commented.

'What's that?' asked Amber.

'You look much too happy. You're supposed to be his prisoners.'

Amber pulled a face. 'We haven't started acting yet.'

Mack Swain turned his head and said, 'Listen, Amber, when those guys get the paddy wagon on the move, we won't need to act. The only question is who's in greater danger: them or us.'

'Thanks,' said Amber, laughing. 'Nice to have such a confident driver.'

'Forget the driver,' Swain responded. 'Just hold on to the kid. His mother is out there somewhere.'

'I wouldn't worry about Arnold,' I advised them. 'He looks to me as if he's going to like this as much as sitting on a roof.'

'Push off, Keystone,' muttered Swain.

I winked at Amber and moved on. When I reached the paddy wagon I was sorry I had stopped to speak. It was already full. It was an old six-cylinder Chevrolet with the back seat removed, but the presence of eight Cops accounted for all the space available.

Chester Conklin was one of those aboard. 'Room on the running-board,' he told me with an evil grin.

'Thanks. I'd rather watch.'

'Scared?'

'No. I'm not needed.'

'But you are! Someone has to ride the running-board. Haven't you seen a Keystone chase before?'

'Why me?'

'Last man aboard,' Frank Hayes explained.

Conklin added, 'If you fall off when we skid, don't worry. It's like skating — you don't really hurt.'

At that moment Roscoe Arbuckle lumbered over after a conference with Murray Brennan. 'Sorry, guys,' he announced. 'Murray says I have to be aboard this wagon.'

'That means three more riding on the side,' decided Hayes. 'Charlie, Al.' He took his time. 'And one more. Chester, do you mind?'

'Do I mind?' said Conklin in a horrified voice. 'I was laid up for a month last time I hit the street.'

'You told me it was like a skating rink,' I pointed out.

'Frostbite,' said Hayes casually.

Murray called the first rehearsal and we took up stations on the wagon.

'Isn't someone missing?' I asked Conklin.

'Who's that?'

'Slim Summerville. He was in this picture.'

Conklin put a finger to his lips, so I returned a nod and said no more about it. Presumably we covered up for absent colleagues. I wondered if they would have done the same for me.

We rehearsed the opening sequence. Figueroa Street

was brought to life with vehicles and extras moving and criss-crossing. Mack Swain drove the Model T steadily down the centre, with Amber calling frenziedly for help as she unravelled Arnold's woollen jumper, scattering the trail. Arnold, as anticipated, ruined everything by smiling.

'Fine,' said Murray, with his usual calm. 'We'll do a take on that.'

Amber told him. 'But the baby didn't look alarmed.'

'Don't worry, sweetheart. I've taken care of that.'

When everyone was in position for the take, Murray gave a signal. From somewhere on the sidewalk, Arnold's mother ran towards the model T and gave her beaming offspring a stinging clout across the leg. Arnold bellowed, Swain drove off and the scene was played without a hitch. After it, Murray slipped five dollars to the mother.

They went on to film our overloaded paddy wagon, solo first, then in pursuit. The rehearsals were at little more than walking speed, the takes at 30 miles an hour. By cranking slowly, the cameramen could produce the illusion of much higher speeds. I clung grimly to the side and stared ahead.

'So far so good,' said Murray. 'Now let's try the tricky stuff.'

This was the routine when vehicles shot out of inter-sections and avoided pile-ups by the narrowest of margins. Three automobiles at three different inter-sections were to pass between the Model T and the pursuing paddy wagon. We rehearsed it smoothly at 10 miles an hour. Murray decided on a take.

Mack Swain revved the Ford and drove away. Arnold was still howling in Amber's arms.

The paddy wagon followed, those with free hands brandishing their nightsticks. We picked up speed. The first tin lizzie passed across us. The second was already moving out. It crossed the street desperately slowly. We missed it by perhaps a yard. The third appeared in view.

Then I heard Roscoe Arbuckle shout, 'Oh, my God!'

From the wrong side of the street a fourth motor car had unexpectedly materialised. It was a bright red Brush with beautiful brass lamps.

'That's my car!' I yelled. 'For God's sake, it's my car!'

There was no doubt of it. Slim Summerville was at the wheel. If he had not turned to wave, the Brush would probably have crossed the street untouched.

He waved.

The driver from the opposite direction swerved. The paddy wagon veered a yard off course and shoved the Brush aside. Metal crunched on wood.

In strict accordance with instructions, our driver kept the paddy wagon cruising in pursuit of Swain and Amber. We had to pass another camera. When we halted, Murray shouted, 'That was beautiful, but I didn't schedule it. Where the heck did that red buggy come from?'

I didn't stay to hear the answer. I had already leapt off the paddy wagon and sprinted up the street to inspect the damage.

Slim Summerville stood beside the damaged Brush. He scratched his head. 'Seems like my joke misfired,' he explained with an apologetic grin.

I didn't trust myself to speak. I stood with my arms crossed in front of me and stared at what had been a perfect motor car.

The point of impact was the trunk. The paddy wagon's mudguard had detached it from the chassis. Wood fragments lay around the street.

Summerville asked nervously, 'Was anything inside?'

I shook my head, then remembered the things from Amber's carpet-bag. I stooped to pull aside some of the broken slats of wood. Amber's things were there: the shoes, the *Saturday Evening Post* and the paper parcel with her cooking pans. So far as I could see, they were undamaged. Except that the brown paper round the parcel had been torn, to reveal not saucepans, but what was unmistakably the metal casing of a magazine, the box of film that fitted on a movie camera.

Amber had lied to me.

I was shaking, but I rearranged the paper to cover the magazine from Summerville's view. I don't know why. At that moment, I felt I owed no-one any favours. I said with an effort to stay calm, 'I suppose I can get another trunk.'

'We'll all chip in.'

'You certainly will. I don't intend to foot the bill myself. Whose wonderful idea was this?'

Summerville gave a shrug. 'No-one's in particular. We thought of it together. I volunteered for driver.'

'On this evidence, that's not what I would call you. How many more of these puerile practical jokes am I expected to endure?'

'I guess this wraps it up.'

'That had better be a promise.' I added with a glare, 'I don't have much more property for you to damage.'

'Easy, Keystone — I said we'll pay for the trunk.'

I snapped back, 'And my apartment, my accordion, the bed I sleep in?'

Either Summerville was a better actor than I took him for, or he knew nothing about the wrecking of my apartment. His face showed blank incomprehension.

I didn't tell him about my night in the bathing hut, but I described what I had found when I got home.

He assured me earnestly that the Cops were not the

offenders. 'Hell, smashing up a guy's apartment isn't funny.'

'Is smashing up his motor car?' I asked him icily.

But the denting of a single private vehicle could not long delay a Keystone shooting schedule. At the far end of the street, propmen were rolling out the barrels of liquid soap. Murray ordered us to our positions. There was a chorus of apologies as I climbed aboard the paddy wagon, but no-one felt so conscience-stricken as to offer me a place inside.

Our driver was a madman called "Skid" Rowe. He took the wagon screaming, slipping and careening across the oily intersection in eleven terror-stricken takes. I managed to cling on, but others hit the road. Conklin ripped his trousers and got a ten-inch burn along his thigh. Another man lost a tooth.

When Murray finally called a halt, Mack Sennett was on hand to lavish tributes. He was mounted on a black Arab stallion. Apparently he had ridden out from Edendale to see the fun.

'Nice work, fellas,' he said companionably. 'We cranked some fine stuff there. No casualties, I hope?'

Some instinct told me to keep quiet about the damage to the Brush. Conklin was not so wary. He complained about his burn.

'Let's see, Chester,' said Sennett sympathetically.

Conklin pulled aside the torn part of his trousers and said bitterly, 'I'll never lose that scar.'

'Yup,' said Sennett with a grin. 'You're just another cancelled stamp in the post office of life.' He dismounted and gave the reins to one of Murray's assistants. 'Roscoe, can we talk?'

I caught sight of Amber up the street looking at the damage to my motor car. She was alone.

'It's too bad!' she said as I walked towards her. 'It

was in such beautiful condition.'

'They promised to meet the cost of the repairs.'

'And so they should — the hooligans! They don't behave like adult men at all.'

I studied her face as I said mildly, 'You realise that your property was in there?'

She caught her breath and frowned. Then she opened her eyes wider.

I went on, 'It's undamaged, as far as I can tell.'

She felt for one of her blonde ringlets and twirled it around her finger in an unconvincing effort to seem casual. 'That's good. My fault if it *had* been damaged. I should have moved it out.'

I kept my eyes on hers, as I asked, 'Would you like to have the articles back now?'

'No!' She said it with such force that she decided to repeat it in a calmer voice. 'No, Keystone, if it isn't too much trouble, I'd like to leave them with you. It's kind of reassuring to me, if you understand.'

'I'm not sure that I do.' I didn't spare her. I meant to get the truth this time. 'Why did you tell me there were cooking-pans inside the parcel when it was actually a magazine of film?'

'You know that?' She went white.

'The paper wrapping came undone.'

'Did anyone else . . .?'

I shook my head. 'Nobody but me.'

She grasped my arm. 'I can't talk about it now. Please, darling, keep it for me.'

'This was the reason why my apartment was broken into, wasn't it? They were looking for the film.'

Amber closed her eyes and made a whimper of distress. I said, 'Don't you think I'm entitled to an explanation?'

She said, 'Keystone, whatever am I going to do?'

I couldn't disguise my irritation as I said, 'Amber, how can I answer that without the first idea of what is going on?'

Tears were forming at the corners of her eyes, but she was determined not to tell. 'Darling, I feel so bad about this. I don't know what to say. I had no idea that I would cause you all that trouble. But this is something I must handle by myself.'

I shook my head. 'That's ridiculous and you know it.'

'If you want to help me, keep that film in some safe place until I ask you for it.'

'All right — but only if you tell me what is on it.'

She gripped my arm more tightly. 'Please don't press me any more. When it's safe to talk, I promise you I will.' She turned at the sound of Mack Sennett leading his horse towards us. I swore. She let go of my arm and repeated in a voice that only I could hear, 'I promise.'

Sennett took his horse on a round tour of the Brush, assessing the damage. He grinned at me. 'Why look so down in the mouth? It could have been a whole lot worse.'

I met the grin with a blank stare. 'It should never have occurred.'

'Yup, I heard. Keystone, I'll tell you something interesting. I had a premonition this was going to happen. I have a very acute sixth sense. You know what that is?' Sennett laughed so loud that it unsettled his horse. 'My sense of humour, buddy, my jolly old sense of humour!'

I said acidly, 'Thank you for being so concerned.'

'Shucks, man, don't be such a stuffed shirt. We'll see to the repairs.' Having dealt with me, Sennett turned to Amber. 'Well, honey, what's the matter with you? I'm damned if I'll have every member of my company looking like the world just ended. It's bad for business.

Listen, your movie's in the can now. I'll have the rushes by this evening. Come out to my villa tomorrow afternoon and have a preview in my projection room. Bring your bathing-suit: we'll get some swimming in.'

Amber looked embarrassed. She stammered, 'Mr Sennett, I'm not sure that I —'

'Christ! I forgot I am the big, bad wolf. It's okay, sweetheart. Roscoe will be there with Minta, and some other kids — Murray and Louise. Mae. And Mabel. Keystone, why don't you come too? Take your mind off the lousy automobile.'

'Thank you, but I think I would be rather out of place.'

'Bullshit. Amber, make sure he comes. Around 3.30. Keystone, if you still feel sore tomorrow, you can push me in the goddamn pool.' Sennett mounted and rode away.

Amber said, 'I must change my clothes. Shall I see you there tomorrow?'

'I suppose so. Where are you going next?'

'To have my hair done. It's a mess after all that chasing in the motor cars.'

'And this evening?'

She pressed her mouth together like a child refusing food.

I could see she would say nothing more today, however hard I pressed.

'Tomorrow, then. At Mr Sennett's bathing party.'

She nodded.

'And you definitely want me to keep the film?'

'Please, Keystone — somewhere safe — and I think it's better if you don't tell me where.'

TWENTY-ONE

Roscoe Arbuckle was so confident and agile in the water that no-one else would venture in. He could do marvellous things. He could spring from the edge and arc his whalelike body to cleave the water with such precision that hardly a ripple moved across the surface. Or he could bellyflop and water much of Sennett's garden. This was a popular stunt that splashed the girls and sent them screaming from the poolside. Pretty girls in bathing-suits were not meant to be seen only in repose.

Sennett's villa was Mexican in style, white adobe, with red tiles and wrought iron balconies. The swimming pool was bordered by white arches set at angles that served as shades or sun traps. Sennett himself sat drinking Russian tea with Murray Brennan and Louise. Across the pool, under a striped sunshade, I shared a table with Mack Swain. Amber, Mabel Normand, Mae Busch and Minta Arbuckle dangled their slim ankles in the water at the deep end, waiting for another splash from Roscoe. The Sennett servants in black ties and white shirts kept us all supplied with drinks.

'Isn't Keystone going to take a dip?' Mabel Normand called across the pool.

'Keystone is not equipped for aquatic exercise,' I answered with the touch of self-burlesque I had adopted in America. I was in shirt and white flannels. I hadn't brought a costume. If I was honest, I hadn't come to enjoy the party. I was there because of Amber. She still fascinated and exasperated me. I felt that I deserved her trust, yet she stubbornly withheld it. Why? The only way to find out was to stick with her, watch her. And watch the people around her. Any of them might have had a hand in the ugly events of recent weeks.

'Keystone can borrow a costume if he really wants to swim, can't he, Mack?' called Mabel, bent on making mischief.

The prospect of Keystone in a bathing-costume was overtaken by a more distracting spectacle. Roscoe Arbuckle had used the conversation to swim unperceived below the water to where the girls were sitting. The first they knew of it was when Mae Busch gave a shriek as Roscoe grabbed her ankles and dragged her into the pool.

Mae was in a two-piece costume consisting of a pink wrapover jacket and red and white striped drawers. The costume was attractive, but not designed for bathing. In the water it became diaphonous. Roscoe, below the surface, was oblivious of this. He expected Mae to wriggle, and she did. It was part of the amusement. He held his breath and stayed submerged, still holding on to her ankles.

Mack Sennett heard the commotion. He stopped his conversation with the Brennans and came closer to the pool in time to see Roscoe let go of Mae.

Mae did the only thing she could, swam on her front towards the shallow end. Under the stripes of red and white, her bottom bravely flexed and bobbed. Sennett held his sides and laughed.

The other girls were on their feet, safely out of Roscoe's reach. Minta had been trying to shout through five feet of water to her husband. Amber had her hands pressed to her mouth. Mabel's initial peal of laughter died away. She had her eyes on Sennett. She shouted, 'When you've seen enough, she might appreciate some help.'

Sennett gestured to a waiter to bring a bathrobe over. His laughter still reverberated round the pool. He took the robe to meet Mae at the shallow end.

Mae struggled upright and waded the last yards, using hands and arms to keep a modicum of decency. She matched the laughter with a sporting grin. Sennett put out a hand to help her. Perhaps from desperation, she grabbed the hand and pulled him in.

Sennett was fully clothed in an expensive linen suit. He toppled on to Mae and they both went under. He had his arms around her and he kept them there. He and Mae stood up. He was not annoyed. He still shook with laughter. He stooped and picked her up and climbed unaided from the pool.

'A dry robe for the lady and a cigar for me,' he called to the waiters. 'Hey, boys and girls, I really asked for that, didn't I?' He set Mae down, patted her backside and took the robe and placed it round her shoulders. She gave him a sidelong smile.

'You bet!' said Mabel bitterly as she came towards them. 'I don't know which is the bigger ass — Mae's or the one that I'm engaged to marry.'

Mae made a sound that was something like a war cry.

'Come on, come on,' said Sennett tersely. 'It does no harm to spill a little soup on dignity. That's my guiding principle, and it pays. How do you think I got to be the world's most eligible bachelor?' He put his hand out to Mabel, but she jerked away.

'I don't want you touching me. You're wet.'

'Christ, so I am — has it been raining?' asked Sennett, playing to the gallery. He turned to Mae. 'You and I had better get into some dry things, my dear. I guess our charming audience will excuse us after the entertainment we provided.' He took Mae's arm and started walking up the steps towards the house.

Mabel was about to say something, but Minta came close and touched her arm. In the pool, the perpetrator of the incident lingered guiltily.

Minta said, 'Roscoe.' With a jerk of her head, she told him what to do.

He nodded, shouted after Sennett, 'Wait for me,' and clambered out and followed them.

Minta sighed. 'Just like some dumb kid out of school.'

Mabel commented, 'I wish I could believe that,' but her mind was clearly not on Roscoe.

The Brennans had been left alone during the diversion. They got up and spoke to Amber. Then they walked around the pool to the table I was sharing with Mack Swain. We greeted them.

Louise Brennan said, 'Good afternoon,' and in those two conventional words conveyed her absolute distaste at what had just been happening in the pool. She was in one of her enormous hats, pink to match her dress.

Murray was more relaxed. 'Looking forward to the screening, fellas?'

Mack Swain grinned. 'Haven't we had enough slap-stick for one afternoon?'

'How does it look?' I asked.

Murray shrugged. 'How would I know? Mack does all his own cutting.'

I turned to Louise and what I thought was a safer subject. 'Where are your little girls this afternoon?'

She softened slightly. 'It's their riding afternoon. We left them at the stables on our way here.'

'Mack invited us to bring them,' added Murray.

'I'm glad we didn't,' said Louise.

'Maybe we should join the other ladies,' suggested Swain.

'Ladies?' said Louise.

No-one followed that. We strolled across and got into an easier conversation with Minta Arbuckle. Mabel was unusually subdued. She kept glancing at the house.

After what seemed an age, Roscoe Arbuckle called down from the terrace, 'Anyone coming to see the rushes?'

Sennett and Mae Busch were already in adjoining armchairs in the projection room. They were in matching yellow bathrobes. Sennett got up to greet his guests.

'We'd better have the players of this little masterpiece along the front row.'

'I feel so nervous, I'd rather hide,' said Amber.

Swain said, 'Hide behind Roscoe. Let's all of us hide behind Roscoe.'

'Why are you nervous, Amber?' Mae enquired.

Mabel Normand said casually as she moved into the seat Sennett had vacated, 'She knows it's make or break.'

Minta Arbuckle said, 'From what I heard, she has no reason to be nervous.'

Mabel turned in her chair and said with a charged quality in her voice, 'What exactly did you hear?'

Minta gave a puzzled smile. 'Why, that the rushes are very good.'

Mabel turned to me, 'I should explain that Amber's elevation to leading actress surprised us all, or all but one.' Her eyes fixed on Sennett. 'Quite a lot that goes on here is going to have to be explained some time.'

Sennett said, 'Keystone, would you kindly press the light switch?'

The picture show took over. It was at once apparent that the footage from the previous week was already cut and spliced. Even without titles, the pictures told a story. They also told how skilful Sennett was inside the cutting room. The film had pace and visual impact over and above its comic content. No-one would describe it as a classic, but it would not disgrace the name of Keystone Films. It roused sufficient laughs to ease the tension in the audience.

The chase was on another reel, still in its fragmentary form, although the poorer takes had been removed. When the paddy wagon started up the street, Sennett called, 'Hold on to Keystone, Amber. Here it comes!'

We watched the Brush emerge sedately from the side street and take its mortifying bump as Slim Summerville turned to wave.

'That stays in,' said Sennett. 'It's a howl!'

Amber placed her hand softly on my rigid arm.

When the last frame ran through the gate, Sennett said, 'Congratulations, everyone. I like it. We'll ship it to New York this week.'

Mabel switched on the light and said, 'Do you really think that's wise?'

'Mabel, what's gotten into you?' demanded Sennett. 'I like the picture. That's enough.'

'Sure. It's up to you, Mack. It always is.'

Sennett scowled and chewed a piece off his cigar. 'That's one opinion. How about the rest of you? Not the front row, the uncommitted. Mae, you've been quiet. What's your verdict?'

Mae looked along the row and caught Mabel's eye. 'If you want my honest opinion, Mack, it could be improved by reshooting some of the scenes.'

Suddenly the two antagonists were allies.

Mabel nodded. 'Like the scenes with the nurse.'

At this, Amber was on her feet. 'I'm not taking that from you!'

'Ladies, ladies!' Sennett cautioned. 'Let's keep this civilised.'

'Can't you see they're ganging up on me?' cried

Amber. 'They don't want competition. They want all the leading parts for themselves.' She thrust her finger accusingly at Mae. 'She was a throwout from a two-bit musical that flopped. She wouldn't rate a walk-on if she wasn't Mabel's friend.'

Mae stood up and was immediately yanked back into her seat by Sennett. She still said, 'So what's *your* trump card, Amber Honeybee? One thing's sure — it isn't talent!'

'Shut up the lot of you!' ordered Sennett. 'Jesus, what a Sunday afternoon! Listen, while my name is over the front gate of Keystone Studios, I'll hire the dames I please, and, by hell, I'll fire them, too. Try me. Let's hear one more bleat from any of you.'

Amber's eyes still blazed. She turned and quit the room.

Sennett commented, 'Not so easy to make the big exit in a bathing-costume.'

It broke the tension.

'We could all use a little sunshine, I guess,' said Murray, getting up.

Sennett rested a hand on my shoulder. 'By the way, we got a replacement trunk for that buggy of yours. Take it into the auto shop in the morning and you'll be on the road again tomorrow evening. Now see what you can do with Amber, will you? I prepared a barbecue, and I refuse to eat all those damn spare ribs myself.'

TWENTY-TWO

'Bitches!'

'Prize ones.'

'They wouldn't get a prize from me.'

'Just bitches, then.'

'Ugly bitches.'

'Utterly revolting.'

Amber smiled through her tears.

I said, 'Better?'

She lifted her face to receive a kiss. I didn't disoblige.

'I think you'd better change now.'

'I'm not cold.'

'I know.' I slid my hand slowly down the length of her back.

She put her two hands on my face and kissed me hard. 'You've persuaded me.'

I raised my eyebrows.

'To change my clothes,' said Amber. She took my arm and we returned to the house.

Sennett was on the terrace singing the drinking song from *Traviata* as the food was served.

'This smacks of desperation,' Mack Swain commented to me.

The party carried on. There were smouldering looks across the terrace, but the only flare-up was the barbecue itself. The evening was still light when the Brennans excused themselves on the grounds that they had to collect their children. Amber took this as her cue to leave as well. I offered to drive her back and she accepted.

Murray Brennan's Packard was parked in Sennett's drive in front of my damaged Brush. While his chauffeur cranked the engine, Murray came over to Amber, already seated in the Brush. 'My dear, I didn't speak up in there for obvious reasons. Don't let those things they said discourage you. You're going to whip them all.' He raised his hat. 'That's all I wanted to say. Good evening to you both.'

'Thank you,' said Amber. 'You're really kind.' She turned to me. 'I feel better for that.'

'Yes,' I said. 'I'll start her up.'

Murray came back while I was wrestling with the handle. 'I just had a word with Louise. Why don't you two drive over and have dinner with us tomorrow evening?'

Thus it was that next evening I drove the Brush, fully renovated by the studio mechanics, along the Pacific Coast Road to Malibu. I had borrowed a tuxedo, and Amber was in a long black velvet dress with a large mother-of-pearl brooch worn close to the left shoulder. She had warned me to expect formality, and she was right.

The house was white as the President's and trying to be whiter. A butler stepped from the colonnaded entrance.

'He's stumped,' I said to Amber. 'He's never seen a motor car without a door to open.' As we drew up in front of him, I asked, 'Shall I leave it here?'

'If you leave the motor running, sir, one of the staff will take care of it.'

I murmured to Amber, 'He means put it out of sight.'

The butler led us across a tiled floor that clattered under our shoes. The whole place evoked Louise. Pastel pinks and blues. Rosewood furniture. A small rococo fountain playing in the centre.

The Brennans were waiting in the room beyond. They got up from a high-backed, cushioned sofa. Louise extended a lace-gloved hand. Uncertain whether I was expected to kiss it or shake it, I found myself making the uneasy compromise of holding it a moment and dipping my shoulders in a rudimentary bow.

Murray kissed Amber on the cheek. 'Good of you both to come.'

Louise said, 'I don't know what you must think of us, inviting you to dinner with no-one but ourselves to meet.'

'It was my idea,' admitted Murray with a smile.

'He's so impetuous,' said Louise. 'How could I raise a dinner party almost overnight?'

'So we have you to ourselves,' said Murray.

Amber asked, 'Won't we meet your daughters?'

Louise shook her head. 'Children don't eat dinner.'

'That's not to say we keep them hungry,' said Murray with his knack of cushioning his wife's remarks. 'Who's for a drink?'

Over dinner, served in a panelled dining room by a waiter in black tie and tails, Amber talked earnestly about her Boston childhood. Louise, probably remembering Sennett's party, was slow in warming to her, but by degrees she did.

'How sad for you that your parents aren't over here to share in your success.'

'My mother was,' said Amber, and she hesitated.

I explained, 'There was an accident last month. Mrs Honeybee was killed.'

'How terrible! My dear, I didn't mean to —'

'It's all right,' said Amber quickly. 'People have been very kind.'

'They're not a bad crowd at Keystone,' said Murray, adding as an afterthought, 'Most of them.' He gave a sly smile. 'Darn it, you get occasional injured feelings among professional people any place. Actors are highly strung individuals.'

'You mean actresses?' said Amber, smiling unself-consciously.

'I think we are all the same,' I put in. 'None of us likes to be belittled by a jealous rival.'

'Right,' said Murray. 'Why should you take it on the chin?'

Later, over coffee, Louise said, 'We've given some lovely parties here. Nobody ever misbehaves. My belief is that the host and hostess should set the tone. If you expect people to respect your standards, they will.'

'Mack Sennett, for example?' Murray asked her, a twinkle in his eye.

Louise answered, 'That person is beyond the pale of decency.'

Murray explained, 'He asked for the spittoon. Louise thought it was some Irishism for the bathroom.'

Louise said, 'I had never heard of such a thing.'

'She had the butler show him where to go,' chuckled Murray, 'and the best of it was that Sennett went!'

Louise glared at her husband and Amber tactfully nudged the conversation in another direction. 'I don't suppose all your dinner guests are movie people.'

'Most of them tend to be,' said Murray. 'That's the way it is in this business. You need to know people. The social round is almost as important as what happens on the studio floor. I guess the only friends I have outside the business are real old buddies from San Francisco days. That's going back a bit.'

'Eight years,' said Louise.

'We keep in touch. They look us up occasionally.'

'Were you happy living in San Francisco?' Amber asked.

'Happy to get away,' said Louise.

'The earthquake?' I ventured.

'No,' said Murray. 'Me. She was happy to get away with me. Isn't that right, sweetheart?'

Louise lavished a long smile on Murray. However oddly matched they seemed, there was unmistakable, at times embarrassing, love between them.

'Do you know Frisco, Amber?' Murray asked.

'I've never been there.'

'How about Keystone?'

'I played at the Empress for a fortnight earlier this year.'

'I forgot you were in vaudeville. See much of the city?'

'Not enough. What I saw I liked.'

'You should take Amber for a trip up there in that red buggy of yours.'

Louise said sharply, 'That's not a nice suggestion, Murray. It would be too far to make into a day trip.'

Murray winked at me and said nothing.

Amber, unperturbed, said, 'Keystone doesn't want to spend his wages on a trip to San Francisco. He's going back to Europe to fight the war.'

'Really? That's patriotic. When do you plan to go?'

'When I've earned enough to pay my way. I borrowed some to buy the car. I should have enough in six weeks to clear my debt, sell the car and buy my passage home — provided Mr Sennett doesn't sack me.'

'He won't do that. You got talent.'

'I haven't got a contract.'

'None of us has. It's a point of pride with Mack that no-one has a legal obligation to work for him. He lost some good people that way: Ford Sterling, Chaplin, Marie Dressler. One day he'll lose Roscoe, but he'll never learn. The only player he's sure of keeping is

Mabel. She's tied to him emotionally. Always will be.'

'More coffee, Amber?' Louise asked.

'Amber is a case in point — if I may, Amber?' Murray went on. 'She's come up by the Sennett route and now she is a leading lady. *Kidnap in the Park* is being shipped this week. Pretty soon we'll get reactions. My guess is good ones.'

Amber went pink with pleasure.

Murray grinned at her and said, 'But Amber isn't too crazy about playing comedy. She'd rather be in dramatic roles. Pretty soon she'll get an offer from another company and she'll take it, because what is there to keep her at Keystone? Certainly not Mack's charming personality.'

'Or his manners,' said Louise.

'Let's face it,' Murray said. 'Not one of us is in it out of loyalty. I happen to have a few ideas myself about the kinds of picture I would make if I went independent. This is confidential, but I don't want to go on making comedies much longer. When I can raise a production team of real talent I'll be ready. I have the finance and I'm damn sure Tommy Ince can lease me some studio space. I've asked around a bit, and I figure I can raise a crew from Keystone who would be delighted to tell Sennett to go —'

'Murray!' said Louise in a shocked voice.

'So you see,' said Murray, smiling. 'Mack Sennett is his own worst enemy.'

While this all too obvious sales pitch had been going on, I had studied Amber. Her eyes were shining. She asked exactly the question he had fed her.

'You said you have ideas outside comedy. What do you have in mind?'

Murray stirred his coffee. 'That's kind of a secret, Amber.'

Louise looked quite severe. 'Now, Murray, that's not fair. You've kindled Amber's interest. You really can't bite your lip at this stage.' She turned to Amber. 'He wants to make pictures of the great classic stories of the Greeks. Real pictures, four and five reels long.'

'How marvellous!' said Amber.

'For God's sake, keep it quiet,' said Murray. 'I'm terribly afraid someone else may get in there first before I'm ready.'

'They will if you delay much longer,' said Louise.

'Okay,' said Murray. 'I'll have to phrase this carefully. I don't want to be accused of leading a revolt at Keystone. If circumstances made it possible, Amber, would you consider moving to another company?'

'Tomorrow, if you like!' said Amber, flushing all over her fair skin. Then she looked at me and said, 'Well, I guess it couldn't be so soon as that.'

'I'd ask you too, Keystone, only I figure you're not looking for a long career in movies.'

'He's going to be a soldier,' said Louise.

'Yes,' I said, and added cynically. 'Not Alexander the Great, however.'

'That's one picture we definitely won't make,' said Murray.

'Why?' asked Amber.

Murray glanced at his wife. 'Louise had a previous marriage to a guy called Alex, and he was a real son of a gun. Debts. Booze —'

'All right,' said Louise. 'You made your point, Murray.' To Amber she explained, 'My first husband was a victim of the fire that followed the earthquake. It was a short, unhappy marriage.'

'To come back to my pipedreams,' said Murray, 'you were asking what ideas I had. Back of my mind, I have this movie almost ready. It's called *The Siege* and it's the story of the Trojan War. Without going into details, there's a certain part I think you could play better than any actress this side of America. But unlike Mack, I intend to work with contracts and if you were interested we would have to enter delicate negotiations first.'

'I understand,' said Amber in a whisper. From the way she held her head and looked into the distance, she was already launching ships.

TWENTY-THREE

It was after midnight when we left. The Brush was ticking over and the lamps were lighted. It was drawn up at the steps below the entrance and the butler waited in attendance. His only function was to assist us in stepping up to our seats.

'I feel like royalty,' Amber told me as I drove away. She took out her handkerchief and waved it to the Brennans, standing arm in arm to see us off. When there was no more cause to wave, she settled into her seat with her head against my shoulder. 'What an enchanting evening!'

'Yes, I'm sure you would have found it so.'

She missed or overlooked the emphasis of my remark. 'Isn't Murray one of the most charming men you ever met? And Louise was very sweet when she relaxed. At first I wondered why he married her, she seemed so starchy.'

'I expect she married *him*.'

Amber gave a giggle of incomprehension. 'What's the difference?'

'Murray has two priceless assets that Louise was sharp enough to recognise: dedication to the job and a way of putting people at their ease. So she married Murray to realise her ambition.'

'What's that?'

'To become what you Americans call a socialite. Didn't that house strike you as insufferably pretentious, with its columns at the entrance and the stupid fountain and the butler and the waiter obviously hired for the evening?'

'I think that's a little unfair, Keystone. I quite enjoyed it.'

'But you must admit it reflects her tastes and aspirations more than his.'

'You're probably right. Keystone, you're deeper than you seem.' She made a murmur of pleasure. 'Don't the lights ahead look dreamy? How would you like to stop and enjoy them for a while?'

'It's late.'

'I know. Is that important?'

I had other matters on my mind than the lights ahead, however dreamy. 'As you wish.' I steered off the road on to a slab of rock that overlooked the ocean, and switched off the engine.

Amber nestled closer to me and said, 'I'm happy.'

I did not reply.

She passed her hand across my shirt-front. 'You're warm.'

'Yes.'

'Tell me what you're thinking, Keystone.'

'That I shouldn't have switched off the engine. I'll only have to get out and crank it in a minute.'

'That's not too romantic.'

'No.'

There was another period of silence before she asked, 'What's biting you?'

'I'm sorry.'

'That isn't really an answer. We had a delicious meal in a beautiful house with charming people and here we are looking at the moonlight on the ocean and you think about cranking the engine. You've got to admit it isn't going to make my heart beat faster.'

I stared ahead in silence. 'If you really want to know, I feel depressed.'

'But why?'

'A combination of things. Unlike you, I didn't enjoy the evening, and I feel hypocritical for pretending that I did. That's one thing. Then there's you.'

'Me? Do I depress you?'

'Yes.' I turned to face her. 'You see, I care about you, Amber.'

She said in a whisper, 'But that's nice. That's what I was hoping you might say.'

'Ah, yes,' I told her in a hard, ironic voice. 'Also that I find you beautiful and fascinating and unique?'

She caught her breath with a sound that might have been a sob. 'Don't say it like that. You sound resentful.'

'I am: resentful that against my soundest instincts, I care for someone who will not be frank with me.'

She moved away and stared at the city lights. 'That again. You think I have some secret you should know.'

'I'm certain of it. It's connected with that damn parcel of film that was hidden in this car.'

'It doesn't matter any more.'

'Amber, it does. Someone broke into my apartment to look for that film.'

'Keystone, I said I was sorry about that.'

'He also entered your bungalow the night your mother died, while you were at the Arbuckles'. He searched your room. He went to your mother's room without expecting to find her there. He pushed her against the washstand. He killed her, Amber.'

She blurted out, 'Don't say that! It was an accident.'

'I don't believe it was.'

She put her hand up to my mouth. 'Please. I know what you are trying to say, but I don't want to hear it.'

We were both silent for a moment.

'You see?' I told her. 'How can I be romantic, as you put it, when you won't trust me enough to let me help you? You could be in danger.'

'Not any more. *Really*, Keystone.'

'Why not? What has changed?'

'This evening altered everything. Murray's plans. I'll be leaving Keystone for good. Once I've quit, there will be no reason for anyone to hurt me.'

'The danger stems from someone in the Keystone Company — is that what you are saying?'

She gave a shrug and said off-handedly, 'If you insist.'

'Who? Mack Sennett? Mabel Normand?'

She turned her face away. 'I don't know. I can't be sure.' Then she looked at me again. 'But don't you see, if I work for Murray, I'll be out of everyone's hair at Keystone.'

'Is that why you practically fell into his arms when he mentioned the possibility?'

Her mouth tightened. 'That's not true, and not fair, either.'

'It was hardly the manner in which a leading lady should receive an offer to join a rival studio.'

'I was taken by surprise.'

'You shouldn't have been. You must have realised that something was behind the invitation to dinner.'

'You can't take anything for granted in the movie business.'

'You didn't have to make it obvious that you were ready to jump at any offer.'

Amber said acidly. 'Since when have you been my agent?'

I picked the crank-handle off the floor. 'I'm going to drive you home.'

'You're jealous, aren't you?'

'Jealous of whom?'

'Murray. He's taking me away from you. He clicks

his fingers and I come running and that really puts your nose out of joint, doesn't it, Keystone?'

'Don't be ridiculous.' I stepped out, went to the front of the car, engaged the handle and swung it hard. The engine roared. I removed the handle and got in beside her. 'I like the man. And I respect his wife. She has a head for business.'

'Meaning I haven't, I suppose?'

'I didn't say that. You are determined and ambitious and you got all you wanted from Mack Sennett, so why shouldn't you succeed with Murray and Louise?' I reversed the car into the road and drove it fast to Santa Monica.

Outside the bungalow, before she left the car, Amber turned to me and said with an effort at control, 'Believe whatever you like about me, Keystone, but I'm telling you one thing: I swear to God I haven't let Mack Sennett take advantage of me, or any other man — and I think you know what I mean. As for Murray Brennan, it may surprise you that he actually loves that insufferable snob of a wife. A woman can tell, you know.' Her voice broke into sobs and she stepped out of the car and ran up the path to the bungalow.

I didn't go after her. I sat still for a long time.

TWENTY-FOUR

I spent the next few days ignoring Amber. Or trying to. It was childish really. I would not go cap in hand to her when she didn't trust me enough to share a secret with me. It wasn't easy. I still felt a strong attraction to her. I told myself it was merely an appetite of the flesh. I tried feeding it with the poison of her faults: selfishness, stubborness, blind ambition, self-delusion, paucity of talent. I knew I was only demeaning myself, yet I would not relent. I could be stubborn too. And at the back of my mind was the comforting conviction that she would have to come to me. Because only I knew where her can of film was hidden.

On the following Monday morning, I reported with the Cops to make a Keystone comedy called *Traffic Duty*. It was to be filmed entirely on the studio lot. This was because the genuine policeman with the hapless duty of patrolling Edendale had filed his twentieth report about the Keystone company creating mayhem on the public streets, and this time the Deputy Commissioner had acted. He had spelt it out to Sennett that the next time there was trouble it would bring official retribution on a scale as stringent as was possible within the limits of the law. He had added that the kind donations from the Keystone company to the Police Widows and Orphans Fund could in no way be permitted to divert him from his duty.

The remedy was Sennett's usual one when things got difficult outside. He sent a cameraman to shoot stills of one of the intersections along Allesandro Street and had them enlarged many times to make enormous backdrops. They were erected on the studio street. To a movie audience, the rapid movement of the automobiles would distract the eye from the deficiencies in perspective.

The scenario called for each of the Cops to take a turn directing traffic. We were told to improvise some 'business'. Summerville, Conklin and the others earned their laughs by being tumbled over by vehicles they misdirected. When my turn came, I used a music-hall routine based on economy of movement. I stood stiffly to attention on the traffic officer's stand and started gently swaying from the ankles. Presently I was tilting back and forward to angles that looked funny and physically impossible. Muscular control had a part in it. So also did the ridge of metal under which I had wedged the welts of my boots.

As a further gag, I pretended to be tired. I balanced on one leg and swung the other gently, like a pendulum. With each swing, the leg appeared to shorten slightly, until when I put it down, it was six inches shorter than the other and I fell sideways off the stand. The director liked it. He said he would shoot the scene immediately after lunch.

On the way to the restaurant I noticed Murray Brennan's Packard parked in front of the tower. I nodded to the chauffeur and walked on.

A short time later, Murray himself appeared in the restaurant. He came to the table where I was eating with the other Cops.

'Excuse me breaking in like this, fellas. Keystone, is Amber anywhere about?'

I gave a shrug. 'I really wouldn't know. I haven't seen her.'

'I'd like to find her if I can. I fixed to meet her for

lunch on Friday. She didn't show up. No message. Nothing.'

I put down my knife and fork. 'I find that difficult to understand.'

'Have you spoken to her since the other evening?'

'No, we haven't seen each other.'

'I'd like to find her,' said Murray. 'That, er, project we discussed — I'm ready to talk business now if Amber is still interested. I planned to mention it to Mack this afternoon, but I'd like to speak to Amber first. You don't think she could have changed her mind?'

'That's highly improbable.'

'Here's my card. If you see her will you ask her to call my home tonight?'

As soon as Murray had moved off, Chester Conklin asked, 'What's this, then? Amber joining another outfit?'

'I really couldn't say. Have any of you seen her?'

Summerville said, 'Not since we shot the chase last week.'

The others shook their heads.

'Maybe she is sick,' suggested Conklin.

I took out my watch. 'I think I've got time to drive down to Santa Monica.'

'Want some company?' offered Summerville, possibly in atonement for the damage to the motor car.

'No thank you. I'd rather go alone.'

I had parked the Brush in the street outside the studio gates. I headed through the dust of Beverly Hills along the Boulevard to Santa Monica.

The bungalow had no windows open. I knocked and got no reply. I walked around the outside looking in. The place was tidy and uninhabited. I saw a woman watching me from the bungalow next door. I knocked to ask her when she had seen Amber last. The woman shook her head. She could not remember. It must have been some time the previous week. I got into the car and went back to work.

During a break in filming in the afternoon I called at Wardrobe and asked the effusive Winnie whether she had news of Amber. That was a miscalculation.

'Why — is something wrong?'

'Not as far as I know. Have you seen her today?'

'Can't say I have.' She grinned at me. 'You two are getting kind of close, aren't you?'

I ignored that. 'Do you remember when you saw her last?'

'Some day last week. Oh, it was way back. Hey, is anything the matter?'

'I don't think so.'

'This hasn't anything to do with the old man's grouchy mood today, by any chance?'

'Do you mean Mr Sennett?'

'Who else? The office girls say he's been acting like his bath was cold. He chucked a boot at Abdul the Turk and he told his gagmen they were a bunch of illiterates and sent them home. They don't know if they're sacked or not, and no-one likes to ask. We've had black Irish moods from Mack before, but this must be one of the worst. If he comes this way, I'm out and through the back, I promise you.'

'Murray Brennan went to see him. Perhaps they had a row,' I mooted.

Winnie shook her head. 'The fur was flying long before that. It looks to me like something happened over the weekend. I would have got the inside story from Mabel, only she ain't here today. Neither is Roscoe, nor Minta. And now you tell me Amber isn't here. The way things are going, nobody will be left except that madman in the tower.'

'I think I'd better get back to work.'

'Quick as your long legs can carry you, Mr Keystone.'

Late that evening, I again drove past the bungalow. There were no lights inside. I stopped and walked back slowly. I knocked, with no result.

There was a mailbox by the gate. I opened it. There were two letters in there, both bills by the look of them. One was datemarked the day Amber and I had visited the Brennans.

TWENTY-FIVE

There was still no news of Amber at the studio on Tuesday. She had not communicated with the office, but as she was not required for filming that week, no-one except me displayed more than a passing interest in her absence. I tried several times to see Mack Sennett, but the word was that the boss was seeing no-one except Abdul.

Thanks to a good run of first and second takes, the morning's schedule on *Traffic Duty* was got through by 11.30, so I took the opportunity to drive down to the coast to Roscoe Arbuckle's house. My knock was answered by a maid, who asked my name and left me standing in the porch. In a moment Minta came to the door. She looked strained and tired. Her auburn hair hung loose around her shoulders as if she had not had time to pin it up. From the way she kept her hand on the door she made it plain that she did not intend to invite me in.

'Hello Keystone.'

I raised my cap. 'I apologise for calling unannounced like this, Minta. I would have spoken at the studio to Roscoe, but I haven't seen him there.'

'No, Roscoe is quite well.' She added with the same tight quality in her voice. 'Did Mack Sennett send you?'

'He isn't ill?'

'No, Roscoe is quite well.' She added with the same tight quality in her voice, 'Did Mack Sennett send you?'

I shook my head. 'I haven't spoken to Mr Sennett this week. This has nothing to do with him, so far as I'm aware. I am trying to contact Amber.'

'Amber?' Minta's features softened as she frowned. 'She's not here, Keystone.'

'You see, she hasn't been home for days. No-one has seen her. I thought, as you and Roscoe took an interest in her, you might know where she is.'

'I didn't know she was missing. You'd better speak to Roscoe.' She bit her lip. 'This may seem inhospitable, but would you mind waiting here while I fetch him?'

In a minute Roscoe appeared wearing a hat and with a brown and white terrier on a leash. He closed the door behind him, put an arm around me and guided me firmly away from the house. 'I'll put you in the picture presently. Now what is this about Amber?'

I repeated what I had told Minta, and added, 'I'm beginning to feel concerned.'

'Let's walk Luke along the beach. Could she have gone to visit with her father in Boston?'

'It's unlikely,' I replied as we started down the wooden steps to the Santa Monica State Beach. 'They don't get on so well. After her mother's funeral, they decided to go their different ways. And there's another thing. This is in confidence. Murray Brennan is thinking of leaving Keystone and making his own pictures. He invited Amber to lunch to talk about a leading role. She was very excited at the prospect. Roscoe, she didn't turn up.'

'That is a queer thing,' Roscoe agreed. 'Did she tell Sennett about the offer from Murray?'

'I don't believe she did. But Murray called at the office yesterday. He was planning to raise the subject with Mr Sennett. He was really surprised not to have heard from Amber.'

'And of course you tried the bungalow?'

'She hasn't collected her letters since Thursday.'

Roscoe shook his head. 'It *is* a mystery, and I don't know what to suggest. You say you haven't talked to Sennett?'

'I tried, but he is incommunicado. I was told he was in an evil temper yesterday.'

'I can believe that,' said Roscoe. He bent to let Luke off the leash, then stood up facing me. 'This, too, is confidential, but I figure you ought to be wise to it before you go see Sennett. The reason Minta didn't invite you into the house this morning is that we have Mabel with us and she's in a pitiful state.'

'Mabel? Why? Whatever has happened?'

'It's a messy story, Keystone, and I guess we should have seen it coming. Last Sunday afternoon Mabel and Minta went for a drive with Anne Harvey. Do you know Anne?'

'No.'

'She's on the Keystone payroll. Tall girl. Dark, curly hair. Anyway these three are friends off the set, and they like to meet and gossip, as girls do, so they borrowed my chauffeur and took a picnic hamper to the forest out beyond San Fernando. On the drive back, there was some joshing about men in general. It was all lighthearted and amusing until Anne dropped the bombshell that she happened to know Mack Sennett had lately been dating Mae Busch.'

'Somewhat tactless.'

'Not only that,' said Roscoe. 'She told Mabel that if she went to Mae's apartment that afternoon, she would find Sennett there.'

'That was downright nasty.'

'Maybe Anne didn't understand how serious Mabel is about marrying Mack,' said Roscoe charitably. 'Their romance has been going almost as long as motion pictures. Most times you can tease Mabel a little about it, only there's a difference now. Sennett has actually named the day — July 4th — and Mabel has bought the wedding dress.'

'Yes, I was there when she told him. I suspect that the naming of the day was precipitated by the purchasing of the dress.'

Roscoe gave an indulgent smile. 'You could be right. After all this time, Mabel can be forgiven for trying to force his hand. He flirts with every woman who walks into the studio, but he really loves Mabel. She thinks marriage will straighten him out.'

I raised my eyebrows sceptically.

Roscoe nodded. 'Yup, I know exactly what you're thinking. You saw what happened at the bathing party. Mabel was humiliated in front of all those people, but she forgave him.'

'She appeared to forgive Mae Busch as well.'

'You mean when they joined forces to pan Amber's acting? That's a fact, they did. You must understand that Mae is one of Mabel's closest friends. It goes back years, before Mabel went to Biograph. When she was thirteen, she was put to work in the pattern department of a women's magazine. She had a nice figure even at that age, and they persuaded her to model the dresses. By fifteen, she was well known as an illustrators' model. You've heard of Charles Dana Gibson, the artist of the Gibson girls?'

I nodded.

'Mabel posed for Gibson and James Montgomery Flagg — the two top painters of girls in America. That was when she met Mae. They were just two pretty little girls in Brooklyn who appeared on the covers of magazines, and they became good friends. When Mae came out west last year with a road company musical she looked Mabel up. And when the musical folded,

Mabel rescued her. She let her stay in her apartment and found her a job at Keystone. So you see why she couldn't credit that Mae would steal the man she loved and worshipped?'

'And is that what has happened?'

'Mabel had to be sure. While she was in the motor car with the others she laughed it off, but after she got back she went to call on Mae, who came to the door herself and invited her in. There was no sign of Sennett. Mabel confessed that she felt ashamed to mention it, but she asked Mae straight out if she was having an affair with Sennett. Like you would expect, Mae denied it. She seemed shocked and deeply hurt by the suggestion. But they talked it through and parted on good terms, with Mae promising to come to the wedding. Mabel went home in a much happier frame of mind.' Roscoe paused. 'The next part of the story is the way Mabel tells it. Possibly like me, you may suspect there was something more going on in her mind than she admits. Her version is that when she got home she discovered she had left her purse at Mae's place.'

'She went back?'

Roscoe nodded. 'It was only a couple of blocks. She went around to the back door, like she had often done before. It was not locked. She could hear voices — Mae's and a man's. She had to know. She opened the door. This room back of the house was a bedsitting room.'

'Sitting was not the activity in progress?'

'You've got the picture. Mae stark naked; Mack in his undervest caught climbing out of bed in a state you rarely see outside a stud farm. Keystone, if I didn't care about each of these two people as much as I do, it would be a howl. It was pure slapstick after that. Mabel asked what the hell was going on, as if it wasn't standing out a mile

158

— well, you know what I mean. Mack said he and Mae had been discussing Mae's next movie role, for God's sake. Even Mae appreciated that this wasn't going to wear with Mabel, so she panicked. She grabbed a china vase and smashed it over Mabel's head. Poor little Mabel staggered out of the apartment and somehow found her way to my place. We heard a sound and found her lying on our porch semi-conscious and bleeding from the head. Minta took her in and I went for a doctor. The injury to the head fortunately isn't serious, but the shock to her nervous system is. She's numb, Keystone, quite numb.'

'I'm profoundly sorry. And she is still at your house?'

'We couldn't leave her. She won't see anyone except the doctor and ourselves. That's why we couldn't let you in.'

'I understand.'

'But I doubt if this has anything to do with Amber's disappearance,' Roscoe went on. 'Some people thought that *she* was Sennett's lover, but this makes it seem unlikely.'

'Utterly unlikely.'

'Unless . . .'

'What?'

'. . . she heard what happened and was terribly upset the same as Mabel.'

'No,' I said emphatically, 'that is impossible. But thank you for telling me what you have. I had better go now. It looks as if you ought to claim your dog.'

Roscoe stared along the beach to where Luke was straddling a French poodle, oblivious of the lady owner. 'Oh, no! Why does it happen to me? Luke! Come here, you brute! Luke!' He lumbered after him, a fat, beleaguered victim of the fates.

TWENTY-SIX

So Mack Sennett's ugly mood had nothing to do with Amber. I still meant to see him. His philanderings and his guilty conscience didn't interest me. But Amber did. I was worried. She had admitted to me that she felt threatened as long as she remained at Keystone, but she hadn't told me why. If anything had happened to her, Sennett bore some responsibility. He had stirred up jealousies and dark suspicions when he had given her the leading role in *Kidnap in the Park*. I wanted explanations and they were going to start with Sennett.

I drove back to Edendale and stopped in Allesandro Street two hundred yards beyond the studio gate. Now that the Brush had been repaired, I was taking no more chances with the doubtful humour of the Cops. It was safer on a public street.

I was walking through the usual crowd of would-be extras waiting at the gate, when the studio sentry hailed me. 'Hey, where you going, Mr Keystone?'

'To the players' building, for some lunch, I hope. Why, is something wrong?'

'Better grab a sandwich and run. Two cops are looking for you.'

'Real ones?'

'Genuine flatfoots.'

'Are you sure? Where are they?'

'In the tower with you know who. What you been doing — holding up the bank?'

My reception in the office would have been flattering in other circumstances. The girls stood up and pointed at me.

'Here he is!'

'Mr Keystone, we looked *everywhere* for you!'

'Go right in. They're waiting for you.'

I knocked and entered Sennett's office. The King of Comedy was slumped morosely in his leather armchair facing two empty chairs brought in for the visitors. The Chief and his assistant, Chick, preferred to lean against the bathtub.

'That's our man!' barked the Chief before I said a word.

Chick slipped quickly and professionally behind me, to cut off my escape route.

Sennett voided chewed tobacco into the spittoon. 'Where the hell you been?'

'I drove down to Santa Monica for an hour. I understood that I would not be wanted until this afternoon.'

'Santa Monica, huh?' said the Chief with a rising note of interest.

'Have I violated studio protocol?'

'What were you doing in Santa Monica?' pressed the Chief.

I decided this was not the time to mention Roscoe Arbuckle.

'Walking by the sea. Why are you asking me these questions? So far as I am aware, I am perfectly within my rights to go off the studio premises for an hour.'

'You took the automobile?' The Chief was on the scent again. Where there was a motor car there was usually a crime.

'I doubt whether I could have walked it.'

The Chief stabbed a finger at me. 'I told you once before — don't smart-mouth me. Where is the vehicle right now?'

'I parked it in Allesandro Street.'

'Why didn't you bring it in?'

'For personal reasons.'

The Chief's blood pressure showed. 'What did you say?'

Sennett said, 'Keystone, they aren't messing.'

'Very well. Last week my motor car was appropriated without my knowledge or permission and used in the filming of a car chase. The damage that resulted has since been made good, and now I park the vehicle out of temptation's way.'

The Chief said, 'Anyone see you in Santa Monica?'

'I expect so.'

'You know the Honeybee residence is down there?'

'Yes.'

'Call there today?'

'No.'

'Seen anything of Amber lately?'

'Not for several days.'

'When precisely did you see her last?'

'In the small hours of Thursday morning. We had dined with friends in Malibu. I drove her home.'

'Who were these friends?'

'Mr and Mrs Murray Brennan.' My eyes briefly locked with Sennett's.

'The director of the movie she was making?'

Sennett said, 'That's the guy.' He told me, 'Don't sweat, we all know about Murray's offer to Amber.'

'I'll handle this, if you don't mind,' the Chief told Sennett without taking his small, accusing eyes off me. 'You say you drove her home from Brennan's place. What happened then?'

'Really,' I objected, 'I fail to understand why I should be obliged to submit to questions of this sort.'

I felt a hand curl over my shoulder from behind and Chick muttered something quite inaudible.

The Chief said, 'She invited you in?'

'No, she did not.'

'So you invited yourself?'

'Certainly not. That's an odious suggestion, and I repudiate it.'

'You telling me you drove this beautiful blonde actress back to the bungalow after midnight and didn't go in? Is that what you're asking me to believe?'

'We had a difference of opinion.'

The Chief's eyebrows twitched. 'A fight, huh?'

'I wouldn't describe it as that. On the drive back we discussed Mr Brennan's suggestion that she might work for him. I thought she had made her eagerness too obvious and I told her so.'

'You were jealous?'

'Disapproving.'

'And she resented it.'

'We begged to differ.'

'So what happened?'

'Nothing *happened*. I drove Amber back to the bungalow and she got out and I went home to bed.'

'And you haven't seen her since?'

'No.'

'Have you tried to see her?'

'I have been to the bungalow on two occasions, but she was not at home.'

The Chief nodded. 'So you know she's missing. Any idea where she might be?'

'None whatsoever. Someone suggested that she might have gone to Boston to see her father but I consider it unlikely.'

'She ain't in Boston. We checked this morning.'

This simple statement shocked me. If they had wired Boston, they really were in earnest. 'Why are the police involved in this?'

'Information,' answered the Chief in a way that made it clear he would not be giving any more himself. 'Okay, let's go see that automobile of yours.'

'Why? What is your interest in my motor car?'

Chick flung open the door and the Chief gestured me on my way.

Mack Sennett yawned and said, 'I figure you don't need me any more.'

With a detective at each shoulder, I strode along the studio street stiff-limbed, but nonchalant in expression, nodding at anyone who recognised me. By the entrance I told the gateman, 'I should have taken your advice. I didn't get that sandwich.'

Allesandro Street basked in the enervating heat of early afternoon. Even the luckless extras had stopped parading and four-flushing and were lounging in the shade.

I pointed to where I had left the Brush and attempted to make conversation with the Chief and Chick as the three of us marched up the street towards it.

'There she is, then.'

'Who? Where?'

'The motor car, officer. Like ships, they are usually assumed to be feminine.'

With a grunt of displeasure the Chief made a circular tour of the Brush and then stepped on the running-board and looked at the seats and floor. He stepped down and moved to the rear and rapped his hand on the new wooden trunk.

'What's in this?'

'You are welcome to inspect it.'

It was secured with two leather straps. Chick stepped forward and unfastened them. He pushed up the lid. 'Chief.'

The Chief glanced in and said to me, 'You want to

know what it is about your automobile?'

I looked inside the trunk.

I shuddered.

At the bottom was a mass of fine, blonde hair in ringlets.

TWENTY-SEVEN

At police headquarters I was handed through a relay of detectives for the rest of the day and into the night. I doubt that I would have slept if they had let me, but they did not. They kept me alert with bright lights, black coffee and sharp questions, endlessly repeated. My story did not materially alter from the version I had given the Chief in Sennett's office.

I asked a number of times to see my lawyer. Madison eventually appeared the following morning at 10.30.

'You look bad.'

I was as sallow as the wall of the interview room and I didn't need him to tell me.

'I feel bad.'

'Cigarette?'

'No thank you. Wouldn't you feel bad if this had happened to a friend of yours?'

'You and Amber were pretty close, then?'

I had listened to insinuating questions all night long. I snapped back, 'It's bad enough when the police put words in my mouth but do I have to take it from my lawyer as well?'

'Mr Easton, I have to get background on the case.'

'Let's say it once and for all, then. Amber is a friend, no more.'

'You can't deny that you acted protectively towards her. Even I observed that for myself.'

'Yes, I helped her when her mother was killed. No-one else appeared to show much sympathy or interest. I was friendly to her because I cared about her. I care very much that someone has treated her so savagely. But I was not her lover in a physical sense, and I'd like that understood for her sake.'

Madison persisted, 'You admitted to the police that you disapproved when Murray Brennan offered her a part in a motion picture. You also admitted that you quarrelled on the drive back from the Brennans'.'

'They assume I tore her hair out in a jealous rage, is that it?'

'It was hacked off with a knife.'

Up to that moment nobody had told me anything. They had only asked me questions.

I was silent, picturing it. I shivered.

'Some of the hairs were torn out at the roots,' Madison went on, 'But most of them were severed. From the way the curls were lying in the trunk, still pretty well in shape, they presume it happened in the close proximity of the automobile. The hair was dropped straight in. Which doesn't look good for you.'

'And where is Amber supposed to have gone after I attacked her?'

'Nowhere.'

'What do you mean?'

'They think she's dead.'

'Dead?' My eardrums roared. The blood was rushing from my head.

'Put your head down a moment,' suggested Madison.

I did.

'Coffee?'

'No.'

'Shall I go on?'

'Of course.' I sat up again and gripped the chair. 'What you're telling me is that they suspect me of murdering Amber, isn't it?'

He nodded.

'What sort of madman do they take me for?'

'People do bizarre and peculiar things, Mr Easton. You have to admit that you made sure nobody went near that automobile.'

'I explained the reason for that.'

'They have a theory that you were connected with the death of Amber's mother.'

'That's preposterous.'

'Maybe, but not impossible. You visited the house the night before Mrs Honeybee died. So you got to know the layout and she got to know your face. You claim to have spent the evening of her death alone in your apartment. No alibi, you see?'

'Why on earth should I have wanted to harm Mrs Honeybee?'

Madison put out his hand to me. 'Take it easy. You've been through a difficult time. They suggest that Amber resented her mother putting the brake on her social life. It was a pretty strict set-up, I understand. The theory is that you and Amber conspired to murder Mrs Honeybee and fake an accident. You got away with it. Everything was hunky-dory until out of the blue Amber made arrangements to quit Keystone with Murray Brennan. You quarrelled. She threatened to put the finger on you for her mother's death. You got mad and murdered her. Don't look at me like that, Mr Easton. I'm just repeating a theory.'

I sighed heavily and leaned back in my chair, 'Mr Madison, I would like you to know that I am not mad, not in any sense of the word. I am tired and confused. I can't understand what has happened to Amber. I can't accept that she is dead. I don't understand why her hair was in my motor car. I don't understand how the police seemed to know it was there.'

'I can answer that. They were tipped off. Someone

called them on the telephone.'

I jerked forward. 'Who was it — a man, a woman?'

'Man. The call was taken by the switchboard girl. The caller said something like "If you want to know what happened to Amber Honeybee, find an English guy called Keystone and look in his automobile". Then he hung up.'

I stood up and looked through the metal grille across the window. 'Mr Madison, I'm beginning to wake up. I've been bombarded by so many questions that I was — what's the expression? — shell-shocked. This man who called the police on the telephone: let's consider him a moment. He certainly had some inside knowledge. He told them to look inside my motor car, have I got it right?'

Madison nodded.

'So it's fair to presume he was a witness to the attack. I wouldn't go round telling people I had cut off Amber's hair and put it in the trunk, now would I?'

'Fair point.'

'So if the attack took place on the evening I drove Amber back from the Brennans', we're talking about some man well enough placed to see what was going on after dark between two people whom he recognised and named.'

'Could be one of Amber's neighbours,' Madison pointed out. 'They hear a scream, look out the window, recognise the automobile. You visited there before, remember. Maybe Amber is friendly with her neighbours, told them about her current boyfriend.'

'Has anyone actually asked them?'

'I'll check.'

'You might also check whether the police have been inside the bungalow to see whether Amber returned home that night.'

'How would they know that?'

'I can tell you what she was wearing. Black velvet. A full-length dress. And a mother-of-pearl brooch. The Brennans will confirm it. If that dress is in the bungalow — and it should be, because I watched her go inside — surely it proves that I didn't attack her in the street where a neighbour could have seen us.'

'You could have let yourself in and taken the dress inside.'

I gave him a withering look. 'Stripped it off her in the street? All right, Mr Madison. Let's postulate even that. If the dress is there, isn't it almost certain that some of the hair that was cut from her head will be found sticking to the velvet?'

'Okay,' he said. 'I'll mention it.'

'You might also mention that it's worth making an effort to find this person who made the telephone call, because if he wasn't a witness to the crime he almost certainly committed it himself.'

'Right now, they're much more interested in you,' said Madison.

'But they haven't charged me yet. Don't they have to charge me?'

'I wouldn't put significance on that. It's usual to wait for the forensic people to put in their report.'

'Wonderful!' I said. 'In the meantime, is anyone looking for Amber?'

TWENTY-EIGHT

Harassed and exhausted as I was, I didn't tell the police about the magazine of film that Amber had entrusted to me. Call it loyalty or plain pigheadedness, I clung to the conviction that I alone was capable of acting in her interest. I gave answers to their questions, but volunteered no information. I said nothing about the night I had spent trussed up in the beach-hut, or about the damage to my apartment. I didn't have a high opinion of the Chief, but I reckoned even he would eventually conclude that I was innocent of harming Amber. And when I was released, I knew what I would do.

I had to wait until the afternoon. He had me brought into his office at 1 p.m. Madison was already in the room. He gave me a sly smile. The Chief didn't even look at me. He was leafing through a set of files. He said, 'We got no more questions just now, Keystone.'

'May I go?'

'We're holding your automobile for further examination.'

'That's inconvenient.'

'Balls.'

Madison said, 'The Chief is saying, in effect, that he is legally entitled to impound the vehicle.'

'When can I reclaim it?'

'When we tell you,' said the Chief.

'I'll drive you home,' offered Madison.

'Don't get anxious,' the Chief advised me without a trace of genuine concern. 'I won't forget you, Keystone.'

On the drive back to Edendale, Madison said, 'You saw the look in his eye? He still believes you're guilty, but there are too many gaps in the evidence to book you. He'll be working on that.'

'Did they search the bungalow?'

'Yes.'

'And they found the velvet dress?'

'No.'

'The brooch?'

'No.'

'I don't understand.'

'Get this in your head. She went missing the night you brought her back from the Brennans'. She was wearing those things.'

I grappled wearily with the implications. 'Well, why have they released me?'

'I had to give my personal assurance that you would stay inside their jurisdiction.'

'In other words, they haven't finished with me.'

'I think you'll find they put a tail on you.'

'I take offence at that.'

'Take anything you like, Mr Easton, but if the Chief in his wisdom decides you ought to be watched, you've got a tail.'

'I see. They got nowhere with their inquisition, so they think setting me at liberty will lead them somewhere.'

'Standard police procedure,' said Madison. 'What do you propose doing now?'

'Having a sleep — if it's permitted.'

'I won't argue with that.'

The look he gave me as I stepped down from his limousine in front of my apartment was not reassuring. He didn't say, 'I'll see you soon,' but he might as well have done.

I went indoors. I suppose if I had given it any thought, I would have expected what I found. This time the sacking of my apartment was more systematic. They had pulled back the carpet and taken up a number of floorboards. In the bathroom they had dragged the bathtub from the plumbing and ripped out the plywood panelling and several boards. They had stolen nothing. They had not found what they came for.

It was not a break-in. As before, they had entered through the front door with a key, presumably a copy made from an impression of my own. I had meant to change the lock, but other matters had taken my attention. If any doubt lingered that my attacker and Amber's were the same, this removed it.

I didn't sleep. I stepped across the gaps, washed, shaved, changed my clothes and left the apartment. As I started up the street I was conscious of someone in a light grey suit following thirty yards behind.

At the studio entrance, the gateman was surprised to see me.

'Thought you were down at police headquarters, Mr Keystone. What a Godawful thing this is.'

'Yes.'

'You answered all their questions?'

'I did.'

'And they didn't keep you there?'

I spread my hands to indicate the obvious.

'So it's back to work as usual?'

I nodded. 'There is one thing. I expect you heard about the ban on filming in the streets?'

'Sure, but who's worried about that after this has happened?'

'Quite. It's just that it occurred to me that the police might use it to gain unrestricted access to the studio. They could send in plain-clothes officers to look for

173

things that smear the studio's reputation. From all I hear, it wouldn't worry them if we were forced to close.'

'Jesus, Mr Keystone!' The gateman buttoned his uniform. 'Thanks for the tip. No dick gets past me without authority.'

I nodded and moved on and when the man in the grey suit reached the gate, he got no further.

It was the end of lunchtime. The movement back to the stages had begun. Suddenly I was spotted and surrounded by a crowd that, if not a lynch mob, was by no means well disposed. Their questions — so rapid and so many I couldn't answer them — were loaded with suspicion. Why had the cops released me? How did Amber's hair get in my automobile? Why hadn't she been found yet? Was she dead, or what?

I backed against a wall, shaking my head and mouthing words. Someone with a penetrating voice appealed for quiet. I launched into a statement about my concern for Amber and my total ignorance of what had happened to her.

I don't think they believed me, but I kept repeating it until they started to disperse. It must have been twenty minutes before the last of them moved on.

I snapped my thoughts together and went to look for Murray Brennan. What I planned could not be done alone. If I trusted anyone at the studio, it was Murray.

They told me in the office that he was with Del Lord, the ex-racing-driver with the awesome job of devising chase sequences and stunts. Not wishing to share my plan with Lord, one of Sennett's inner circle, I sat down to wait among the battered Fords that comprised the Keystone fleet. It seemed appropriate.

Murray emerged towards 3 p.m. He came over right away and asked what news I had of Amber.

We took a slow walk up the studio street and I told

him everything that had happened, not just in the previous twenty-four hours, but since that afternoon Amber had asked me to drive her home from Griffith Park. His blue eyes grew huge behind the pebble glasses, but he let me finish.

Then he whistled.

I waited.

'Let me get this clear,' said Murray. 'Amber told you someone broke into the bungalow the night her mother died?'

'Yes.'

'But she didn't tell the cops?'

'She didn't tell me until I virtually forced her to admit it.'

'Why keep it to herself?'

'Murray, you know Amber. Her heart is set on becoming a famous motion-picture actress. She had a strong suspicion who was behind this tragedy. She thought if she spoke out, it would ruin her career.'

Murray nodded. I didn't need to be specific. He understood. 'What about the cops? Didn't they suspect a break-in?'

'There wasn't any evidence of one.'

'No forced entry?'

'It was a warm night. There were probably windows open. And before the police arrived, Amber tidied up — threw the things inside the drawers and closed them.'

'Cool-headed.'

'Quick-thinking, anyway.'

'And you believe the same hood — or hoods — cracked you on the head, tied you up and ripped up your apartment?'

'I'm sure of it.'

'They figured you and Amber were going out together, so if she didn't have what they were looking for, maybe it was at your place.'

'Right.'

'Only it wasn't there at all: it was sitting in your automobile.'

'In the trunk — until that madman Summerville tried to drive it through a Keystone car chase.'

Murray nodded. 'But let's give Slim his due. If he hadn't hit the paddy wagon, we still wouldn't know what was inside Amber's parcel.'

'All right,' I said. 'I saw that it was a magazine of film, but, really, Murray, I'm no wiser. How can a reel of film be so important that people go to these extremes to get it back? It's lunacy.'

'You think they cut Amber's hair to make her talk?'

I tensed. Each time I pictured what had happened my stomach lurched. 'Actually I don't.'

'They did it out of spite?'

'Yes. They abducted her to force the truth from her. But she couldn't tell them where the film was hidden because she didn't know. She made me promise not to tell her.'

'I get it,' said Murray. 'All she could tell them was that you had it and it was in the trunk up to the morning of the smash.'

'Yes. I believe they brought her out at night to search the motor car in the street outside my apartment. When they found nothing they cut her hair and threw it in the trunk. Sheer bloody malice, Murray. It's cruel beyond perversity.'

'They're bastards. Someone's got to stop them, Keystone.'

'I mean to.'

'Only how?'

'By finding out what is on that film.'

'You want some help developing it?'

'Could you?'

'Sure. I told you I know movies from top to bottom. All we need is a darkroom. And the film. How soon can you get hold of it?'

'As soon as you like. It's here.'

'On the studio lot?' Murray grinned. 'You're smart.'

'But can we get a darkroom where we won't be interrupted?'

'Around seven this evening, we can. The labs are clear by then.'

'No earlier than that?'

Murray shook his head. 'Wouldn't be safe. The drying can't be done in less than an hour. When that film is on the rack, anyone could walk in and take a look at it.'

I knew he was speaking sense, but that didn't help my state of mind. Three and a half hours!

Somehow we got through them. Murray asked me when I had last eaten and I honestly couldn't remember. After so much noxious coffee at police headquarters I didn't want to think of food. He insisted that we drive downtown and look for a restaurant. As anything was better than killing time at Keystone, I didn't argue. I sat in the rear of the Packard ducking under the canopy in case the plainclothes man was still on duty.

We had to go as far as Wilshire Boulevard to find a place that served hot meals in mid-afternoon. By then I was ready to tackle the steak that Murray ordered. I ate, while he drank whisky sour and talked about Louise, their daughters, his early life and his career in motion pictures, from the San Francisco nickelodeon to the absurdities of Keystone. He made it sound like a lament. He was definitely quitting. He had talked to Sennett and this picture he had been discussing with Del Lord would be his last. He was planning a spectacular finale with a chase involving a locomotive and the destruction of six or seven cars. I made a show of interest, but really I was watching the clock above the door.

I explained that I would need to get to Edendale by six to collect the film. Murray looked surprised, so I said I understood the storeman worked an eight-hour day and locked up when he finished.

'You're speaking of the studio film store?'

'Yes,' I said. 'If you wanted to hide a book, where would you put it?'

He laughed. 'Okay. Let's go.'

In a little over an hour we started work. The Keystone developing plant was fully mechanised. Sennett had been one of the first in America to go over to Bell and Howell continuous printers. But there was one old prehistoric darkroom kept in case of breakdowns and this was where Murray had brought me. It stank of dust and chemicals.

'Do you know the rack and tank system?'

I shook my head.

'Too late to learn now. Just pull down the blinds, would you?'

He took the film from its can and slotted the first few feet between the pegs on the developing racks. He worked fast and expertly. I gave assistance when I could, but there was not much I could do. I think my hands would have shaken if he had asked me to handle the film.

After twenty minutes of concentrated work, Murray said, 'Seems the film was only partially exposed. It stops here, see? Shall we cut it?'

'No, if you don't mind, I think we should develop all of it, in case there's something further on.'

'Okay, but I don't see how there could be.'

He was right. When the entire film was developed, fixed and in the washtank we were certain that only the first 150 feet, perhaps a minute and half of running time, had gone through the camera.

'You can let up one of the blinds now. Let's see what we got.'

We held a length of negative up to the light and examined it together. 'Looks like a fairground.'

'Exposition Park,' I said.

'How do you know?'

'I recognise it. I was there. The film was never made because of the accident to one of the Cops.'

'Sandy Sullivan,' said Murray. 'It was my good fortune to be working on another picture when that happened. I heard about it when everyone got back.'

'Why did Amber have this piece of film?'

'Soon as it's dry we'll make a print and run it through a projector. Then maybe we'll get wiser.'

But late that evening, when we finally saw the film, we did not, in fact, get wiser.

TWENTY-NINE

Mack Sennett liked to be alone when he watched rushes. He would settle into the rocking-chair that was the only piece of furniture in his private projection room and chew at a cigar. It was a well-attested truth that the action of that rocking-chair was as conclusive in its verdict as the Emperor Nero's thumb. When the King of Comedy was not amused, he rocked his chair. Men and women destined to be giants of the motion-picture industry had been known to stand in the adjoining room in terror of the rasp of wood on wood.

Today nobody expected favours. Sennett had not smiled all week, let alone discharged that huge guffaw that telegraphed approval of a gag. Some people doubted that it would ever be heard again. If rumour were reliable, his seven-year affair with Mabel Normand was at an end. The wedding had been cancelled. Loyalties in the studio were strained to breaking-point. Roscoe and Minta Arbuckle had taken Mabel's side. So the two leading Keystone players, Arbuckle and Normand, were not on speaking terms with the man whose name was over the studio gate.

As if that were not enough, the fates had floored him with another uppercut: the abduction of Amber Honeybee. He had shrugged off the death of Amber's mother; it had not hurt the studio's reputation. But Amber was on the Keystone payroll. He had given her a leading role. She had visited his house. Her clipped hair had been discovered in an automobile belonging to a Keystone Cop. These were facts impossible to duck.

On the screen appeared the silver square of light. Sennett had his elbow resting on the left arm of the chair, his chin buried in his hand. He was so still he might have been asleep. The leader was threaded through the gate. The screen went dark except for tiny streaks of light. A picture followed.

It was not the scene from *Traffic Duty* that Sennett was expecting.

It was a long shot of a fairground. The big wheel. A carousel. Machinery revolving. Cars hurtling round the rollercoaster ride. It was Exposition Park.

Sennett did not react. The rocking-chair was still.

A close shot of Mabel Normand in a white bonnet and white lawn dress walking happily among the crowds. Tilting her head to watch the rollercoaster. A car hurtled overhead with people waving. Mabel smiled.

Sennett shifted in his chair. He rested both hands on the chair-arms and his head against the back.

A top hat, the universal emblem of the heavy, momentarily blocked out the screen. The wearer was Harry Gribbon, equipped with a villainous moustache, and watching Mabel with lascivious eyes.

Mabel was still looking at the rollercoaster. It was a retake of the earlier shot. Gribbon was seen again in close-up.

The action moved on. Mabel opened her handbag and took out a coin. She approached the kiosk where tickets were issued for the rollercoaster ride. Ahead of her in the line were Harry Booker and Amber Honeybee. They purchased tickets and went through. Mabel bought her ticket. As she moved on, Harry Gribbon stepped up to the kiosk.

The picture blurred briefly. Then the sequence was repeated.

About a minute had elapsed.

The screen went dark.

Sennett had sprung up and blocked out the beam of light. His empty chair rocked violently. His face was livid with the images filtered through the film. He advanced on the small square that housed the lens and shouted through the space, 'Turn it off and get your ass in here.'

The projector motor stopped, putting the room in darkness. Sennett groped for the light-switch.

When the light went on, I was standing in the room.

Sennett croaked, 'You? Jesus, what is this? What in the name of sin is going on?'

I said, 'I took the liberty of letting your projectionist sit in on a poker game.'

'He's fired,' said Sennett. 'You're fired. Where did you get that piece of film?'

'Did you recognise it?'

Sennett flexed his arms and shoulders like a wrestler. 'Boy, I don't take lip from anyone.'

He was going to get it from me. 'Exposition Park,' I went on doggedly. 'The fairground. The picture you were making in the week I started here. The picture that was never finished, Mr Sennett.'

'You threatening me?'

'Quite the contrary. If anyone is uttering threats, it is yourself. I am seeking information, Mr Sennett — the truth about that piece of film. Are we to have a civilised discussion?'

'Will you get out of here, or shall I throw you out?'

I folded my arms. 'You see? Who is threatening whom? Let me put it plainly. Amber has disappeared and her hair has been discovered in my motor car. That concerns me, Mr Sennett. I like Amber. She put her trust in me. The film you have just been looking at was in her possession. She asked me to take care of it. She felt that she was under threat. I am convinced that her disappearance is connected with the film. She hasn't got it, and she's been made to suffer for it.'

Sennett was wide-eyed. Things were happening to his face that would have earned spontaneous applause for an actor playing Dr Jekyll. He slapped his hand dramatically against his chest. 'Are you suggesting I'm responsible?'

'That isn't what I said.'

'You think I wanted my pesky film back, so I kidnapped her? And when she didn't have it, I hacked off her hair? I know what this is. The cops have chased you up a stump, so you want to put the rap on me.'

'Rubbish.'

He jabbed an accusing finger at me. 'Where have you put her, Keystone?'

I stared back and answered coldly, 'What sort of man do you think I am?'

'You want to know? You're off your head. The quiet guys with nice manners are the craziest killers — that's a fact. And most of them are English. That doctor who cut up his wife — Crippen.'

'He was American. This is leading nowhere. I think we should resume the film show. You haven't seen the rest of what was filmed in Exposition Park.'

'Nuts. I directed the damn movie, for God's sake.'

'But you haven't seen it.'

'How do you know that?'

'The film was not developed until yesterday evening.'

Sennett's mouth gaped. 'By you?'

'By Murray Brennan, with some help from me.' As Murray had already handed in his notice, I wasn't putting him in trouble. But I added, 'Amber trusted Murray. I decided I could trust him, too. Sit down, Mr Sennett. I'll go behind and start the projector again.'

'The hell you will! I just fired you, Keystone.'

'You're going to watch the film.'

He shoved one massive fist between us for me to look at. 'See the white marks there? Molten iron made them, fella. Don't mix it with an ex-iron-worker unless you want scars yourself.'

I said mildly, 'Are you afraid to watch it?'

For a second I expected him to punch me. His grey hair was deceiving. I knew for a fact he was not more than thirty-five, and regularly sparred with Abdul.

I hadn't come to fight him. I kept my two arms limply at my side.

It seemed to give him second thoughts. He turned his head away and sent a great blob of spit into the corner. 'You don't need to tell me the film was a fiasco. Movie comedy is like war. People get hurt. But when a guy gets killed, believe me, I take note. I don't need to see that.'

'But you will.'

My obstinacy finally broke through. He said, 'You got more brass than a pawnshop. But you're still fired, understand?' He sank into the rocking-chair.

The projector whirred again. There was another take of the line for rollercoaster tickets. Then a shot of Amber getting into one of the cars, twitching her skirt to reveal a glimpse of shin and calf. She was followed by Harry Booker. Next, Mabel prepared to climb aboard. She planted her foot on the ornately decorated side. As she put out her hand for balance it was held and supported by the villain, who helped her in and climbed in beside her.

The sequence was repeated. Then the screen went blank.

The film ran on, but there was no more on it.

After half a minute, I stopped the projector and went

back. I switched on the light.

'What happened to the rest?' asked Sennett.

'That is all there is.'

'Don't push me, Keystone. The whole sequence on the rollercoaster is missing. The accident to Sullivan. You been messing around with that film?'

'It's exactly as it was. There is no rollercoaster sequence.'

'Come on,' said Sennett, getting out of his chair. 'What's this crap you're giving me? I made the god-damn movie. I had the camera on a scaffold tower beside the track. It was the main shot of the day. The Cops running up the rise to meet the car and being scattered. Sullivan turning and running for his life.'

'And dying in the attempt.'

'Right. You saw it too. It's got to be on the film.'

'It isn't.'

'Bull. You cut the sequence out.'

'Impossible.'

'Yeah?' He flung open the door to the projection room. 'Let's take a look at this lousy film. I'll show you where they took the cut and spliced it.'

Sennett unhitched the film from the projector and put the reels on to a winding-frame and turned the handle. He let the film run between his thumb and finger. 'Sure way to detect a splice,' he told me, but in four minutes he had not detected one, and the film was totally wound through. He was still not satisfied. He reversed the process until he reached the section where the filmed sequence ended and the blank frames began. He inspected it frame by frame until it was beyond dispute that the film had not been cut. Then he laughed.

It was a laugh that started with a shudder, as if it were painful to produce. It gathered strength with a couple of convulsive shakes and ended in a bellow.

I waited for an explanation.

Sennett, red-faced with the effort, shook his head and said, 'Terrific! To think I hit the roof when that piddling piece of film went missing! I blasted the cameraman. I had sleepless nights. If one of our competitors had gotten his paws on a film of a fatal accident at Keystone, he would have run it as a news item in every picture house across America.'

'Would that be bad for business?' I asked blandly.

'Would it! Mister, if it got around that I had sacrificed men's lives for laughs, I'd be finished.'

'Would it be untrue?'

He glared at me. 'Listen, any damn fool knows that if you horse around with automobiles, you're going to get some casualties. We take reasonable precautions. But it's no good telling that to the public if they see a sequence of an actor being killed. Yeah, I was sick with worry.' He grinned. 'And now I find the goddamn sequence isn't on the film!'

'How do you explain it?'

'Simple mechanical failure, I guess. Jake Harper cranked the camera, but the handle must have turned without engaging the shaft, so no film went through. Cameras are like women — you can hope they give you what you want, but don't ever count on it.'

'Has it happened before?'

'Not for some time.' He chuckled. 'It's hellish funny when you think about it. Harper didn't know — he got bawled at by me. I didn't know — I was leaned on by Amber. And Amber didn't know —'

'And she could very well be dead by now,' I interjected. 'What do you mean when you say you were leaned upon by Amber?'

Sennett looked startled. He had obviously said too much.

'Forget it — that's my business.'

'Also mine,' I said with something extra in my voice. 'Let's face the truth, Mr Sennett. We both know she had possession of the film. Did she use it to secure her role in *Kidnap in the Park*?'

Sennett admitted it with a shrug. 'So what? Amber wouldn't be the first extra who found a way to hoist herself above the rest.'

'She threatened to sell the film to your competitors unless you offered her a leading role.'

'Christ, you make it sound like blackmail,' protested Sennett. 'Amber was intelligent. She didn't threaten me. We had a civilised discussion, a few laughs, too. Matter of fact, it appealed to my sense of humour. Mabel and Minta and some of my leading ladies were getting too complacent. I figured it would do no harm to let them find they had some competition. I was damn sure Amber didn't have their talent, and I was right, but with Roscoe and Mack Swain to carry the picture, we got by. We made the movie, didn't we?'

'However it was done, the threat was there,' I pointed out. 'Amber had the reel of film. You didn't know it was innocuous. You believed she had it in her power to destroy your reputation.'

'Okay, so I played ball,' Sennett conceded. 'I let her be a leading lady. You've got to be crazy if you think I have her hidden some place.'

'Someone has.'

'Not me, buster.'

'Someone made repeated efforts to obtain that can of film. They searched Amber's house the night her mother died.'

'You sure of that?'

'They may have killed her mother. When they suspected me of having the film, they knocked me out and

187

locked me in a beach-hut while they ransacked my apartment.'

'You *are* nuts.'

'I tell you someone is desperate to get the film.' I was becoming desperate too, because, contrary to all my expectations, I was being persuaded that behind the bluster and bad language, Mack Sennett was telling me the truth. 'If it isn't you, who would go to lengths like this?'

'Harper?' suggested Sennett.

'The cameraman?'

'He was the guy who took it in the first place.'

'And had to answer to you. Have you been threatening him?'

Sennett sniffed. 'Keystone, if you'd been around here longer than you have, you'd know that's not my style. I don't harbour grudges. If one of my employees louses up a job, I deal with it right off. I roast him. Or I fire him like I just fired you. Harper I roasted.'

'Has he been with you long?'

'Harper? Ever since we got here. He's Californian. A dozy hick like most of them are, but useful with a camera. I'll be sorry to lose him.'

'He's leaving?'

'With Murray Brennan. This new company Murray is setting up. Five-reel historical dramas.' A fleeting smile moved across Sennett's lips. 'Not many pratfalls there.'

'Amber is joining them too — or was, before this happened.'

'Murray told me.' He gave a shrug. 'It's okay. We didn't fight about it. You don't stop people moving on if they get itchy feet.'

'Was Harper the only cameraman at Exposition Park?'

'Yeah. Generally we have two or three filming chases, but I knew exactly the shots I wanted, so Harper was enough.'

'Why did the accident happen?'

'Human error. In rehearsal, it worked fine. In the take, it didn't. Sullivan missed his jump. The car smashed into him. He fell.' Sennett looked at me with a challenging expression. 'There was nothing anyone could do.'

'But what did you do?'

'Ran towards him. He was dead, of course. Covered him and called an ambulance. Spoke to the cops. Fixed for Mabel to be driven home. She was pretty overcome. Remember she was sitting in the car that hit him.'

'So was Amber.'

'Right.'

'And Harper — where was he?'

'On the camera tower. He came down and made a statement.'

'What happened to the camera?'

'That was brought down and stacked in one of the automobiles. Soon as we were all packed up, we got out fast. I was the last to leave, Harper and me, that is. I gave him a lift in my Packard.'

'So Harper didn't have the camera with him?'

'No, that went before.'

'Do you recollect who drove it back?'

'I couldn't tell you. It was in one of the automobiles.' Sennett scratched his head. 'But I can tell you who was in the back beside the camera. Two girls. A dresser and one of the bit-players — your friend Amber.'

'With all the journey back to Edendale to devise a way of becoming something better than a bit-player,' I reflected. 'Poor Amber, poor misguided Amber.'

'Everyone makes mistakes,' said Sennett philosophically. 'Just like you did, taking over my projector. I guess you'd like me to overlook the error.'

'As you wish.'

'I don't. Get out, you jerk. You're fired.'

THIRTY

Murray was waiting for me in the players' cafeteria, his eyebrows inching up his forehead in expectation.

I shook my head.

'No progress?'

'Precious little.'

'Did he look at the film?'

'Eventually.'

'What did he say?'

'He laughed.'

'Laughed?'

'And he gave me the sack.'

'Jesus.'

I filled in the gaps for Murray. I also told him that Sennett's version of events had impressed me. 'The way he justified giving Amber her leading role. It was just as he would do it, Murray, side-stepping the suggestion of blackmail and laughing it off as a chance to take Mabel and the others down a peg or two.'

'He laughs a lot,' said Murray, 'but, underneath it, Sennett is a ruthless character.'

'Also shrewd. He knew this was just a stepping-stone as far as Amber was concerned.'

'He still wouldn't want the film getting in the wrong hands.'

'But that's no reason to kidnap Amber and treat her vilely, Murray. It would be as damaging as the piece of film itself.'

'He could hire people to do his dirty work,' Murray pointed out.

KEYSTONE

'Well, if Sennett *is* behind it, he's got the damn film back now, and there's no reason to hold Amber any longer. We'll see if she's released.'

Murray said gravely, 'If she's left alive. Did Sennett have any theories of his own?'

'He mentioned the cameraman, Jake Harper.'

'Jake? He wouldn't do a thing like this.'

'He lost the film in the first place. He got what Sennett termed a roasting. If he felt aggrieved —'

'Listen, I've known Jake for years. I got him his job at Keystone. Sure he's a surly son-of-a-gun, but a kidnapper — no, sir!'

'Have you any suggestions?' I asked.

'If I had, I'd come up with them, I promise you.'

We sank into a troubled silence.

'Care for a coffee?'

I nodded.

When Murray came back, I said, 'We've been so preoccupied with our suspicions of Mack Sennett that it's cluttering our minds.'

'You think there's something else?'

'I'd like to look at the film again.'

'We rolled it five or six times last evening, Keystone.'

'Yes, but we were so mesmerised by what wasn't there that we haven't applied our minds to what was.'

Murray tried to be positive. 'Maybe you're right. Where is the film right now?'

'Still in Sennett's private projection-room. Let's run it through again.'

He goggled at me. 'You must be off your head.'

'He isn't there now. He went out when I did.'

'Swell!' he said with heavy sarcasm. 'And if he comes back and finds me sitting in his rocking-chair, I tell him sorry, no more seats in the house.'

'The worst he can do is fire us. I'm fired already, and

191

you're working out your notice anyway. Come on, I saw an old hand-cranked projector in there. We can look at it frame by frame.'

Murray muttered, shook his head and followed me. The blob of still-white spittle in the corner of the projection-room and the cigar-butts on the floor were no help to Murray's nerves. He refused my invitation to try the rocking-chair, so I settled down to watch in style while he worked the projector.

I tried to be sure of missing nothing, searching the shots for anything of significance. Some incident in the background, perhaps, captured by the camera. The long shot of the fairground, every individual on every ride. The crowds surrounding Mabel Normand. The roller-coaster seen from her position. Harry Gribbon in his hat. We compared the first and second takes.

Then the next sequence, the queue for tickets at the kiosk. The first glimpse of Amber, glancing at the camera, her moment to be noticed.

I felt the force of her eyes on me. I stopped trying to analyse the film and responded to her personality instead. In that glance, her strengths and failings were projected as clearly as her beauty: lovely, impetuous Amber, driven by ambition, determined to be noticed and innocent of where it would lead her. I could not suppress the memory of the last words she had spoken to me, that evening I had motored her home from Murray's and she had wanted me to be romantic. I had disappointed her, jealous and annoyed that she had so readily agreed to work for Murray. Amber, before she had run from me in tears, had rightly pointed out that Murray loved his wife. '*A woman can tell, you know.*'

Amber might have been right about Murray, but she was mistaken about me.

I loved her.

On the screen the images had flickered into the second take. Amber and Harry Booker bought tickets for the second time and went through the gate. Followed by Mabel. And Harry Gribbon.

Followed by the empty screen.

'If I missed something, tell me,' said Murray, 'but I really cannot see what makes this piece of film so special.'

'Let's run it through once more.'

At the end of another showing, I was forced to admit that we were no wiser.

'Let's get out of here,' Murray appealed to me.

'It's so damn frustrating,' I complained. 'I saw the accident to Sandy Sullivan. I have a vivid picture of it in my mind. Yet it isn't on the film.'

'You told me Sennett explained that — about the crank handle failing to engage,' said Murray. 'What other explanation is there? He had only one camera, didn't he?'

'Only one that I saw. One camera and one cameraman, Jake Harper.'

'And when the scenes on the ground were finished, Harper had the camera winched up to the tower to film the Cops running towards the rollercoaster car?'

'Right.' I snapped my fingers. 'Murray, I wonder . . .'

'What?'

'Whether Harper changed the film.'

'For the rollercoaster sequence?' Murray didn't look too impressed. 'I see what you're driving at. If Harper changed the magazine, the accident would be on another reel of film.'

'Exactly. Is it a possibility?'

'I guess it's not impossible, but it's unlikely. How much film had he shot? Not much over a minute. he had another three minutes in the can. No cameraman wastes film on that scale. It's an interesting theory, Keystone, I give you that.'

'It's all we've got,' I said. 'There's only one way to find out — by talking to the cameraman himself.'

THIRTY-ONE

We were turning out of the studio gate when Murray said suddenly, 'Keep your head down. Grey sedan just pulled out behind us.'

My shadow from the police department must have learned that I had teamed up with Murray.

'Is he following?'

'Like we're towing him.'

'Confound him!'

'Don't worry. We're not breaking any laws.'

Jake Harper had rooms in a house on Vine Street, so Murray drove us up Hollywood Boulevard as far as the silver buildings of the Lasky Studio standing among the pepper trees, and there turned right.

'You've met Jake?' he asked me.

'Yes. First impressions can be wrong, but I thought him truculent.'

Murray smiled. 'That's Jake. Likes you to know he's a real tough guy.'

'He can't be too ferocious if you're offering him a job.'

'Good cameraman,' said Murray.

'How did you meet him first?'

'Must be all of five years ago, before I came to Keystone. When our second daughter was born, Louise had the nice idea of shooting some movie film of the babies. I made enquiries at some of the studios and Jake agreed to do it. Did it well, too. We had him back next birthday to shoot more pictures and now it's a regular thing. Part of the birthday ritual. The girls love it.

Would you believe he brings candies in a box tied with a ribbon?'

The house was a half-mile up the street, one of a group of detached brick buildings brownish-yellow as the hills behind them. As I got out I noticed the grey sedan go slowly past and halt some fifty yards further on. No-one got out.

Murray's knock was answered by a woman with gaunt, Slavonic features. She had her hand on the collar of a snarling boxer dog.

'Mr Harper at home?' Murray asked.

'I don't know. Who are you?'

'Friends of Jake.'

'Movie people?'

'Yes.'

'You can go up. Left at the top and first on your right.'

Murray led us confidently past the dog and up the stairs.

He tapped on the door.

No answer.

'Must be out.'

'Is it open?' I asked.

'You can't go walking into people's rooms, Keystone.'

'Murray, we don't have time to be good-mannered.' I turned the handle.

There were definite signs of occupation. A check shirt hanging over the iron bedframe. A copy of Photoplay Magazine open on the chest.

'That's odd. He left his wallet,' I said, picking it off the bed.

A voice from behind me said, 'Drop it.'

I turned. I obeyed.

Jake Harper was standing in the doorway we had just come through. He had an open cut-throat razor in his hand. He held it rigidly in front of him. He was bare-chested. He had never seemed to me to look companionable. Now he looked murderous.

'Jake, it's us,' Murray blurted out. 'Just thought we'd look you up.'

'We happened to be out this way,' I added in an effort to sound casual.

Harper kept the razor pointing at us. 'Don't give me that. What are you doing in my room?'

'Looking for you, Jake,' said Murray, adding tamely, 'How are you?'

Harper ignored that. He took a step towards us and we both backed against the window. He was not so tall as I was, but he had the torso of an acrobat.

He fixed me with his dark, suspicious eyes, 'I thought you were being held at police headquarters.'

'Well, you can see that I am not.'

'That Honeybee dame — they found her hair in your automobile.'

'It doesn't follow that I put it there.'

'Jake, be reasonable,' said Murray.

'The dame is missing. It's in the papers.'

'That's why we're here,' I told him, ignoring the offensive way he spoke of Amber. 'We mean to find her. We need your help.'

Harper didn't look convinced. His grip on the razor tightened. He said accusingly to Murray, 'I thought you were my friend and now I find you in my room with this guy the cops arrested.'

Murray spoke in the eminently reasonable tone that he put to use in heated moments on the movie stage. 'It's okay, Jake. Nobody is threatening you, so why don't you put down that thing and talk to us?'

'Talk about what?'

'A piece of film you shot.'

'Film?'

'The rollercoaster.'

Harper's hand twitched dangerously. He said, 'I don't have it.'

'We know that, Jake,' said Murray. 'It was taken off your camera on the day you shot the film.'

'Mack Sennett bawled me out for that. Isn't that enough?'

'Jake, Sennett didn't send us here.'

The hand with the razor was lowered a comforting inch or two.

'Keystone was fired this morning,' Murray went on. 'And you and I are going to be making movies together in a couple of weeks, unless you changed your mind, so shall we trust each other?'

Harper slowly dipped the razor, to hang less threateningly at his side.

'Thank you,' said Murray. 'You thought we had come to look for the film, is that it?'

Harper nodded.

I asked, 'Why do you think the film is so important?'

'I told you. Sennett lambasted me,' answered Harper.

'That's not the point.'

'Okay, I screwed up the job, but I couldn't see why he was so mad at me, considering he stopped work on the picture anyway.'

'You found out later,' Murray prompted him.

'Right, I saw the schedules for *Kidnap in the Park*. Roscoe Arbuckle billed opposite this unknown blonde called Amber Honeybee. You don't have to be a Pinkerton detective to figure out who had gotten possession of the film and found a use for it.'

'Did you take this up with Amber?' I asked.

The hand around the razor tightened. 'What are you driving at? I didn't hurt the dame. You got the wrong guy, Keystone.'

'Did you talk to her about it?'

'What for? Sennett knew she had the lousy film. Even if I grabbed it back from her, it was too late to make my peace with Mack. I was quitting anyway. No sir, there was no credit for Jake Harper in recovering that film.'

'But you believe Amber is missing because of it?'

'No question. She overplayed her hand. She got her leading role, but she wouldn't hand back the film. I guess she had it hidden some place.'

'Are you suggesting Mack Sennett is behind this?'

'Draw your own conclusions.'

I wasn't ready for conclusions yet. I pressed the conversation on a stage: 'I think I ought to tell you that we've seen the film, Harper.'

He stared at me and for a moment I thought I saw panic on his face. His mouth gaped in a kind of rictus that he contrived to curve into an unconvincing smile. 'It's been found?'

Murray took up the explanation. 'Yes. You're right, of course. Amber had it and was using it to further her career. Mack Sennett decided it was safer to co-operate and offer her a leading role than risk the film being sold to a rival company. What neither he nor Amber realised was that they were dealing with an empty threat.'

I added, 'The film had not been developed. Neither of them knew for certain what was on it.'

The forced smile changed into an impish grin. Harper said, 'What you mean is neither of them knew what *wasn't* on it.'

'Precisely.'

'It didn't show the accident to Sandy Sullivan.'

'As we discovered,' said Murray. 'Now, Jake, how about telling us what happened?'

199

'You know what happened. Sullivan fell off and was killed.'

'What happened about the film? Did you shoot the scene at all?'

'Yup. I cranked it.'

I asked, 'Did you change the magazine?'

'No. Why should I do that? There was plenty of film left to use.' He gave me the look of an expert dealing with an ignoramus. 'I had a second camera on the tower. It was easier that way. That's all there was to it.'

'So there *is* a sequence of the accident?'

'Not any more. When people started making trouble, I exposed the film. Destroyed it. I didn't want Sennett on my back. It wasn't needed any more. He axed the whole production.'

The more I heard from Harper, the less I believed. If he had a film of the accident, he wouldn't have destroyed it. Once he had cut his ties with Sennett, he would sell it to the highest bidder. *If* the film existed. I was not convinced of that. 'Mr Sennett told me you used only one camera.' Actually, he hadn't but I wanted to test Harper.

Unfortunately, Murray cut in diplomatically. 'You know Mack. His notion of directing is to bellow orders at the actors. He expects the cameraman to get on with the job.'

Harper picked it up at once. 'That's true. It doesn't bother him which camera is in use so long as you're in the right place ready to grind when he shouts "camera".'

'So you filmed the accident, but it was never printed?' I said.

'I told you. I exposed it.'

'From what you can remember, did you catch the actual moment when Sullivan was hit?'

'The whole damn thing. The Cops climbing up the track just as the car came over the top. Then everyone getting out of the way except Sullivan. I had him in profile running in the path of the car, then getting hit because he missed his jump. He was carried on the front of the car. I'm not sure if I caught the moment he fell off. He may have been taken out of shot by then.'

'Apart from the people in the car, you must have been closer to what happened than anyone else.'

'Guess so.'

'Why do you think it happened?'

'Who can say? He got his timing wrong. It was a dangerous stunt.'

'I heard that he failed to make any attempt to jump for the arch.'

'He must have panicked. I don't know what was in his mind. Didn't even know the guy.'

'Sandy was okay,' said Murray. 'Popular with all the Cops.'

'We were shattered when it happened,' said Harper.

I didn't believe him. He had just denied knowing Sullivan. Now he was telling me he was shattered by his death. It was just too glib to be believed. He didn't convince me as being a compassionate man. He hadn't expressed a syllable of concern for Amber. Nor, frankly, could I picture him playing the benevolent uncle to Murray's little girls.

'If you're through,' he told us, 'I'd like to finish dressing.'

'Going out?' asked Murray.

'No. I generally put on a shirt and necktie.'

The sarcasm rolled off Murray. He thanked Harper and apologised for our intrusion.

On the stairs the rasp of rapid canine breathing carried up to us, scotching any thoughts I might have had of secretly returning to make a search of Harper's room. When the growling started, Harper's landlady came from the kitchen to hold the boxer's collar for us to pass.

'Fine dog, ma'am,' Murray remarked to her as we edged by.

'Henryk wouldn't bite you,' she informed us. 'He is trained. Very clever animal. My name is Swatowska, Irina Swatowska. You think there is chance to get into movies?'

Murray exchanged a glance with me. Mrs Swatowska was not ugly, but she was fifty, and there were not many openings for small, middle-aged ladies. 'It doesn't pay well,' Murray told her. 'A dollar a day if they use you, but it isn't regular. You'd do better working in a foodstore.'

Mrs Swatowska laughed. 'Not me! I mean Henryk. Wonderful actor. Make growls. Listen.' She ordered the dog to growl and it bared its teeth and obeyed at once. 'See?'

'He's talented, I give you that,' said Murray with a wink at me. 'Too bad you wouldn't hear that in a motion picture.'

'But you have dogs in Keystone pictures. I see them,' persisted Mrs Swatowska. 'Quiet, Henryk! He can beg, lie down, fetch and carry, pretend to be dead.'

Murray nodded. 'Only it isn't up to us, ma'am.'

We opened the door, but she came with us into the street. I looked up at Harper's window. He was watching us, still without a shirt, but I reckoned he was out of earshot. I said to Mrs Swatowska, 'I dare say he's content to be a house dog.'

'Yes — and he could act in movies, too.'

'Would he attack a burglar?'

'Sure, he would.' She took hold of Henryk's muzzle

to display his teeth. 'You like?'

'How about your house guest, Mr Harper? When he comes in, does Henryk go for him?'

She shook her head. 'He knows Mr Harper.'

'But suppose he came in late at night, after you had gone to bed?'

'Henryk is used to it. One bark or two, no more.'

'Mr Harper often gets back late?'

'Most nights. One in the morning. He drinks much beer at the Sunset Inn or some place. I don't mind. He's quiet coming in.'

'I'd like much beer right now,' said Murray.

'Can you get my dog a movie contract?'

Murray said, 'Lady —'

I interrupted him. I wanted more information before we cut this conversation short. 'Have you ever seen Mr Harper with a young lady, blonde hair in ringlets, pretty face, about twenty years of age?'

'No lady visitors. Rule of the house.'

'Do you know who I mean?'

'I never seen such a lady.'

'Keystone, we'd better be on our way,' said Murray.

Mrs Swatowska gave a cry of surprise. 'This is Mr *Keystone*?'

I said 'Yes.' I was not sure how to convey to Murray that I was about to take a gamble on getting into Harper's room. He looked on in blank amazement as I said to Mrs Swatowska, 'I'd like to test the dog. Has he ever been driven in a motor car? Keystone dogs have to be good passengers.'

'Try him,' said Mrs Swatowska confidently.

'We might be able to arrange it.'

'Sometimes Mr Harper take me shopping and Henryk ride with me.'

'Harper has a motor car?'

'Across the street,' Mrs Swatowska informed us, pointing to a Ford Model T, a new one with front doors, a sharply superior cousin to the tin lizzies used in Keystone chases. 'You want to test Henryk now?'

I glanced up at Harper's window and then along the street to where my police escort was still waiting in the grey sedan. 'Later. This will have to be done in secrecy. We could have trouble from the studio animal trainer, so don't mention this to a soul, will you? When is Mr Harper going out?'

THIRTY-TWO

With conspiratorial nods, we took temporary leave of Mrs Swatowska and Henryk and drove off in the Packard. As we drew level with the waiting sedan, I deliberately turned to look at the plainclothes man. He tried to look uninterested, but he already had his engine running. We left the street at the next block and turned the car in the road to face the way we had come. With all pretence of subterfuge abandoned, our escort performed the same manoeuvre.

Murray looked bemused, but he had not asked what this was about. I was grateful for his forbearance. Nine men out of ten would have asked me what the blazes I was planning. Now I told him.

When I had finished, he patiently enquired, 'What do you hope to find, if you get inside? The film Jake claims to have destroyed?'

'Murray, I'll be looking for *anything* that points us to the truth.'

'You don't believe him?'

I had to remember we were talking about a man Murray had trusted enough to welcome to his home and join his new film company. 'Let me put it this way. His story doesn't square with Sennett's.'

'The two cameras?'

'Yes. Sennett clearly believes only one camera was used. He talked of a fault in the mechanism — the handle failing to engage the shaft.'

'That's just his theory, Keystone.'

'Of course. And if it actually happened, Jake Harper

wouldn't have known. He would assume he had cranked the scene and captured the accident on film.'

Murray's eyes widened as he saw the point. 'But he *did* know! We didn't have to tell him the scene was missing. He told us before we mentioned it. Doesn't that prove that Sennett is wrong?'

'Yes.'

'And Jake is right?'

I lifted an eyebrow. 'If he *is*, it raises an interesting question about his conduct. If he *knew* the accident wasn't on the film that Amber had in her possession, why didn't he enlighten Sennett? He could have saved himself that roasting, couldn't he?'

'You're right,' said Murray, rubbing his chin. 'That's very odd.'

'Unless he decided the roasting was worth the profit he would make.'

'By selling the actual sequence to one of our competitors?'

I nodded. 'He must have made a tidy profit somewhere recently. A new car. Drinking every night.'

Murray gave another of his long, low whistles. 'Christ, I trusted that guy! Louise will never believe this.'

I tried to look sympathetic, but my thoughts were not of Louise. I couldn't, wouldn't displace from my mind a crudely shorn blonde head and a pair of green eyes looking for help and seeing none . . . if they saw anything at all.

Please God, she was still alive.

Each time I groped towards an explanation of Amber's disappearance, it flashed out of reach like an image in a hall of mirrors. Jake Harper may have double-crossed Mack Sennett, but he had no reason to persecute Amber. If he knew the film in her possession had nothing of interest on it, he certainly wouldn't have ransacked her apartment and mine, and committed bodily assault and kidnapping to get it back.

Think again.

I didn't get the chance. Harper's Model T Ford passed across the end of the street, heading towards Hollywood Boulevard.

'Action!' said Murray.

He started the engine and we drove back to Mrs Swatowska's house. 'How long do you need?' he asked.

'Just keep driving round the block and praising the dog.'

'I've done some dumb things in my time, Keystone —'

'Thank you, Murray.'

Three minutes later, Mrs Swatowska had taken my place beside Murray, who sat resignedly at the wheel with Henryk in the back seat breathing hotly on his neck. I had informed Mrs Swatowska that it would not be necessary for me to join them, and she had obligingly offered me the hospitality of her drawing room.

I stood at the window and watched the Packard move away. Henryk at once began the howling that he would continue as long as the vehicle moved.

There was no fooling the plainclothes man. He remained staunchly in his sedan on the other side of the street, keeping the house under observation.

I went upstairs and tried Harper's door. It was locked. I tried the keys from a couple of other doors but I was unlucky, so I went downstairs to search for Mrs Swatowska's set. I found it eventually in the sideboard. When I got into Harper's room, twenty minutes had gone by.

I was looking for anything that would throw light on

Amber's disappearance. Whatever Harper might or might not have done himself, he had been alarmed to find us in his room. He was afraid of something.

I had the wild idea I might find a few blonde hairs attached to his clothes. I opened the closet and examined each of his jackets. Took out the trousers. Got on my knees and searched the floor. Dust. A few hairs of his own. Not one that could have belonged to Amber.

Something else, then. An address book, a diary, a letter. I went through pockets, drawers, cupboards, cases. Apparently, he kept nothing more personal than a few loose coins and keys that I scattered on the bedside table.

I was getting desperate. I rolled back the carpet. Without exception, the boards were firm and pinned. There were no telltale marks along the edges.

Still on my knees, I examined the underside of the bed. It was an iron frame with a wire grid to support the mattress. Nothing was hidden there. I stripped the bed and looked for an opening in the mattress. I ran my fingers under the corded edges. No sign of a cut in the fabric.

Something broke my concentration. The sound of Henryk's howling.

I glanced through the window and saw the Packard drawing up outside. The search was over. I had failed.

I whipped the covers across the bed and tidied them. Shut the drawers and cupboard. Moved to the door. Took a last look round and spotted the coins I had spread on the bedside table. And the keys.

Two keys, one tarnished by much use, the other obviously new.

On an impulse, I took my own keys from my pocket and compared them. The new key was a duplicate to the key of my apartment.

I pocketed it, swept the coins into the drawer where I had found them and raced downstairs to open the door.

Mrs Swatowska was in tears. 'Mr Keystone, he never cry before today. Never.'

'He didn't jump out,' said Murray to console her.

'You think he still has chance?' said Mrs Swatowska.

'We'll let you know if we need him,' I assured her, moving fast towards the Packard. 'Remember to keep this to yourself.'

'Sure! You like to see him beg?'

'Another time. Tell me, where did Mr Harper go?'

'To eat, I guess. He hadn't eaten nothing today.'

'Where does he generally go?'

'Sometimes Benny's on Lexington, or that new place further up, next to the hospital. Lemon Tree. Why you want to see Mr Harper again?'

THIRTY-THREE

As we drove downtown, I told Murray about the key.

'Smart spotting!' he commented. 'Only where does it get us?'

'On Jake Harper's heels, I hope. Can't we go any faster?'

'We're doing nearly forty, Keystone.'

To stiffen his resolve, I told him precisely why Harper was the man we were hunting. The key had clinched it. A brand new key identical to mine. Harper had taken mine the night he had attacked me on the cliff. He had entered my apartment and searched it, without result. After my escape, I had found the key left casually among the wreckage of my possessions. Or so it had appeared. I hadn't appreciated that Harper was about as casual with keys as Harry Houdini. He had taken an impression in soap or wax ready for his next visit: the night I had spent at police headquarters.

Harper was dangerous. He had killed Mrs Honeybee, admittedly by accident, but everything that happened since that night pointed to a fanatically single-minded man. And now he had kidnapped Amber.

'Harper killed Amber's mother?'

'Probably by accident. I reckon she surprised him and he gave her a push. She had a thin skull.'

'Keystone, isn't there a flaw in this?'

'I don't think so.'

'All these things that happened. Why did he do them?'

'To recover the can of film that Amber had taken.'

'The film of the rollercoaster ride?'

'Yes. It's an obsession with him.'

'Maybe,' admitted Murray, 'but there's got to be a reason.'

I knew what he meant. An hour ago we had both agreed that the film had no interest for anyone because Sullivan's death-fall wasn't on it. Of all people, Harper knew that.

I didn't answer Murray. Like him, I didn't understand. I wouldn't until we caught up with Harper.

I just said, 'Can't you go any faster?'

We screeched to a halt outside the restaurant called Benny's, a more formal establishment than the name suggested. Before going in, I looked up and down Lexington Avenue for Harper's Model T Ford. It was nowhere in sight. There was only the inevitable grey sedan.

I spoke to a waiter. He confirmed that Harper was a regular customer. He hadn't seen him that morning.

'The Lemon Tree?' said Murray as I climbed back into the Packard.

I nodded.

The manageress at the Lemon Tree knew Harper. She had not seen him for a week.

'Another dead end,' said Murray.

'Let's not speak of death.'

'At least we know he didn't eat at the usual places today. I guess our visit made him nervous. I wouldn't mind betting he's taken it on the Arthur Duffy to some place safer than this.'

'Which way would he go?'

'Search me,' said Murray.

'You know the man,' I snapped back. 'Come on, Murray! Amber is helpless somewhere. We *must* catch Harper. What do we know about his past? Where does

211

he come from?'

'Lived in Los Angeles all his life.'

'Has he got any family? Parents? Brothers?'

'Never mentioned any that I recall.'

'Any places he visits?'

Murray thought for a moment and shook his head.

There we sat in one of the most powerful motor cars in production. Stationary. Because we had nowhere to go.

In a Keystone picture, when the villain in his motor car crosses the railroad and the Cops are compelled to stop for a train, they stand on their patrol wagon and jump up and down in frustration. I was close to doing the same.

'If *you* wanted to flee from justice, where would you go?' I asked Murray over the throb of the engine.

'Some other state, I guess.'

'Some other country!' I said. 'How far is Mexico from here?'

'Hundred and fifty.'

'He could do it inside five hours.'

'I wouldn't bet on it. The road isn't so good.'

'We could catch him in this.'

'If he really went that way,' Murray agreed with a clear note of doubt, then added more positively, 'We'll need some more gas.'

We had the tank filled at the gas station on Santa Monica Boulevard and Vermont. I asked the attendant if he had served the owner of a new Model T in the past hour. He shook his head.

Out of the corner of an eye I saw a familiar grey shape. It occurred to me that we had set our police escort a problem. He had no idea how far we planned to drive. Perhaps he remembered the parable of the wise and foolish virgins. He had decided to get some fuel.

KEYSTONE

I slipped the attendant ten dollars extra and told him, 'Take your time filling the one behind. If he should ask, we're heading up the coast to Santa Barbara.'

It was the last we saw of the grey sedan. Wise virgins shouldn't believe everything they're told.

We took the main route south through Norwalk and Buena Park, pushing the Packard steadily up to forty to make the most of the tarmacadam before we struck the dirt roads of El Camino Real further on.

'How far to the next gas station?' I asked Murray.

'Thirty, thirty-five. There's one at San Clemente.'

'And after that?'

'Maybe one at Carlsbad. Can't recall now.'

'That's halfway to Mexico, isn't it?'

He nodded.

'Do you see what I'm thinking?'

'Yup. It makes sense.'

The rumble of the Packard's tyres gave way to a crackling, uneven note as we joined the coast road. This was at Huntington's futuristic landscape of oil-derricks extending to the mesa above the ocean. Ahead of us something was moving in its own cloud of dust. A truck, we discovered, as we came alongside. We were to have three more disappointments like that in the next twenty miles.

At San Juan Capistrano, we mounted a rise that treated us to a spectacular view south to San Clemente, but no sight of the Model T. If Harper *was* ahead, he was pushing his car to the limit.

The gas station at San Clemente was on the far side of town, a shack with a single pump beside it. The attendant was on his back examining the leaking underside of a Pierce Arrow, one of several victims of the coast highway pushed into the forecourt after breaking down God knows how many miles away.

213

'You want gas?' he asked without showing his face.

'Just information. Have you seen a new Ford Model T?'

'You trying to sell me an automobile?'

'We're trying to find one,' said Murray. 'The latest model, with doors. The driver's a muscular guy, dark features.'

'That's nothing special. Mexico is down the road.'

'A blue suit. Grey and white check cap,' I said.

'What did he do? Force you off the road?'

'We just want to know if you've seen the man.'

'Yeah. I saw him, forty minutes back. Five gallons and keep the change. Three lousy cents. Wouldn't wait to have his rad checked. He'll be sorry. The hood was getting hot.'

We fairly screeched out of that forecourt and back on the road. A flock of gulls winged off in a panic from the roof of the shack. Curiosity finally got the better of our informant. The last I saw of him he was on his feet staring into the dust we had raised.

For a mile or more we overtook things we had passed before. Then there was just the empty road cleaving to the mesa, with the ocean away to our right and San Onofre Mountain looming on Murray's side.

Forty minutes to make up. About a hundred miles to the border. The Packard had more speed than the Ford, but on this uneven road it was asking a lot to keep going, let alone make up time. The strain showed on Murray's face as he braced to steady the steering each time we hit a rut. I would have offered to take over, only we both knew we couldn't afford to stop.

Instead, I was priming myself for action when we caught up with Harper. Action it had to be. He was on the run. His instinct would be to turn and fight. I intended to take him on. This time he wouldn't be

214

coming from behind us with a cut-throat razor.

A fight, yes. By God, I was ready for one. But words still mattered more than blows. The answer to one vital question: where was Amber?

'What's that up ahead?' Murray asked.

I put my face close to the windshield and caught the flash of the sun on another vehicle. No dust cloud behind it, so it was stationary. A car at the side of the road three hundred yards ahead.

'Could you slow up?'

'Looks like a Ford.' Murray started to brake.

From behind, it certainly appeared so. Black, high suspension, the four-square look of the coachwork, with the overlapping canopy. A Model T.

But it was an old doorless model and the owner was kneeling beside it, changing a tyre. We drew alongside and spoke to him. A Mexican. A new Model T had passed him not twenty minutes before, with steam rising from the radiator.

'What's up ahead?' Murray asked.

'Not much. Twenty miles to Oceanside.'

'No garage?'

The Mexican spread his hands. 'Senor, would I be here on my knees if there was?'

Murray yanked down the throttle lever and shoved hard with his foot and we roared away. The low sun of late afternoon sharpened the scene like a lens in perfect focus. An idyllic composition of sky, sea and mountains. All it wanted for perfection was a broken-down Ford on the road ahead.

Ten minutes more and it was there.

We came to the top of a rise. Nothing too steep or sudden, but too much for an overheated, overworked engine. Harper's Model T had made it to the top and freewheeled down as far as it could go. Now it stood empty and still hissing steam in the long grass that fringed the road.

Not a sign of the driver.

We drove slowly past to confirm it, then halted half-way between the Model T and the only building in sight, a stone one-story house with a red tiled roof, probably built as a holiday home.

'He could have gone there for water,' said Murray. 'Shall we check?'

I was in charge now. 'Wait here,' I told him. 'I'll go and see.'

'Hold on.' Murray delved under the seat and came up with a large wrench. 'Just in case.'

I took it and strode towards the house. There was no point in subterfuge. The grass was six inches high and that was all there was as far as the white palings around the place.

No movement inside or out.

There were outbuildings at the back: a shed and a privy. I stepped over the fence and checked that they were empty. That left the house itself.

I tried the back door and found it locked. Walked around the side, looking through windows. There were dustsheets over the furniture.

I called out, 'Harper, are you there?'

If he was, he didn't answer.

I made my way round to the front and knocked on the door.

Harper wasn't answering and nor was anyone else.

Yet where else could he logically have gone? There wasn't another building in sight. On one side of the road, acres of parched grass extended to the hills. On the other, a ridge of sand. Below that, the beach and the sea.

Had he decided to abandon his new car and get a lift

across the border from some passing truck? If so, we had lost him by now.

I thought about Harper. He worked with cameras. Mechanical things wouldn't throw him into a panic. An overheated radiator wasn't a serious problem provided no damage was done to other parts. He would know that a refill of water would get him on the road again.

Here was an empty house with a ready supply. I knew it was there because the privy was built with a flushing system. Harper could have taken the water from there.

But he hadn't.

I couldn't believe he would have gone for sea water, but I had to check. I climbed the ridge for a full view of the beach.

At once I saw what had happened. Below the ridge the drop to the beach was steeper than my quick inspection had led me to suppose. Two hundred yards back, practically opposite the Model T, but obscured from the road, was another stone building, obviously provided for bathers to use for changing. It was a reasonable bet that it had a supply of water.

My skin prickled. I slithered down the slope to the beach and started walking towards the bath-house. I had gone perhaps sixty yards when something exploded ahead of me.

Harper was armed.

A second shot cracked and whined past me before I did anything about it.

I heard Murray's voice yell, 'Keystone, get down!'

I completed that front fall more rapidly than any I had performed in theatres. I rolled over and over like an actor in a Wild West picture. I saw sand flick up as a bullet impacted itself in the ridge above me.

I had no cover at all. I scrabbled soft sand into a heap in front of my face.

Another bullet screamed over my head. I fully expected to be shot.

Two more in rapid succession, but they were not so close. Harper's aim was off target, thank God, unless he wasn't firing at me. Murray was closer to him.

I lay on my stomach waiting, calculating my chance of getting up the ridge and out of sight. How many bullets had he fired? Five, or six?

I squirmed in the sand with minimal movement, trying to get deeper. For the present, I was staying put. My hand touched something hard and metallic. The wrench. Two minutes ago it had seemed a serviceable weapon. I buried it.

Three or four minutes went by with no more shooting. I risked raising my head to look at the bath-house and spotted the window from which presumably the firing had come. Instead of glass, a fine wire mesh was provided for decency, only the indecent had poked three holes through it. Each was large enough for the muzzle of a revolver.

A sudden movement above me caught my attention. Someone was on the ridge, peering over. If it was Harper with the gun, I was finished. I groped for the wrench.

'Keystone.' A stage whisper.

The sun glinted pinkly on a pair of pebble glasses. Murray. He backed out of sight again. 'You hurt?' his voice asked.

'No. He missed, thank God.'

'Can you get up here?'

'I'd rather not chance it.'

'I counted six shots. I don't think he has any more.'

I waited another half-minute, weighing the odds. If Harper had more ammunition, I had given him time to reload. Staying on the sand had saved me from the first round, but there was no guarantee he would miss with six more. I reckoned I could scramble up the slope to Murray in the time it took to aim and fire two shots.

I wasn't here for safety first. I was here to find out about Amber.

I got up and sprinted for the ridge.

The sand slipped sickeningly under my feet at each step up the slope. Murray reached down towards me and I grabbed his hand and scrambled to the top.

'He didn't fire a shot,' said Murray triumphantly. 'He's out of bullets.'

'Let's not count on it.'

Without another word, we ran back along the road past the Packard towards the point closest to the bath-house. Harper's Model T still simmered gently there.

'Let's surprise him,' I said. 'Give me a hand.'

I released the emergency brake and held the steering wheel, and we pushed the car to the edge of the slope. We stopped it on the angle, poised to career down the ridge and hit the building by the window he had fired from. If Harper were still inside, he couldn't possibly see us at the height we were.

I picked up a sizeable stone. 'I'm going down,' I told Murray. 'Give me ten seconds and heave the car over.'

It involved getting down the slope and around the bath-house at the opposite end to the entrance on the ocean side. The first part was reasonably safe. There were no windows at the back. What I would find at the front, I could only guess. More mesh windows. Probably two doors, to segregate the sexes. If so, I wanted the second door. I hoped to God it was open.

'All right?'

Murray nodded and braced himself against the back of the Model T.

I set off down the slope, past the side window and

219

reached the front. Two windows and two doors, as I expected. Dipping low, I got into position by the second door. It was slightly open. My movements had been muffled by the sand, but I was breathing hard. I tried to control it, wishing Murray would push the damn car on its way. Was it too heavy for one man to move?

The Model T made a sound like a groan and a split second later I heard it hit the wall.

I burst into the room.

I froze.

Jake Harper was there and he had the revolver in his hand. He was not at the window. He was below it, propped against the wall. A bullet had passed clean through his head.

THIRTY-FOUR

Murray was speechless. We stood together in the cool of that shaded room with the powder fumes still in the air and stared at the corpse of the man we had come to question. Harper's face was unmarked. The lips were parted in what must have been a grimace, but had somehow fixed into a meaningless smile.

I looked away. Beside the body was an empty can on its side. On the end wall was a tap, dripping water.

I said without confidence, 'Perhaps there is something in his pockets.'

I went forward and searched them. Coins, a ring of keys, a watch, a penknife, a lens cap and a handkerchief.

'Maybe we should look in the automobile,' Murray suggested.

I said, 'I think he's wearing a body belt.'

Between us, we got the shirt apart and loosened the clothes sufficiently to unfasten the belt. There was money inside, a wad of hundred-dollar bills.

'Holy smoke!' said Murray. 'He could have bought himself a Cadillac with this.'

'We'd better replace it.'

When we had straightened the clothes, it was a relief to go outside and search the crashed car. Although the front was badly impacted, the interior was undamaged. Under one of the seats I found an envelope containing documents relating to the car. Harper had bought it three weeks ago from a garage on Lexington Avenue. According to the receipt, he had paid just over nine hundred dollars in cash.

'Where could he have got all this money?' I said.

Murray shook his head. 'The race-track?'

'What time is it, Murray?'

'Just on seven o'clock.'

'I'd like to get back to Los Angeles.'

His blue eyes widened. 'How about, er . . .?' He pointed towards the bath-house.

'If we report it now,' I said, 'we'll be questioned all night. And it won't help Amber at all.'

He understood. 'You still think she's trapped somewhere.'

'Murray, I've got to believe it.'

'Okay, I'm with you. But this time you can drive.'

I covered the seventy miles to Los Angeles in barely an hour and a half. While Murray sat wide-eyed and white-knuckled beside me, I wasn't really thinking of the driving. I was plumbing my memory for anything that would lead me to Amber.

I refused to accept that because Harper had shot himself, everything came to a stop. It raised other questions that had to be answered now. Why had he done it? Why had he shot so wildly when Murray and I were unarmed? He could have waited in the bath-house and shot us both as we entered.

He had panicked. I had seen it in his eyes the moment he had found us in his room that morning; seen it in the way the razor had twitched in his hand. If Murray had not been there speaking reassuring words, I would have had my throat cut. Instead, Harper had made a run for the border. We had pursued him. And now he was dead.

For a piece of film.

Extraordinary.

He had left Los Angeles with a car, a gun and a

beltful of money. He had been on his way to freedom.

Unarmed, Murray and I had stampeded him into shooting himself.

He knew we were only chasing information. I had told him we were looking for Amber. We weren't the police. We weren't a posse got up by Mack Sennett.

We would have asked him to take us to Amber. I suppose we might have handed him to the police, but that wasn't the end of the world.

For Jake Harper, a bullet was.

I had to face it: nothing I knew or suspected about Harper warranted suicide. Unless he were guilty of murder.

I asked Murray, 'Are you awake?'

'Keystone, the way you're driving, I wouldn't care to close my eyes.'

'Sorry. Tell me, how can we find out whether Harper was speaking the truth?'

'About what?'

'The second camera. He said he used two cameras when he filmed the rollercoaster sequence.'

'I wasn't there, Keystone. I was directing another picture.'

'I know. What happens about cameras? How can we check whether he had two cameras with him?'

'On location, you always have spares, in case of a fault.'

I lapsed into silence for a mile or two, then added, 'When a picture is made, someone must keep a record of all the shots.'

'Sure. That's continuity.'

'Wouldn't that tell us how many cameras were used?'

Murray thought for a moment. Then he nodded. 'Yeah, it would.'

'How can we get hold of the continuity script?'

223

'The director.'

'Mack Sennett.'

'Oh, Christ,' said Murray.

'But where would he keep it?'

'Locked up in the office.'

'Do you have a key?'

'Sorry.'

'But they must have one at the gate. The janitor. Security. Someone. They know you, Murray. If you tell them you need to see a script, they'll let us in.'

THIRTY-FIVE

The gateman was not surprised to see us, even at a quarter to nine in the evening. The entire studio, from Sennett down, appeared to have spent the day demanding to know where Murray was. He was due to start shooting his last Keystone picture next day, and there were queries about scripts, costumes, stunts, and sets that no-one but the director could answer.

'They can see me tomorrow,' he promised as he accepted the main office key.

'Is he going with you?' the gateman asked with a jerk of his head towards me.

'Is there a problem about that?' queried Murray so mildly that it actually sounded menacing.

'No problem, Mr Brennan.'

Nor was there any problem in finding the script we were looking for. It was one of a stack in the outer office. I turned up the rollercoaster sequence.

Each take was recorded there. So was the time in seconds and the camera number. Camera One had been used for every take from the long shot of the fairground to the rollercoaster ride. The words *Accident. Shooting abandoned* were scrawled under Take One of the shot described as *Cop pursued by Car*. It was noted clearly as Camera One.

Jake Harper had lied to us. There had been no second camera.

'So there was only one film,' said Murray, 'and that was the one we developed ourselves?'

'Yes.'

'Without a damn thing on it.'

'Without the accident on it, anyway,' I said.

Murray took out his watch. 'Keystone, it's nine in the evening. I haven't been home all day. Louise gets a little touchy when I don't appear for dinner.'

'I understand.'

'I'll put you down at your place.'

'I'd appreciate it more if you'd take me to Santa Monica.'

'Fine, it's on the way, but what do you want to go there for?'

'To call on the Arbuckles.'

'Roscoe? Can he help with this?'

'Murray, I've got to keep trying.'

'If you need any help . . .'

I nodded my thanks.

I didn't enlarge on my reason for visiting the Arbuckles because I was certain Murray would have tried to discourage me. His help up to now had been indispensable, and I didn't want it to end with an argument.

When I pressed the bell in the Arbuckles' porch, the Packard was already disappearing up Palisades Beach Road.

The same maid I had seen on my first visit opened the door. This time, I was ushered through a panelled oak hall hung with landscapes of the Barbizon School, across a Louis Quinze drawing room into a billiard room where Roscoe was in shirtsleeves, practising.

I said, 'I'm sorry to come unannounced like this.'

Roscoe grinned and said, 'That's okay. We out-of-work actors better stick together. What's new, Keystone?'

'Is Mabel Normand still here?'

He looked away. 'She isn't seeing anyone just now.'

'It's about Amber. She's still missing.'

'That's bad, but I don't see how Mabel can help you.'

I told him my conviction that Amber had been kidnapped in an attempt to get possession of the film of the rollercoaster ride. At first he didn't believe me, but when I told him how Amber had compelled Mack Sennett to give her the leading role in *Kidnap in the Park*, his eyes popped, just as they did in his comedies when the pretty girl appeared arm in arm with the heavy. It was a revelation to him. For a moment he was silent, no doubt recalling his experience playing opposite Amber. Then he muttered, 'Hell's bells.'

I was halfway to convincing him. 'That isn't all,' I went on. 'It has led to violence and death. I'm not sure whether Amber herself is still alive. 'I've got to find her, Roscoe. And only Mabel can help me now.'

'Why Mabel?'

'She was in the rollercoaster car that hit the Cop, Sandy Sullivan.'

'She wasn't the only one, was she?'

'She's the only one I have a hope of finding tonight. I just want her to tell me what she saw. You see, I've reached the conclusion it wasn't an accident at all. I think Sandy Sullivan was meant to be hit by the car.'

'That would be murder, for God's sake.'

'And for God's sake, won't you let me see Mabel?'

He took me across the hall and pushed open a door. His wife Minta came forward to block our way, saying, 'Roscoe, I told you!'

'It's an emergency,' said Roscoe, placing his hands firmly on her shoulders and moving her aside. 'Mabel, my dear, you remember Keystone? He needs your help — urgently.'

She was in a white bathrobe, seated in a winged arm-chair holding a cup in both hands. Her face bore the dark marks of suffering. There wasn't a flicker of response to Roscoe's words.

I went forward and put myself on a footstool in front

of her.

I said, 'Miss Normand — Mabel — I want you to remember the day you were filmed in Exposition Park. The ride on the rollercoaster. The Cop being killed.'

She had the glazed stare of a waxwork.

'Sandy Sullivan,' I said, seeking some spark in her memory. 'You remember? You were in the front of the car with Harry Gribbon. Amber Honeybee and Harry Booker were behind you. As the car came over the rise, you saw the Cops on the track. They all got clear except Sullivan. The car rushed down the slope. You saw him running ahead of you.' I paused.

She had shaken her head.

'But you did!' I told her. 'You were there, Mabel. You saw him hit the car. You screamed. I was watching from below.'

Behind me, Roscoe said, 'I don't think she remembers.'

I ignored him. I concentrated on Mabel's eyes, willing her to help me, picturing the sequence of events as she must have seen it. 'First, a trial run, a rehearsal. It goes without a hitch. You get out. Someone tidies your hair. You take some puffs on a cigarette. And then Mr Sennett orders a take.'

At the mention of Sennett's name, her eyes flickered.

'You must have made a joke, because everyone laughs. Then Mr Sennett ruffles your hair and draws you towards the boarding stage. He kisses you.'

She nodded. Her brown eyes were watching me now, reacting to my memory of that morning when filming was still a joy and comedy was fun.

'As the car moves away, you blow a kiss to the crowd. You are starting to climb. You can feel the machinery hauling you up. Then you're up there and into the ride. A small dip. A rise. Picking up speed. Harry starts to wrestle with you. You are racing up the track to the highest point. As you reach it, Harry's silk hat flies off. The car dips and you see the Cops. Sandy Sullivan holding his hand up like a traffic cop. He turns and sprints ahead of you. You can see the arch he is meant to pull himself up by.' I stopped.

She was shaking her head again.

I was sure I had lost her. I took a long breath and tried to contain my frustration.

Then she spoke. Flatly, as if each word were an effort, she said, 'I didn't see it happen.'

I said gently, 'Mabel, you were there.'

'Yes.'

'In the car that hit Sandy Sullivan.'

'But I didn't see it on account of the sun in my eyes.'

I shook my head. 'The sun was behind you, Mabel.'

'No,' she insisted. 'I was dazzled.'

I pictured the scene as I remembered it. The ride soaring above me with the high point on my right and the steep dip towards the left where the car had crashed into Sullivan. And somewhere to my left, the ocean. The sun couldn't possibly have been over the ocean at that time of day.

Then I remembered the sun reflectors.

Four-foot discs faced with tinfoil to catch the sun's rays and highlight the action.

I said, 'The sun was reflected into your eyes when you reached the bottom of the slope?'

Mabel nodded.

I thanked her. I had nothing else to ask her. I knew how Sandy Sullivan had died. Between the rehearsal and the fatal take, Jake Harper had adjusted the reflectors. I remembered seeing him do it. He had fixed them so that the reflected sun shone in Sullivan's eyes. In a stunt of such precision it meant Sullivan would certainly miss his jump and his handhold.

It was no accident either, and the proof of that was that Harper had deliberately omitted to crank the camera. He had made sure there was no record of what happened.

A neat, undetected murder. Until Amber had picked up the film. From that moment, Jake Harper was in trouble. If it were developed, someone was bound to ask why the accident had not been filmed. His efforts to get it back had been characterised by desperation mounting to panic. Finally, he had cut and run.

Explanations. But was I any nearer to finding Amber?

In the hall I asked Roscoe, 'What can you tell me about Sandy Sullivan?'

He scratched his head. 'Sandy? Can't say I knew him too well. I heard he wasn't much over thirty, but he looked ten years older. Lived hard. Every pay day he went on a bender and the rest of the week he was skint.'

'Did he make any enemies?'

'Not that I heard. He took on the dangerous gags, and the boys appreciated that.'

'No trouble with Sennett?'

'They got along fine.'

'The ladies?'

'Sandy behaved himself. He married young, but it wasn't a success and they drifted apart. Once bitten, huh? After he died, Sennett found a marriage licence among his things and the office tried to find the lady. No dice. The funeral had a Keystone cast.'

'What happened to Sullivan's possessions after the funeral?'

'They fitted into one tin trunk. Far as I know, It's still at the studio.'

'Where is it kept?'

'Wardrobe. Anything we haven't a place for is given to Wardrobe.'

THIRTY-SIX

'Thursday,' said Roscoe. 'There's only one place Wardrobe Winnie will be, and that's the Hollywood Hotel. Dance night.'

'Does she dance?' I insensitively queried.

'Fat people can be smooth movers, Keystone.'

'True — but isn't this a public dance?'

'It's very respectable. No liquor. No late admissions. Mrs Hershey who runs the hotel won't let you in this time of night. In fact I'd better come with you.'

I was grateful. It meant not only that I was driven there in Roscoe's Pierce Arrow, and admitted without question, but I also had his assistance with Winnie. She was there in the lobby dancing a supple Turkey Trot in a mauve crêpe de Chine and lace creation that she had probably made for Marie Dressler. Unaided, I would never have enticed her off the floor, let alone out of the hotel. Roscoe had only to crook a finger and she came.

'Couldn't we wait until the dance ends at midnight?' she asked when we had finished explaining our mission.

Roscoe said, 'Sweetheart, if we go now, we'll be back by midnight and you and I shall have the last dance.'

'That had better be a promise.'

He gave her a wink and we drove out to Edendale.

The studio gateman gave me a long look, but in such company he didn't presume to challenge me. Roscoe stayed at the gate talking to him while Winnie collected her keys and took me to Wardrobe.

Sandy Sullivan's tin trunk was doing service as a bench in one of the changing rooms. Winnie swept off

231

the cushions and unlocked it.

'Not much to show for thirty-odd years of life,' she commented as she started removing the contents and heaping them on the floor. 'A couple of shirts frayed at the cuff. Two pairs of beat-up shoes. One suit stinking of tobacco. Socks. Underpants. A necktie. Overcoat. Cap. And this.'

'May I see?'

She handed me a flat, square biscuit tin. Inside, I found the few things Sandy Sullivan had counted as precious: a carte-de-visite photograph of a small lady with an ostrich-plumed hat, presumably his mother; some newspaper notices of vaudeville shows; a printed prayer to St Francis; a bottle-opener; three brass buttons cut from a soldier's uniform; and a marriage licence. I unfolded it.

The licence had been issued in San Francisco on 8 October, 1904. Alexander Sullivan, bachelor, occupation stevedore, 20, had married Louise May, spinster, 19.

Louise.

My heart pumped harder.

Murray's wife?

I dredged my memory for the things she had mentioned in our conversations at the studio and in their house at Malibu. Her two daughters, Louise and May. Louise had been given her first name and May was her family name.

Louise May, spinster.

'*Louise had a previous marriage to a guy called Alex and he was a real son-of-a-gun.*'

Alexander Sullivan, bachelor.

Alexander the Great had been the one film Murray definitely wouldn't make when he started his historical pictures.

But according to Louise, Alex had died in the fire that followed the San Francisco earthquake in 1906. She had married Murray a year later.

What if Alexander Sullivan, stevedore, son-of-a-gun and victim of the fire, had miraculously risen from the ashes as Sandy Sullivan, the Keystone Cop who dared do anything? What if Louise had spotted him on the set?

His survival would invalidate her marriage to Murray. Their position in society, their ultra-respectable, butlered existence would crash around their ears. Their daughters would find themselves bastardised. For Louise it would be insufferable.

There had to be a remedy, and there was. To arrange what the earthquake and fire had failed to achieve: the extinction of Alexander Sullivan.

'The dance will be finished if we don't hurry,' Winnie reminded me.

I returned the licence to the tin and shut it in the trunk and we rejoined Roscoe at the gate. I gave uninformative answers to his questions as he drove us back to the Hollywood Hotel. There, I thanked him.

'Don't you want me to drive you home?' he asked.

'You made a promise to Winnie.'

I walked over to the line of taxis and told the first driver to take me to Malibu.

THIRTY-SEVEN

I stopped the cab and settled the fare on the coast road half a mile short of Malibu. If I had chosen to drive up to the house and asked to see Murray, no doubt he would have received me in his usual disarming way. He would have heard me out and defended his actions plausibly and calmly. He would have shrugged off all responsibility for the three people who had died. He would have denied any implication in Amber's disappearance.

He was not going to get the opportunity. I now knew he was as dangerous as the characters with silk hats and staring eyes we hissed in melodramas.

So I approached his estate by stealth, keeping to the shadow under the trees that skirted the moonlit foreshore. A stone wall and a padlocked wrought iron gate separated the terraced garden from the beach. I climbed over the wall on to a paved area furnished with chairs and benches.

Ahead of me was a wooden summerhouse, solid and large enough to accommodate a prisoner. I tried the door. It opened.

Nothing, except a few canvas chairs.

I moved on, using trees and shrubs as cover. There were no lights at the windows of the house, but I couldn't be certain that everyone inside was asleep, or even in bed. It was barely an hour after midnight.

If Amber were a prisoner in the house, where would the Brennans be keeping her? Nowhere, surely, where the children were likely to find her. I could probably ignore the ground floor. But in a house of this size, there would certainly be a cellar. With luck, it would be accessible from steps at the side.

I found them half-hidden by a eucalyptus trained up the south side of the building. Steps into darkness. I counted twelve and reached the bottom.

A door with a narrow window beside it. I looked in. I could make out the shapes of pieces of furniture. It was impossible to see very far inside.

I drew back the bolts at top and bottom and tried the handle. The door refused to open. There was sufficient movement to indicate that it was held by a strong bolt on the inside.

I peered through the window again, telling myself that it was unreasonable to expect any sign of movement from Amber if she were inside. She would certainly be bound and probably gagged.

The wooden frame of the window was in good condition and the fixings appeared to be firm. I dared not risk the sound of shattered glass. Yet that window had to be my means of access to the cellar, and, I hoped, the house.

Back up the steps to a small building I had noticed at the rear: with luck, a toolshed. I got inside and fumbled in the dark for something to use as a jemmy. On one of the walls was a rack of chisels. I selected two and returned to the cellar window.

The process of getting some leverage took forty-five frustrating minutes. Ultimately I succeeded in chiselling away enough of the frame to get the larger chisel under the window and force it away from the fixings. With a screech like a cockatoo the screws came out of the wood.

I held my breath and listened. I waited half a minute, then put my arm inside and drew back the bolt on the door.

The shapes inside the cellar sharpened into recognisable objects. An upright piano. A sideboard. Several rolls of carpet. Stacks of pictures. A bed frame.

Disappointment number one: I knew from the staleness of the air that I was the first to open a door into that cellar in months.

Number two: steps led up to a door giving access to the interior, but it was locked. I couldn't force it without waking the house.

I took stock. Amber was inside the house; that was my premise for being there, so I refused to consider anything else. As she was not being kept in the cellar, it was a fair bet that she was three stories up, at the top, in an attic or possibly the loft.

I left the cellar and walked around the outside seeking another means of entry. I examined doors, windows, drainpipes and the climbing plants on the walls. My best chance, I decided, was a drainpipe to the flat garage roof, giving access to a bathroom window.

I pocketed the two chisels and tested the drainpipe to be sure it could take my weight. Then I hauled myself hand over hand to the garage roof. As I expected, the window was firmly secured. Another job for the chisels. It would take even longer, because at this level I dared not risk waking the sleepers on the same floor.

Once or twice when I was working to free that window, I fancied I heard a movement inside the house, but after a pause each time I dismissed it as nerves.

Then, when the job was almost done, a sound came up from below with paralysing clarity.

Someone walked round the side of the house.

A short, stocky figure with a slight roll in his gait. The glint of glasses.

Murray.

He couldn't fail to see me if he raised his eyes. All I

could do was hold every muscle rigid.

He walked by. Around the garage to the front. A scraping sound. He was opening the garage doors.

It was 3.30 in the morning and Murray was going for a drive.

I waited for him to start the Packard. He cranked it a couple of times and as soon as its throb began, I put down my chisels, slid down the drainpipe and sprinted for the cover of the bushes that bordered the front drive.

Murray reversed the car, got out and entered the house at the front, leaving the engine running.

I crouched behind a rhododendron and in a moment I saw him come out again. He was not alone this time. Ahead of him a slight figure shuffled towards the Packard, climbed in and sat in the front passenger seat. In that poor light there was no chance of recognising who it was. I would have guessed at an old woman if it were not for the clothes. So far as I could see, the figure was not in a skirt, but bare-legged. The upper half was covered by a jacket slung loosely over the shoulders. And the head was cropped.

I was so intent on the figure, trying to conceive of it being Amber, that I failed to notice Louise come between the columns of the entrance behind Murray. The first I was aware of it was when I heard her voice above the engine.

She had a small gun in her right hand. She was pointing it towards the figure in the car. I couldn't make out what was being said, but she appeared to be giving orders.

Murray got into the back of the car and picked up a length of rope. He wound it several times around the figure in the front seat. There was not a murmur of protest, even when he jerked the rope tight for the knot.

I was in turmoil. Logic suggested that it was Amber they were tying to the car seat, but almost everything my eyes had taken in challenged my confidence. I needed to get closer.

At the near end of the colonnade that fronted the house was a holly bush. I reckoned it was between eight and ten yards from where the Packard was standing, and the only way to reach it was by crossing a twenty-yard strip of gravel. Murray had just struck a match to light the car lamps. Louise had lowered the gun. She was watching him. I seized my chance and dashed towards the holly bush, counting on the sound of the motor to drown my steps on the gravel. I ducked out of sight and waited. Hearing no reaction, I raised my head. They still busied themselves with the lamps. And I had a clear sight of their prisoner, caught in the flicker of the match.

A vision of horror.

The face that stared out from the car was inhuman. It was chalk white. It had a painted line for a mouth and a painted moustache. Thick painted eyebrows. No hair at all, simply a coat of black paint to resemble hair. I had seen it before, the morning the Cops had tricked me with their practical joke on the beach.

A Keystone dummy.

I reeled back, shook my head and looked again. The same lifeless face. The body wrapped in a dark jacket with silver buttons. A Cop's uniform.

It was Amber.

They had shaved her head and painted it. Wrapped tape across her mouth and drawn that crude line where her lips should have been. Whitened the rest of her face. Covered her limbs in some kind of muslin body-stocking.

But I knew those eyes.

I was at a loss to understand why they had done this to her. I was appalled and enraged. And yet elated, because the girl I had agonised over minute by minute ever since she had disappeared was alive. Whatever she had suffered, it was coming to an end. I didn't rush out to do battle with Murray. If I had, I would probably have been stopped by a bullet. I stayed hidden. In a couple of seconds I had raced across the drive. I had spotted the brass lamps of a second motor car through the open doors of the garage.

So when Murray got into the Packard and drove Amber away, I didn't attempt to stop him. I watched him go and I watched Louise return to the house and close the front door.

I dashed to the garage to start the second car. It was a small red roadster, not unlike my own. I checked the handbrake, set the controls and went forward to cold-start the engine. Two turns and she was humming.

As I straightened, I felt a nudge in the small of my back.

'In case you wonder,' said Louise, 'the safety catch is off.'

THIRTY-EIGHT

Louise ordered me to switch off the engine.

I had no option but to obey.

'Through there.'

I turned and saw a doorway from the garage to the house — the way she had used to surprise me. I entered a small square room with shelving laden with plates and pans.

'Face the wall and raise your hands high.'

'Isn't this a trifle melodramatic, Mrs Brennan?'

In fact it was disconcertingly efficient. One hand searched my clothes for a weapon while the other held the gun against my back.

I added, 'Or do I call you Mrs Sullivan?'

I heard her snatch a breath. The gun jabbed hard against my spine. 'Who told you about that?'

I said, 'I think it would be wise to keep that to myself for the moment.'

She gave me a hard shove with the gun, 'I'm not afraid to use this, Mr Keystone.'

'Exactly. That's why I'm being reticent. You wouldn't kill me without finding out where I got my information.'

'I wouldn't need to. A bullet through the shoulder would do the trick.' She moved the gun higher.

Even if I found a way of getting out of this, I needed information as much as she did. I needed to know where Murray was taking Amber. I said, 'That's not your way, Louise. Better kill me outright like the others.'

'Others?' she repeated. 'I don't know who you mean.'

'Sandy Sullivan, Mrs Honeybee, Jake Harper.'

'I didn't kill them.'

'You don't need blood on your hands to be guilty of murder. May I turn round now? I'm unarmed, as you see, and I dislike addressing the wall.' Without waiting for a reply, I turned slowly, still holding my hands high.

Louise took two steps back. She was holding the gun like a sheriff in a wild west film, with one hand supporting the other. The look in her eye was no comfort. Yet she had yielded a little of the initiative to me.

She said, 'I didn't want Mrs Honeybee to die. Or Jake.'

'Only your husband, Sandy?'

'That was an accident.'

I nodded, 'All done with mirrors, so to speak.'

She shifted her ground. 'You can't blame me for that. Jake was responsible.'

'But you and Murray paid him handsomely.'

Louise reddened, clearly disturbed that I knew so much. She launched into a justification, oblivious that it also amounted to an admission of guilt. 'I married Alex Sullivan when I was only seventeen and it was a disaster from the first night until the day eleven months later when he deserted me. He spent what little money I had on drink and earned none himself. He abused me, beat me and tore my clothes. I was left in a filthy hovel that collapsed around me in the earthquake. I was homeless and penniless, yet when I saw the newspaper and found Alex's name among the dead, I was the happiest widow in the world.'

'Sullivan was listed as dead?'

'Do you think I would have married Murray otherwise?'

There was outrage in her voice, and it carried the

conviction of a woman whose paramount ambition was to be regarded as respectable. I was certain that she was speaking the truth. I asked her, 'Was it someone else called Sullivan who died in the earthquake?'

'Alexander Sullivan,' she emphasised. 'Both names were listed. If it wasn't someone else, I can only guess that Alex had cleared out of town and some other body was presumed to be his. I didn't question it then and I couldn't later on. When I saw that list, I just knew that I was free. I didn't want to know anything else.'

'And when Murray came along, you married him.'

'Yes. Both of us had lost everything. We had to claw our way up from the wreckage of the earthquake. Everything in this house was slaved for, believe me. The first eighteen months of our marriage, I swept and scrubbed the floors of three nickelodeons because we couldn't pay a cleaner's wage. But I didn't resent it. I knew we had something to strive for. And we did it. We built this beautiful house and raised two daughters we adore.' Louise paused. She said with her blue eyes fixed in a gleam of resentment. 'You can't imagine what it was like to learn that Alex was alive and working at Keystone.'

'I can understand the shock you experienced, but was it necessary to have him killed?'

She said as if it were the purest logic, 'He was certain to find out I was married to Murray.'

'You thought he would blackmail you?'

'If it had been as simple as that, we'd have paid him. Murray was willing to buy his silence, but I told him it wouldn't work. You couldn't trust Alex. It was the drinking. He'd have boasted about it in every bar in Los Angeles, however much we paid him. He'd have made Murray and me into monsters and our beautiful marriage into an obscenity. Maybe the two of us could

242

have faced that, but we weren't the only ones liable to suffer.'

'Your daughters?'

'Innocent children.' Louise gave me the look of a tigress defending its young. 'They'll never know anything of this.'

I understood. We had come to the real reason why Sullivan had been murdered. His return from the dead meant that those two small girls — so adored by their parents — were illegitimate, the progeny of an illegal marriage. The fact was inescapable. But if Sullivan were to die, and, this time, stay dead, it need never be known.

'So you asked Jake Harper to solve your problem,' I prompted her. I had a new incentive now to keep Louise talking: the logic of what she had said about the children never knowing anything of this was that she intended to silence me as well.

'Jake was one of our closest friends,' she answered. 'Murray had actually gotten him into Keystone. We didn't tell him everything. We just talked about Alex creating terrible trouble for us all. Jake was reassuring. He said he figured he could remove the problem.'

'Which he did — by staging the accident on the rollercoaster. You must have been very relieved to hear that Sullivan was dead.'

'We paid Jake a thousand dollars.'

'And then he killed Mrs Honeybee.'

Louise clicked her tongue at the memory. 'He panicked, the fool. None of this would have happened if Jake had kept his head. Breaking into apartments, tying people up, kidnapping Amber — he lost his nerve completely when that wretched film disappeared.'

'With some justification,' I pointed out. 'It was the only thing that could have made anyone suspicious.'

She was unimpressed. 'If he had kept cool, Murray and I would have dealt with it. We had it under control.'

As she spoke, my thoughts darted back to the evening Amber and I had gone to dinner with the Brennans. 'Your remedy was more subtle. The velvet glove.'

'I understood the girl,' said Louise. 'She was so deluded about her future in the movies that she was ready to eat out of Murray's hand when he offered her the film part. If you had not been present, we would have got the truth from her then. As it was, we delayed, and Jake, curse him, chose that evening to make his own hamfisted effort to get the film back.'

'By kidnapping Amber?'

'Yes. He didn't tell us for days.'

'I know. Murray was as anxious as I was to find her.'

Louise gave a thin smile. 'I can't tell you how grateful we were when you asked Murray to develop the film.'

If it was meant as a taunt, I ignored it. 'Where did Jake Harper keep Amber?'

'In some farm building at Edendale. He brought her to this house yesterday, after you and Murray called on him. Then he fled for the border. Unluckily the motor car let him down.'

'Not only the motor car,' I commented.

'Meaning what?'

'Meaning that his old friend Murray shot him through the head.'

Louise said evenly, 'You know about that as well.'

'Now I do. At the time I didn't realise Murray was playing a very clever confidence game, sitting in on my deductions, watching me grope towards the truth. I really believed Jake committed suicide until I thought it through last night. Like me, Jake trusted Murray. To get so close to him in that bath-house on the beach,

Murray must have crept in there with the gun and told Jake they would shoot me. He fired a few shots at me and then the last bullet into Jake's head. And put the gun into his hand. Aren't you glad he isn't really your husband? Imagine being married to a murderer.'

'No-one except me will ever know,' said Louise.

'You're forgetting your daughters,' I added casually, but with calculation.

'No!'

It came with such vehemence that I knew what I would do as soon as she had told me what I needed to know. I said, 'They don't know their parents are murderers, but they must know you're torturers, and that isn't particularly comforting to a child.'

The effort she made to hold herself in control was clear in her voice. 'If you're speaking of Amber, the children know nothing about her. We put her in the attic above our own bedroom. We treated her decently enough.'

'Decently! Is what I just saw your idea of decency?'

'It was necessary. We couldn't keep Amber here, so we devised a way to get rid of her. Don't look at me like that, Mr Keystone. She knew enough to destroy us. She won't suffer. She's well doped. I had to shave her head and paint her, so I needed her submissive. I think I did a passable job.'

'Turning her into a dummy?'

'Appropriate, isn't it? At last she is given a role that matches her range as an actress. They're shooting at first light this morning, a few miles up the coast from here. An extra stunt for Murray's last Keystone film. It's one of those trick shots. The paddy wagon full of Keystone Cops drives straight over the top and crashes two hundred feet into the ocean. Dummy Cops, naturally. All except one.'

She smiled and I hated her. I dismissed any lingering sympathy for the seventeen-year-old who had married the brute of a husband in San Francisco. I said, 'Why are you doing this to Amber?'

'We had no choice once Murray shot Jake. We'll get away with a verdict of suicide so long as Amber isn't around to tell her story. Her feet will be strapped to the chassis. The ocean is plenty deep enough below Gale Head.' She stopped. 'I wasn't going to tell you that.'

'Gale Head? That's twelve or more miles from here.'

'Pity you won't be there to see it.'

'Oh, I'll be there,' I stated confidently, 'and I'll stop it.'

'I'll kill you if you move.'

'No you won't. If you fire a shot, those daughters of yours are going to wake in terror and come running downstairs to find their mother holding the gun over a dead man. They'll want to know why. And that's the very thing you've gone to such lengths to avoid.' I put down my hands and held them out in a gesture of finality. 'If you fire that gun, Louise, what was the point of it all?'

She glared at me with a concentration of fury I would not have believed possible in those pale eyes. Then she lowered her lids and stared at the gun in her hand. In a low voice she said, 'Goddamn bastard.'

It was all the confirmation I needed. Without waiting to see her put down the gun, I strolled to the door. I tried to be casual, so as not to provoke a panic reaction, yet I was fully alert.

I had reached the doorway when I heard a deep, almost feral moan. I moved my head enough to glimpse Louise in the act of making a lunge at me. Instead of the gun that I expected to see in her hand, she had snatched up a meat knife. She had raised it ready to bury it in my back.

Thank God my reactions had been tested and proved on the stage. I didn't have time to turn. I reached back and grabbed her arm as it plunged towards me. The force of her effort and my forward movement swung her off her feet and over my back.

I felt the jolt as she crashed against the door frame. Her head hit the floor first. Louise, the social climber, would not have been pleased at the spectacle she presented. She was knocked out cold.

I stepped over her into the garage and cranked the car.

THIRTY-NINE

I had no trouble from the motor car. It ran like a ball across a billiard table except that the coast road was not baize all the way. I hadn't lighted the lamps, not wishing to signal my approach to Murray, so I was at the mercy of pot-holes and stones. Fortunately I knew where I was heading. I had never visited Gale Head, but I had more than once passed the sign pointing out a narrow road between the dunes.

Already there was a lighter tinge to the sky. I wasn't going to alarm myself now by looking at my watch. I reckoned the drive would take half an hour, perhaps more.

Louise had talked of filming at first light, but even in California it would be pointless trying to use a camera until an hour after dawn — assuming Murray was serious about filming the stunt. I was prepared to believe he was. There were plenty of worn-out motor cars at the studio that directors delighted to dispose of in spectacular effects. A good smash or a drive off the end of a pier was a cinch of a gag in Keystone parlance. Thanks to the wizardry of the cutting-room, the passengers always sprang out of the wreckage to take up the chase. The audience rocked with laughter, confirmed in the knowledge that nobody ever got hurt.

Who cared if a dummy was ripped apart and spilt its sawdust?

I had been driving at full throttle for perhaps twenty minutes when I spotted the lights of another vehicle half a mile ahead of me, moving fast in the same direction. I

was doubtful whether it could be Murray. By my calculation he was already setting up the camera on Gale
Head.

In the next two miles, I gained steadily on the lights,
occasionally losing them on the winding route, but finding them again on the straighter stretches. I got close
enough to see that it was a limousine with two people
inside. It was definitely not the Packard.

Something about the shape of the passenger began to
make me feel uneasy. He seemed to have no neck. The
head rested on the shoulders like a lump of dough on a
board. He had cropped hair.

It was the Chief. I was following the police.

This was as crazy as a Keystone chase. I was at a loss
to find a rational explanation. I eased the throttle to
increase the space between us and took the next turn off
the highway. This part of the coast was interlaced with
smaller roads and tracks and I reckoned if I kept the
ocean on my left, I would find another route. There
couldn't be much over a mile to go.

The going was rougher here, and I cursed each
chugging ascent that failed to produce a view of Gale
Head. The light was improving all the time, which was
no comfort to me at all. My first sighting of the sea
showed me the sun three parts clear of the horizon.
There was no-one on the headland.

The road wound right again, dipped for a few
hundred yards and then snaked up another hill. I
engaged the lower gear, gritted my teeth and climbed
towards the skyline.

When I topped it, I needed to go no further.

The Packard, with nobody inside, was only twenty
yards away at the side of the road, standing beside two
Keystone Company cars.

Murray was a short way beyond, bending over a

camera mounted on a tripod perilously near the cliff edge. A cameraman was beside him.

Amber was not with them. There was no paddy wagon loaded with dummy Cops.

Murray turned and stared. He gaped, frowned and attempted to smile. It looked more like the baring of teeth.

I got out without cutting the engine and ran across to him.

Behind the pebble glasses his small eyes made rapid nervous movements, yet his voice was as calm as ever. 'What's this, Keystone? What are you doing here? Is something the matter?'

Before he had got the words out, I yelled, 'Where is she?'

He pretended not to understand. He said, 'That's my car you were driving.'

'I saw her, Murray! I watched you drive off with her, for God's sake.'

'You mean Amber?'

I went for his neck. My two hands closed over his throat. 'You killed her, you bastard!'

His fists flailed my ribs. He spluttered incoherently. We fell on the turf and it loosened my grip. I crashed the back of my fist into the blabbering mouth. As my hand moved away, his lip oozed blood.

I felt hands on my shoulders, tugging me off.

I had enough pent-up fury to deal with the cameraman as well as Murray. I got up and flung a punch that sent him crashing against his tripod. He hauled himself up, and I thought he was coming at me again. Instead, he pointed towards the road.

Sensing a trick, I didn't turn to look.

Then I heard the screech of brakes. We all stared towards the black limousine I had followed along the coast highway.

The Chief climbed out and walked towards us. With him was his assistant, Chick, holding a gun.

Murray murmured, 'You and I better stick together, Keystone.'

'Go to hell.'

The Chief strutted the last few yards of turf and eyed Murray. 'Been in a fight?'

Murray shook his head. 'Not a real one, officer. Just for effect.'

'Yeah — like the suicide on the beach at San Onofre?'

'What are you talking about?'

'You and this punk from England forcing a guy named Harper off the highway and putting a bullet through his head. Suicide, my ass. What is it about you movie people? We never had this before you came.'

Murray decided to bluff his way through. 'Would you kindly stand aside? We're in the middle of shooting a scene.' He took a handkerchief from his pocket and waved it above his head.

'I don't care a whoop in high water about your scene,' said the Chief. 'Chick, throw me the cuffs.'

'You don't understand,' said Murray. 'I've given the signal. Look for yourself.'

The Chief fielded the handcuffs and moved towards Murray, who was pointing along the edge of the cliff. My own view, like the Chief's had been obstructed by the rise of the headland. I moved a pace or two nearer the cliff edge to follow the line of Murray's arm.

Two hundred yards away, on a higher promontory, was a police-wagon apparently filled with Keystone Cops. It was moving slowly across the turf towards the sheer drop, pushed by three propmen.

'Jesus!' said the Chief. 'There are guys in that wagon!'

I was already sprinting to the car I had left by the road. I flung myself aboard, yanked down the throttle lever and kicked the clutch. The car catapaulted forward. I released the pedal and moved up a gear.

I heard Chick give a shout and fire a shot that buried itself somewhere in the woodwork behind me. I dipped my head and roared away up the rise. After fifty yards of road, I spun the wheel and sheered across the turf towards the paddy wagon. Twice I managed to sound the horn, but the wheel jolted so violently that I had to give up and grab it with both hands.

The men pushing the wagon didn't look round. They were straining to build up speed, propelling it towards a slight decline where its momentum would carry it on and over the cliff.

My only chance was to block the way.

I was close enough to see the heads of the dummies rocking limply with the movement. I saw the paddy wagon reach the slope. The men gave a final shove and dropped exhausted behind it.

I was not going to be in time.

In those final seconds I strained so hard on the throttle lever that I bent the metal. The roadster gave all it could to cross the path of the wagon, but my sense of timing told me I was asking the impossible. There simply wasn't enough space between the wagon and the cliff edge.

Our front wheels touched.

Instead of ramming the centre of my car, the wagon was shoved to one side as we collided. In that split-second I looked at the dummy heads and saw Amber's eyes wide open, watching me from the back seat.

Then my car dipped. The leading wheel had slipped over the edge. The car poised there a moment. I saw the paddy wagon veer aside and stop a yard from disaster.

But my car gave a sickening lurch and started its plunge two hundred feet towards the sea.

I braced my legs and flung myself clear of the car. Strange how rapid the brain's reactions can be *in extremis*. I had time as I plummeted towards the solid-looking sea to reflect that the saving of Amber had been the purpose of the exercise, and I could be pleased about that, but it was a poor end to the stunt if the next time she saw me was in a coffin. A long way down I had the sense to roll my body into something resembling a dive.

I must have hit the water cleanly, but I have no recollection of what happened next. I may have cracked my head on the ocean bed or it may simply have been the impact of striking the water. I am told that I swam fifty yards through a churning sea to the safety of the rocks, where I was afterwards picked up.

It doesn't worry me to have this two-day gap in my memory. I will settle for the moment I recovered it.

FORTY

I was lying in bed and someone was calling me Keystone. A woman's voice, almost no voice at all really, more of a whisper. Cool fingers touched my forehead and stroked my face.

I opened my eyes and said in surprise, 'Your hair?'

Amber smiled. 'Only a wig, I'm afraid.'

'You're really all right?'

'A little shaky on my feet, but yes. The police got me out of the wagon very soon.'

'Is Murray arrested?'

She nodded, 'Louise, too. She was waiting for them when they went to pick her up. She had managed to get herself dressed, in spite of taking a bad fall. She'd already arranged for someone to take the children.'

'She's very strong-willed.'

'And ruthless,' said Amber. 'She could have taught Lady Macbeth a thing or two. Those ice-cold eyes!'

'Amber, you've been through hell.'

'But you snatched me out of it, darling.' She leaned forward.

I held her and rejoiced in my good fortune. I loved this indomitable girl, her warmth, her optimism, her crazy belief in her talent.

As the kiss ended, she pressed her fingers between our lips and said, 'You know where we are?'

I hadn't looked past her face. I hadn't wanted to. Now I saw unfamiliar gloss-painted walls, that shade of mud-green peculiar to hospital wards. 'Can't I get up?'

'They want to keep you in a little longer, make sure

you're really okay.'

I couldn't disguise my frustration. 'I don't care what they want. I just need to be with you, Amber.'

'That's nice,' she said, but I detected a note of reserve.

'What is it?'

She touched my forehead again and drew a line down my face and neck. 'Could we make it more permanent?'

She wanted to marry me! My pulse quickened to a rate that my doctors were not going to like. I said, 'Amber, my sweetheart, nothing would make me happier, but what kind of life can I give you?'

'I know,' she answered. 'You still have to get back to Europe to fight for your country. I want to go with you. I want you to have someone waiting in England to come home to when the fighting is over — your wife, Keystone.'

I took hold of both her hands. 'That's a beautiful thought, my darling, but I don't think it's possible. I haven't earned enough for my passage home, let alone yours as well. I don't even have a job any more.'

Amber smiled. 'But I'm still on the Keystone payroll.' She hesitated. 'See who else came to visit you?'

I didn't want any other visitors. As Amber drew back, I tried to detain her. I put out my hand, but I was slower and weaker than I had realised. The hand was gripped by another with the muscle of an ex-iron-worker.

'How are you?' boomed Sennett. 'I just dropped in to see the guy who dropped in.'

I summoned a polite smile.

'The best stunt any actor of mine ever pulled.'

'Ex-actor,' I pointed out. 'Will I get my job back?'

He took out a cigar and tested it. 'I'll think about that when you're fit again.'

'Ten dollars a day.'

'Ten bucks?' He spat into the pot of ferns at the foot of my bed. 'Forget it, Keystone.'

I shrugged and looked past him.

Sennett followed the line of my gaze to where Amber was standing staring out of the window at the end of the ward. He said in a subdued voice, 'She's a peach of a girl, but the worst actress I ever saw. What am I going to do with her?'

I said, 'She wants to come with me to England.'

'The best thing that could happen,' said Sennett with enthusiasm. 'She'll never play the lead in another movie.'

I said in a bland voice, 'No?'

His eyes widened.

I said, 'Unless I earned enough in a month to pay both our passages to England.'

'Ten bucks a day?'

'Twenty-five, in the circumstances.'

Sennett heaved a huge sigh. 'Okay — it's worth it to me.'